THE DEAD OF WINTER

THE DEAD OF WINTER

A PIPER BLACKWELL MYSTERY

JEAN RABE

Boone Street Press

© 2018 by Jean Rabe

Cover design by Juan Villar Padron

Interior design by John G. Hartness

Boone Street Press

Name: Rabe, Jean, author

Title: The Dead of Winter / Jean Rabe

First Edition Imajin Books: November 2016

Boone Street Press: June 2018

Identifiers: ISBN 13: 978-1-7320036-8-2 / 10: 1-7320036-8-8

LCCN: 2018905213

Printed in the United States of America

❀ Created with Vellum

For Juliana

ONE

MONDAY, JANUARY 1ST

C onrad Delaney's body leaned against a life-sized stuffed Santa on the seat of a glossy black sleigh. It looked like he was going for a ride with the jolly old elf.

The centerpiece of Conrad's front yard, the sleigh was red the last time Piper saw it. That was more than a dozen years back when her dad drove the family through the county to take in the Christmas lights. Piper had begged to stop so she could sit with Santa, but dad kept driving... on to the next display, and the next.

Large burlap sacks filled the back of the sleigh; artfully spilling from one were boxes wrapped in colorful plastic and tied with red and green bows, everything held in place with fishing line. The ribbons fluttered in the chill breeze that cut across the snowy landscape.

Piper shivered and turned her coat collar up.

For variety sometimes Conrad put big stuffed animals in the mix, and one Christmas he reported a four-foot-tall Teddy bear stolen. The sheriff's department recovered the bear about a month later, hanging from a telephone pole out on Highway 545 near the monastery, fluffy guts spilling out. It had been a hot news item for the town of Fulda, which boasted a population of two hundred.

One hundred and ninety-nine now.

A thin layer of frost had formed on Conrad's face, the spotlight making it sparkle like he'd been dipped in glitter. His lips formed an "O" similar to the expression on Santa's plastic visage, and his eyes, the washed-out blue of a winter sky, were locked open in a perpetual thousand yard stare.

He looked peaceful sitting there in his dark jeans and gray wool sweater, a single line of egg-white reindeers parading across his chest, bright red Merry Christmas mug in his cupped hands that contained, Piper guessed from the look of it, coffee.

"Happy New Year, Sheriff Blackwood."

Piper glanced over her shoulder to see her chief deputy. He cut through the gawkers on the driveway—the people from the farmhouse across the street who'd been celebrating. The owner of the farmhouse had walked over to invite Conrad to the New Year's Eve festivities and discovered the ice cold truth of the tableaux. He called 9-1-1, and then all the partiers came over for a gander.

"Happy New Year, Oren," she returned.

The chief deputy regarded the yard before traipsing over.

"Surprised you're here." Oren checked his watch. "It's only a quarter to one. Surprised you're not out at some bar in Rockport celebrating, a young girl like you."

"The coroner is on her way and—"

"She's an old friend of Conrad's. This'll be hard on her." Oren Rosenberg was the same age as Conrad, sixty-five, though taller at six-four and built like a linebacker, with curly steel-gray hair that stuck out at odd angles from under his hat. "I got here as soon as I could. It was a drive, and I needed to change first." Oren was in uniform, complete with the department-issue leather jacket and boots.

"No one inside," she said. "I checked. Apparently he lived alone."

"Yeah, Conrad had for a few years."

"You knew Mr. Delaney?"

Oren shrugged. "I know a lot of people from working in the department for a stretch."

Piper was a foot shorter than Oren, forty-two years younger and wiry, practically child-sized next to the burly chief deputy. She used the small digital camera in her right hand to take pictures of the sleigh, then close-ups of Conrad, before turning and taking pictures of the partiers on the driveway, the breath trailing away from their faces in miniature clouds. She wore sweatpants, a sweatshirt, and sneakers, hadn't bothered with her sheriff's uniform, rushing here directly from her father's kitchen when she'd got the dispatcher's call at midnight. She'd thrown a pea coat on and now wished she'd gone to her apartment for something more substantial, and—after seeing her chief deputy—to change into her uniform. But she'd thought it would be a simple and quick run.

Oren reached to his side and pulled his flashlight.

"I don't think you'll need that. Got plenty of light." Piper indicated the yard spotlight trained on the sleigh and the front of Conrad's decked-out house. "Probably a heart attack. I saw a little brown bottle of nitroglycerin tablets on the counter in the kitchen."

She heard the people on the driveway talking, the comments swirling together. She could make out:

"Poor Conrad."

"Didn't he have a bad heart?"

"How old was he?"

"Sixty-five, just turned I think."

"Gone to be with his wife."

"Got a boy somewhere around here, right? Maybe in Owensboro? Henderson?"

"Heart attack, I bet. Or a stroke."

"Poor, poor Mr. Delaney."

"Maybe a heart attack," Oren said. He held the flashlight like a baton and gently thumped it against the palm of his free hand. He wore deerskin gloves. "Conrad used to smoke."

Piper rocked from one foot to the other. The cold had burrowed through her sneakers and numbed her feet. "I'm thinking he probably came outside to see the old year off, maybe listen to the folks across the road having a good time." She'd heard their music when she pulled up, loud enough to carry across the county road, moldy-oldies rock, *My Three O'Clock Thrill*. Someone had returned to the farmhouse and turned it off. Now all she heard was their speculative banter and the shushing sound the breeze-tossed pine garland made against the eaves of the house.

"Wish I would've noticed him earlier, might still be alive." This from a man in a green parka.

"You don't know that," a woman comforted.

"It was just his time," another said. "You know, turn, turn, turn."

"The new sheriff is little, ain't she?"

"Looks like a kid."

"I voted for her."

"I didn't. I voted for Oren."

"Poor Conrad."

Piper took another picture. "Mr. Delaney probably figured he'd be out here only a few minutes, so he didn't bother with a coat."

Oren turned on the flashlight and stepped right up against the sleigh, shone the beam in Conrad's eyes. The flashlight deepened the shadows cast from the sleigh, making it look like crooked fingers stretched across the snow toward the blacktop driveway.

"Probably died fast," Piper said. She hoped he did. "Probably didn't feel much. A heart attack."

"Maybe," Oren repeated. Softer: "Maybe a heart attack. More likely murder."

Piper felt what little warmth there was go out of her face. She didn't want this to be murder, wasn't ready to deal with a murder.

"It's in the eyes," Oren said. "See the red spots in the white? Got some red spots on his forehead, too. It's called petechial hemorrhage. When someone struggles for air, it increases the pressure, causes capillaries to rupture. The tiny red spots." He lowered the beam to Conrad's hands. "You can get petechial with some natural deaths, if it's something real sudden. But you'd think if he had a heart attack, he would've dropped his coffee. Big mug, a lot of coffee." The mug in

Conrad's hands rested on his knee. A pause. "Doesn't look like he spilled a drop. In fact, the coffee's frozen solid. He's been here a while."

"Murder," Piper said flatly. *A rural county like this, a saltbox in the sticks, population two hundred...one ninety-nine now.* She sucked in her lower lip. *First day on the job and I'm in over my head. Dear God, don't let this be murder.*

"I'd bet my boat Conrad was murdered." Oren aimed the flashlight at the ground, the snow disturbed all around the sleigh. Boot prints across boot prints. The snow was also disturbed leading from the house to the sleigh. "Damn the lookie loos, messed the yard all up and down."

The flashlight beam returned to Conrad's face.

"Petechial hemorrhage." Oren made a tsk-tsking sound, and Piper had to strain to hear him over the people still talking on the driveway, louder than they needed to be, the volume likely fueled by the alcohol they'd consumed at their party.

"Poor, poor Conrad," had become a mantra.

"But you'd know all about petechial hemorrhage, Sheriff, if you had some experience," Oren said.

Not only was this Piper's first day as sheriff, having won the election in November, it was her first with the department.

"If you're curious, the coroner can tell you all about petechial hemorrhage," Oren continued. "Or a youngster like you, so Internet savvy, you could Google it on your phone." He took a step back. "Most likely strangulation, suffocation. Coffee mug in his hand like that? I'd say someone killed Conrad Delaney and set him up here for the neighbors to see. Posed him all nice and proper next to Saint Nick for whatever sick reason. Petechial hemorrhage. P-e-t-e-c-h-i-a-l. Look it up. Bet my boat on it." He let out a low whistle. "Haven't had a murder in the county in a few years."

"Get the names of those people," Piper said, tipping her chin to indicate the gathering on the driveway. She held her shoulders straight and pulled in a deep breath. Her teeth chattered. "Contact information on all of them. And talk to the guy who found him and called this in. Chris Hagee."

"I'll get right to that, Sheriff." Oren clicked off the flashlight and stuck it in his belt loop. "I know Chris. He's that skinny fellow in the green parka in the middle of the gaggle. Anyone who's lived and worked around here for any amount of time knows Chris and Joan Hagee...and knows most of the other folks standing with them."

Piper bristled and tugged in another deep breath.

"Anything else you need me to do right now, Sheriff Blackwell?"

His patronizing attitude was more biting than the cold. Oren had been her opponent in the election for sheriff; she hadn't won by much, but she had won. Had she made the wrong decision to keep him on?

"You want me to call in the State?" Oren waited for her reply. "If you're not up to this, I understand, you never working in a sheriff's department, never working a murder case. Might be too much for you. I can call the State."

A lot of small towns in Indiana called in the State Police to investigate when the sheriff departments didn't have the resources. If a death wasn't murder, she'd have to pay the State's expenses out of her budget. And if it was a murder, why not direct her department to investigate? Her dad had handled a murder or two, certainly. What was to stop her? How could she pass over her very first case? She'd be sending the wrong message to the people who voted for her if she let this one go.

"Up to you," Oren prompted. "Your call, Sheriff."

Piper had never run from anything.

"No. We can take this," she said. "But call Randy."

Randy was the department's sole detective, had a dozen years of experience at that job, three years before that as a deputy. Piper's experience? She looked at her watch: 12:58 a.m. She'd been sheriff of Spencer County for a whopping fifty-eight minutes.

Piper's olive green eyes locked onto Conrad's sad blue ones.

She broke the stare and took a few more photos, filled the camera frame with the coffee cup, zooming in. She realized that his fingers were kept in place around the mug by fishing line, like what held the presents to the sleigh. The coffee looked dull in the glow from the yard spotlight, heavy and dense-appearing, and when Piper swallowed hard she swore she could taste the bitterness of it.

Piper didn't want it to be murder.

But it certainly was.

TWO

Oren Rosenberg considered himself old fashioned...or maybe just old, given that his new boss was his grand-daughter's age. He pulled out a narrow notebook and a Sharpie and recorded the names and phone numbers of the people shivering and gossiping on the driveway; it was an easy task, he knew most of them. The other deputies used phones and tablets to text in information. But Oren believed electronics could fail, and paper and ink were more reliable, especially in this weather.

"Nobody should die on New Year's Eve, Oren," Chris Hagee said. "You're supposed to celebrate life, you know? Drink, dance. Well, dance if you've been drinking enough. Watch the ball drop."

"Yeah, heck of a way to start off the New Year, eh? Need to talk to you, Chris." Oren's conversation was accompanied by foggy puffs.

Chris rubbed his hands together. "Out here? You're kidding, right? My bony ass is turning into an ice cube, you know. I was a fool to stay out as long as I have. How 'bout we go over to my place with Joanie and—"

Oren pointed to his Ford Explorer parked on the side of the road, flashers going. He wanted to get Chris alone. "How 'bout we talk in my car for a few minutes first? I'll turn on the heater." He directed the rest to the others: "Free country, you're welcome to stay out here, but ain't nothing exciting about watching a dead man in a sleigh. He's not gonna get up and sing. Why don't you head on back with Joan and—"

"I bet it was a heart attack. Conrad used to smoke," someone wearing an Indianapolis Colts jacket pushed. "Two packs a day, he did."

"He quit with the patch," another said. "My cousin quit with the patch, too. Chris, I keep saying you should try the patch—"

"Smokes and weight." The man in the Colts jacket raised his voice. "Darn near as pudgy as that Santa he's—"

"Think he killed himself?" This came from someone Oren hadn't met before, a middle-aged man who bore a strong resemblance to Chris, maybe a relative come for the party. "Wife dead four years now, one kid a loser, the other is who-knows-where. Do you think he was depressed and—"

"Thought I heard you say something about murder, Deputy Rosenberg." This was from Joan Hagee. "Did I hear right?"

Oren figured the gawkers had been chattering too loud to hear his petechial hemorrhage lecture to Piper. He let out a sigh, his breath escaping in a great misty fan. "It's too early to tell anything, Joan. But the facts are, it's late, or rather it's early—too early. And it's cold. Take 'em back over to your house and let 'em sit there until they're sober enough to drive. Fix 'em some coffee while Chris and I—"

"Free country, just like you said," the defiant lookie loo in the Colts jacket cut in. He crossed his arms and watched Piper taking more pictures of the sleigh.

"Suit yourself. Just keep out of the sheriff's way and stay out of the yard. I'm gonna want to talk to all of you. If you go back with Joan, I'll chat with you there and save us all some time and mileage." Oren motioned for Chris, and they walked down the blacktop drive, which looked like a slice of just-washed coal. It had been plowed, but there were mounds pushed up against the sides and ice at the end. Southern Indiana had seen twice as much snow as usual this winter. He called over his shoulder, "And if you take off and we catch any of you

weaving on the road, we'll cite you for DUI, Happy New Year or no."
DUIs were the number one ticketed offense in Spencer County.

"I voted for you," Chris said as he slid into the Explorer. "Just saying, you know. Age and experience trumps youth and...well, I'd say beauty, but that little Blackwell's pretty damn plain looking. Good figure, though."

Oren twisted the key and turned on the heater. The other deputies drove either older Crown Vics or a relatively recent model of Taurus. Oren's was a 2015, newest in the small fleet, and with comfortable leather seats. He'd claimed it a year ago come February when the county caucus appointed him sheriff to fill out Paul Blackwell's term when Paul quit because of the cancer. Oren won the primary and figured he'd take the election in November. Out of respect, no one else in the department contested him for it.

He hadn't counted on a challenge from Paul's daughter, Piper, her coming home from Iraq, putting signs up everywhere, bright neon yellow and screaming red: Vote for Blackwell, Spencer County Sheriff.

And more than that, Oren certainly hadn't counted on her winning.

It was a pity vote, he figured, pity for poor sick Paul Blackwell, the beloved sheriff who'd been with the department thirty years and had held four terms. Name recognition: Paul Blackwell...Piper Blackwell. P. Blackwell. Blackwell Blackwell Blackwell. Probably half the people who voted for her didn't know they were electing a *shikse*...and one the same age as his granddaughter. Twenty-three. The pity vote and ignorance, likely coupled with a hint of anti-Semitism, wanting to elect a Protestant of some stripe.

"*Gornisht helfn*," he muttered.

"Hey...you zoning out on me, Oren? Earth to Oren. Come in, Oren. I said, what do you want to talk to me 'bout? Nice car. What kind of mileage does this get?"

Oren smelled whiskey on Chris's breath, and when the man belched there was a burst of something sharp, maybe spiced sausage.

There was a strong trace of cigarette smoke imbedded in the parka; Chris probably had to do his smoking outside.

"You found Conrad," Oren stated.

"Well, yeah. Was looking out the picture window, saw him in that damned sleigh."

"What time did you see him?"

"Well… let me think. It was heading toward midnight. We were waiting for the ball to drop. Not yet midnight, maybe twenty to, a quarter to, around then, you know."

"Go on… the Delaney place was dark—"

"Except for the spotlight. Yeah, well, I wouldn't've noticed him but for that damned spotlight aimed at that damned sleigh. Actually, Joan saw him first, pointed him out to me, told me I should invite him over, that Conrad shouldn't sit out there in the cold all by his lonesome."

"So you walked over to invite him?"

"Well, I opened a window first and hollered. But then I realized he couldn't hear me over the music. We'd cranked it pretty loud, you know, it being New Year's Eve and a party and all. So yeah, I went over."

"Right away when Joan saw him? Twenty to midnight?"

"Yeah, thereabouts. I wanted to make sure I could go over and back and not miss the ball dropping, time for a cigarette in there, too. So I threw on my coat and walked across the road, lit up on the end of his driveway, you know."

A silence settled, the heater gently purring. Oren glanced out the windshield. Piper had put her camera away and was squatted next to the sleigh, looking at something underneath it. He hoped she had the presence not to pick up anything without properly bagging it.

Oren could have retired after the failed election. He had twenty years with the sheriff's department and twenty before that with the Rockport police. There was a fine second pension ahead of him. But he had helped two of his kids with their money woes, and helped his granddaughter pay for college. Four years ago he and his wife moved into a new, but modest, beachfront house on Lake Noel in Santa Claus, bought a nice boat that he didn't get out on often enough, and had a double-wide second garage built to store it in. He figured he needed the chief deputy salary and wouldn't know what to do with all that retirement time on his hands.

Besides, Piper would have to attend—and pass—the Plainfield Sheriff's Academy this April. If she failed, and he considered that a distinct possibility, Oren was certain the caucus would put him back in charge.

"Slipped on some ice right at the bottom of Conrad's drive, you know," Chris said. "Dropped my cigarette and damn near fell on my bony ass. I called out to him, Conrad, but he didn't answer, just sitting there like a lump in that damned sleigh, and so I went up his blacktop and cut through the yard. I had a bad feeling when he didn't answer me, you know. I knew right then he was dead. I just did, you know." Chris shuddered and reached inside his coat, pulling out a pack of cigarettes. "Dead. Dead."

"Not in here."

"Christ. Bad as my wife."

"So go on. You went over to Conrad, even though you knew he was dead."

He ruefully replaced the cigarettes. "Well, yeah, I thought that he'd climbed up in that damned garish sleigh of his and had the big one. But I figured I should be sure. So I got up close and saw that his lips were blue. Anyway, I went in the house, his front door wasn't locked. Turned on some lights and hollered 'til I was hoarse, but wasn't no one else around. So I called 9-1-1 from the phone in Conrad's living room, and the lady on the other end told me not to touch anything and to wait outside for the sheriff." A pause. "Well, I called Joan, told her Conrad was dead, then I went back out. Christ, I could hear our music all the way over here. I'd forgotten to close the window. Probably still open. Anyway, Joan, she said heart attack right away. Conrad had a heart attack six or seven years ago, you know, that's when he quit smoking. Missed the ball dropping." Another pause. "So you think that's what it was, a heart attack?"

"Nope." Oren was an honest soul. "You didn't see Conrad sitting outside *before* your party? In the sleigh?"

"No, but I was busy with my guests."

"See anybody visiting Conrad's during the day?"

"No. But I wasn't paying attention, you know. I had a party to get ready for." Chris's brow furrowed and he drew his lips forward until his face looked pinched. He let out a low whistle. "Someone killed him? Nobody should be murdered on New Year's Eve. Wait 'til I tell—"

"Did you see—"

"—anybody at Conrad's? No. You need a hearing aid, Oren? No, I didn't see anybody. But like I said, I had company coming, you know, appetizers to put out, lit'l smokies to watch in the crock pot. I make these little cocktail wieners every year, you know. This time I used extra-hot barbecue sauce and doubled the brown sugar."

"When was the last time you saw Conrad?"

"Like I said, just before midnight and—"

"When he was *alive*, Chris. When's the last time you saw Conrad, talked to him?"

Chris scratched at his chin. "Oh, I dunno. I...Thursday? Yeah, last Thursday. I remember. I saw Conrad Thursday, ran into him at the grocery store in Rockport bright and early. I was buying stuff for my party, to make my smokies, getting chips, dips, a couple of bags of them itty bitty carrots. I had a cart heaped full. Conrad had one of them little carry baskets, you know, just a few things in it. Cat food and coffee. I noticed that 'cause we drink the same brand of coffee. Folgers, you know." He shook his head, his chin drooping to his chest. "Oren, can't imagine why anyone would kill him. Not an enemy in the world, Conrad. Who'd want to kill a nice man like that?"

That was the question burning in Oren's thoughts: who would kill Conrad Delaney? Oren liked to work jigsaw puzzles in his den at home, and an investigation was a lot like that, sorting through the pieces, matching the colors, and fitting everything together, building probable cause and finding a suspect.

"So when you cut through the yard to see Conrad, did you notice tracks in the snow?"

Chris scratched his head and leaned forward so he could better look out the windshield. "Well, yeah, now that you mention it, I did see some tracks."

"What did they look like?"

"Like tracks, you know. Footprints. Well, not *bare* footprints. Big ones with tread, like from hunting boots, you know. Going from the driveway to the sleigh, and then from the sleigh to the house. I walked through them, the tracks, stepped right in them 'cause I didn't have boots on and didn't want to get snow in these loafers. I'm wearing dress socks, they're thin and—"

"So you stepped in the tracks you noticed."

"Yeah. Followed the footprints, you know what I mean. Where the snow was already mashed down. I was trying not to get snow inside my shoes."

"Sure, I get it. How many sets of tracks did you see? Before you walked in them? Like, were they from one person, or two?"

"Well, the ones I walked in. One set of tracks. One person. A man. I wear a size ten, and they were a bit bigger than mine." He smiled as if proud of himself for providing that tidbit. Then he leaned even farther forward and pointed. "Can't really see them now, those tracks I walked in. The yard's all messed up. "

"Because of your company."

"My company?"

"The people from your party."

"Well, yeah. Like I told you, after I called 9-1-1, I called Joan and everyone came across to see the body. Didn't none of us get to see the ball drop. I guess we all sort of covered up those tracks I walked in, looking around the sleigh and such, slopped some snow up on that little sidewalk."

"Your guests tromped all over my crime scene," Oren said softly.

Chris leaned back in the seat. "I voted for you, just saying, you know."

Oren saw most of the lookie loos shuffling across the road, back to the Hagee farmhouse, Joan leading them. Two stayed, though, fidgeting to ward off the chill, the one in the Indianapolis Colts jacket occasionally pointing at the sleigh. By the way their breath puffed away it looked like they were engrossed in conversation. So far no one had gotten in their cars and driven away from the Hagee's.

Oren unbuttoned his coat because the heater was a little too efficient.

Twenty-three years old.

He cranked the defroster to take care of the glaze forming on the windshield. The New Year was getting off to a cold and bitter start.

THREE

Piper wrapped her fingers around the cup and cringed, the image of Conrad Delaney holding a bright red Merry Christmas mug in his hands burned in her mind. She set the coffee aside, pulled back from the table, and crossed her arms. She was in her dad's kitchen, right where she'd been when the dispatcher's call came.

"I thought you wanted coffee, Punkin."

"I do, Dad. I'm just—"

"Exhausted?"

"Yeah, that word comes in my size." She offered him a small smile. "Been up thirty-six. Straight. But who's counting?"

"You, apparently."

She laughed. "Listen, sorry I didn't get over here earlier. I'd intended to help you take down the tree, but this murder investigation—"

"I don't need any help. I put it up by myself, didn't I? You really need to—"

"Sorry, I'd just planned on it. I like to look at the ornaments, each one a memory, you know." Her father's tree was an eight-foot tall artificial flocked pine with hundreds of lights and a plethora of Hallmark ornaments. Christmas was a big deal for Paul Blackwell.

His brow creased, the wrinkles reminding her of old bark. "I'll take the tree down when I want it down. In fact, I think I'll keep it up a few more days. Maybe another week. It's pretty and it's not hurting anything. You know how much I like—"

"—a Deck the Halls kind of tree," she finished. "I know. I do, too." What went unsaid was this might be his last Christmas tree, this being his second round of chemo, the first having basically no effect. If this round didn't work, there were a few clinical trials he could pursue, but those amounted to a Hail Mary pass. Uncomfortable, she changed the subject. "I hadn't expected a murder the first day on the job."

"So tell me about it."

Piper took up the cup again, the warmth welcome against her hands. She held it up to her nose and stared across the rim at her father. He looked worn to her, a man of fifty-five who could pass for seventy-five. The Non-Hodgkin's lymphoma and the second round of chemo were responsible for turning a handsome, hale man into this pale, haggard shadow. He had a long, careworn face and a narrow nose, wide-set eyes the color of her coffee. He used to have wavy brown hair like hers, but now he wore a ball cap—even indoors—to cover up the few wisps he had remaining.

"I'll walk you through it," she said.

Piper's first impression: Conrad Delaney's house should be featured in *Better Homes & Gardens*. The exterior was pristine; a white aluminum-sided saltbox with navy blue shutters, pine garland stretched across the eaves and looping down to brush the midpoints between the upstairs windows, pine wreath on the door, a big red bow dangling beneath the mailbox, the sleigh the centerpiece in the front yard.

Piper had set her shoes just inside the front door and treaded lightly through the house. Oren had an evidence kit in his Explorer, and she brought it in with her and bagged the nitroglycerin prescription first, which looked to have about a dozen tiny pills in the bottle. No overturned furniture, didn't look like anything was out of place, no obvious signs of a struggle. Maybe Randy would notice something.

The living room was tidy and seemed to have a feminine feel. She guessed that Conrad's wife had been responsible for the decor. The fireplace mantel was crowded with framed photographs, the largest in the center showed Conrad and Sara in their younger days. A couple of pictures of two boys, grade school aged with a puppy between them; and one of the same boys as teenagers posed by an old car. It appeared that the Delaneys were in their late-thirties when they started having children.

Two socks hung from the fireplace: "Cipín" and "Buttons" were embroidered on the cuffs. Cats? She'd encountered a black and white Hemingway hiding in a corner of the kitchen, and a gray tabby introduced himself by rubbing against Piper's ankles as she explored the house.

The Christmas tree—a real one—was in the den, a wide spruce that scented the air. It was covered with blinking lights and round and pear-shaped frosted glass ornaments. The lights were hot to the touch —they'd been on for quite some time—and the bowl the trunk nested inside was dry. The red velvet skirt had white tassel trim; and silver and green sequins spelled out *Nollaig Shona Duit*, which she Googled on her phone to discover was Irish for Happy Christmas. The many cards Conrad had received were strung across a wall, affixed to a metallic length of yarn by miniature plastic clothespins. She took pictures of everything.

"Mr. Delaney was neat," Piper told her dad. "The place was tidy. He would have put Felix Unger to shame. No sign of forced entry and nothing appeared disturbed. We sealed the scene, couldn't risk someone coming in and corrupting evidence."

"And outside? Around the sleigh?"

"The snow in the front yard looked like a herd of elephants danced a rumba." She took a swallow; the coffee was just the right temperature now, and seriously good. "More than a dozen people were partying at Chris Hagee's across the road, and they traipsed all the hell across the crime scene before I got there."

She'd taken roughly three hundred photographs, downloaded all of them into the department-issue laptop, and had started going through them, printing out two dozen before she called it a day. The coroner also took pictures, and then directed an ambulance crew to whisk Conrad away to the bowels of a hospital in nearby Vanderburgh County for an autopsy that was scheduled for tomorrow morning—if he thawed out enough. The coroner had pulled some strings to move Conrad ahead of the fatalities caused by Evansville's drunk-driving New Year's Eve revelers.

"I had to scour phone directories on the Internet and call around to police departments in Kentucky to find Conrad's youngest son, Zachary, who lives in a rent-by-the-week in Owensboro. That was my first death notification, me calling him."

No luck yet finding the other son, Anthony, who'd left home after high school and moved to someplace in the Orient.

Paul pondered the coffee. "Zach is... was—" He let that thought hang.

"What?"

"Check the department records, arrests. You'll have to go back some years. Zach was a troublemaker when he lived in Fulda. Nothing like his squeaky-clean older brother. A few drug charges here and there. Zach had a fondness for pot from an early age, practically a kid when he started smoking it. I caught him with enough once to send him away for a year and a half. Now pot is a slap on the wrist. Wrong to decriminalize marijuana like they've done."

Paul Blackwell had been with the Spencer County Sheriff's Department for three decades, and received the Sheriff of the Year award from the Indiana Sheriff's Association a few years back for his community work. All those years... he likely knew most of the people in Spencer County, including Zachary Delaney, Piper mused.

"You going to chat with Zach?"

Piper shook her head. "I'm taking the autopsy and giving Zachary to Oren and Randy."

"You'll like working with Randy, he's a solid detective."

She ran her finger around the edge of the coffee cup. "I hope so. I don't like working with Oren."

"Oren's a good man."

"Well, he did take Mr. Delaney's cats, said he has some sort of a forest cat—"

"That would be Freya, a purebred Norwegian Forest Cat—"

"—and said he didn't want Mr. Delaney's cats to go to the shelter, as it's crowded. Said he'd been thinking about getting another cat anyway."

"See? Oren's a good man."

"I suppose." She shrugged. "I've never worked a murder before, you know. Seen plenty of dead men, pieces of dead men. Some nights that's all I see in my dreams, the pieces. But an outright murder—" Piper had been an MP out of Fort Campbell and had witnessed a lot of death from tours in Iraq. She took a few more sips of the coffee and held the flavor on her tongue. "I told Oren I didn't want the State called, said we'd handle it."

"That's my Piper." Paul smiled, and she saw how parchment-like the skin around his mouth and at the corners of his eyes had become. "You *can* handle it." He gave her a wink. "Might want to look into the to-do a few years back when Conrad sold his gas station. A couple different families from the county wanted to buy it, the only station in Fulda, and Conrad sold it to a Vietnamese man living in Owensboro who met his asking price. Bad feelings still lingering. And it wasn't so much about the man's nationality, as that he wasn't local."

"Huh. I'll look into that tomorrow." She fixed her dad with a stern look. "And speaking of tomorrow, what time is your appointment? If it's early enough I'll drop you off, go to the autopsy, come back and—"

"I'm perfectly capable of taking myself. If that poison crap makes me too sick, I'll just pull over and puke." His expression hardened. "I want to show you something. Be right back."

Piper drained the second cup while she listened to him shuffling around. She was in Spencer County because of his dire diagnosis. She'd been all set to re-up at Fort Campbell when her dad called her.

21

Non-Hodgkin's, he'd said, advanced. Spots on his liver complicated things.

She'd moved into the apartment over her dad's garage, the one he used to rent out years ago, complete with orange shag carpet and avocado colored appliances. *Dear God, when did they make refrigerators and stoves in that godawful green?* Piper had been back two weeks when he'd suggested she take a run at the sheriff job, that she'd been working as an MP and so had the "law enforcement chops." It paid sixty-two thousand a year, which made his suggestion more inter-esting—and certainly more appealing than working at the Rockport Power Plant. She figured the campaign would be a good distraction for her dad.

She won the primary on the Republican ticket; Oren won the Democratic primary. Then she clinched it on the final fall ballot... shortly before the doctors told Paul Blackwell that his first round of treatments hadn't knocked out the cancer after all; it was spreading.

Piper knew she had traded on her last name, that her father was well-loved in the county, and that it was the Blackwell moniker that people voted for. She had downplayed her age, touted her military record and MP experience, and had made sure the campaign signs said: Vote for Blackwell.

He returned with a newspaper. "I remembered reading this, Punkin. Good thing I hadn't taken the stack to recycling yet." He spread the paper on the table between them, the headline facing Piper. It was dated December 15. He opened the paper to the middle and pointed.

The picture at the top of the section caught her eye: the sleigh. The reporter quoted Conrad.

"I built that twenty-seven years ago, out of oak, planks from a tree I'd cut down in the side yard. Tree'd been hit by lightning and I put it out of its misery. Painted her Boston Brick Red first, then Merlot Red, and some years after that Million Dollar Red, a little too bright, but the color was on sale at the hardware store. Always bought my paint on sale. About five years ago I painted her Lady Bug Red, which was the best red she had been, but the paint was poor quality, and the next couple of winters were a little harder. She got all chipped and faded, sad looking. I was almost ashamed of her. But right before Thanksgiving I repainted her Midnight Gloss Black and added a little gold trim to dress her up. I thought she'd never looked classier. Should've gone with black years ago. Then I added a row of fist-sized antique bells that my grandfather 'back in the day' I guess you'd call it, used to put on the team when riding into town in the winter. Horse bells. Sleigh bells. I'd saved them too long."

The article went on to say that Conrad had kept the bells carefully packed away in the attic for decades because he feared that if he put them out, the snow and ice would ruin the already heavily-cracked leather straps and diminish their value. He said he put them out this year because he'd turned sixty-five the first of December.

"I thought I shouldn't be saving things anymore," Conrad was quoted.

"Why save anything?" Paul mused sadly. "Why collect anything? It's just stuff your kids will have to throw away."

She looked closer at the photograph, her fingernail tapping against the line of bells.

"Curious," she said. "Those sleigh bells? I looked over every inch of that sleigh. It might not mean anything, but I didn't see any antique bells."

FOUR

TUESDAY, JANUARY 2ND

"You know how it goes. Fell in with the wrong crowd in junior high… not that there was much of a crowd, the school being so small. Hell, everything here is tinier than a flea's fart. But whatever was wrong, whatever was a bad influence… back then I managed to find it." Zachary Delaney sat in his father's living room, in a high-backed chair upholstered in a blue floral fabric. "Drugs, alcohol, you name it, I was into it."

Zachary didn't fit the room, which was done in pastels, the woodwork a creamy birch. But then Oren thought Zachary wouldn't fit much of anywhere, a hippie crossed with a biker wannabe, with a dash of St. Vincent DePaul's Center sprinkled in the mix. Greasy long hair, stubble. He was dressed in navy sweatpants that grazed the tops of his raggedy fringed moccasins darkened from melting snow. His long-sleeved green paisley shirt was complemented with an unbuttoned black leather Harley vest that had seen better years. His winter coat, a hunter's orange nylon parka, was draped over the back of the chair. The coat looked new.

Oren had scheduled the meeting for 9 a.m., but Zachary showed up an hour late and shrugged when given the customary, "Sorry for your loss."

Randy stood in the living room doorway and watched.

"You know, I just saw my old man at Christmas," Zachary continued. "I dunno, guess that was five, six days ago."

"Eight," Oren said.

"Yeah, eight. I came up for just the day." He chuckled. "Hell, I only stayed a few hours. Didn't want to put my old man out. He'd wash sheets, towels, everything after someone used 'em just once, just breathed on 'em. He asked me to stay, though, twice asked me. I should've maybe. Hell yeah, I should've. One more thing in my life I messed up, right? Not spending the night, not watching old Christmas movies with him. Shit."

"If he asked you to stay," Oren posed, "the two of you must have—"

"Been getting along better? Yeah, well, we'd been getting along a lot better since I cleaned up my act, stopped with the drugs."

Oren fought the eyebrow that wanted to rise. From Zachary's outward appearance, it didn't look like he'd cleaned up anything.

"He was doing okay, my old man. Said he'd just been to the doctor, blood pressure was better, had repainted his sleigh, had found a new radio controlled airplane kit at a half-price sale and was gonna put it together after the holidays, fly it in the spring. He asked me if I'd come back some weekend and work on it with him. I was gonna. Shit. I should've stayed Christmas night and started on the kit then. Maybe I'll take the plane back to my place and—"

"Not yet." This from Randy. "We'll let you know when the house is clear and you can take some things."

"Yeah, okay, I guess. Doesn't seem right, though. It's my house, not the sheriff's property." Zach chewed on his lower lip. "I should be able to take that plane kit."

Oren had a notebook ready in his back pocket, but he waited. It was clear the boy—he mentally corrected that to *man*, as Zachary was twenty-six—was going to talk. Bringing out a notebook sometimes caused people to shut down.

"When did you leave home?" Randy asked. "Go out on your own?"

"Fourteen. I started smoking pot when I was fourteen, did some poppers then too, blotter once, maybe twice. Dad caught me with

n't've sat home last night drinking and blaming myself. She should've told me."

"Yeah, she should have told you," Oren agreed. That would have been Piper—and her lack of experience showing.

"Got a clue who did it? Why they did it? Arnie didn't know nothing, and Chris didn't know much. Was it about the gas station? It was about the gas station, wasn't it? He'd gotten threats back when he sold it. Fuckin' gas station."

Oren eased off the couch and walked behind it. Randy took the vacated cushion. "Sheriff Blackwell is with the coroner right now," Randy said.

"Fuckin' Sheriff Blackwell. Put me away for a year and a half. Fuck Sheriff Blackwell."

Neither told Zachary that it was a different Sheriff Blackwell.

Randy cleared his throat. "We won't know anything until the autopsy's over. Maybe it'll be a few weeks to determine the cause of death. Test results take a while. When was the last time you saw your father?"

"Told you already. Christmas. Plank Manor was closed, so I drove up."

Randy's voice was even. "Just trying to find out who saw him last. Where were you yesterday?"

"Work. Eight to five. I punch in. We only close for Christmas."

"And the day before that? New Year's Eve?"

"Work, then a party."

Randy twirled his thumbs. "Anyone vouch for you at that party?"

Vouch for me? Zachary mouthed. "Listen… me and my old man, we were finally getting along. I was here Christmas. I should've stayed, he wanted me to stay, but I didn't, had to get back to work the next day, didn't want him washing sheets just 'cause I'd slept on 'em. And now I'm feeling real bad about that. I fuckin' should've let him wash sheets. I should've watched those old movies. Shit."

"This party on New Year's Eve. Where was it?"

Zachary glared. "Mickey's. It's a bar downtown Owensboro."

"Were you there all night?"

"What is it with you, man? Just 'til midnight. Got a ride home with Buzz, our designated driver." Dez-ig-nay-ted was loud and drawn out. "Buzz. Hah! It was Buzz's night not to get buzzed. He was cool with it. His turn. Though I could've drove myself. I wasn't that bad off. Had to be at work the next day, so I didn't go too overboard. I can give you Buzz's phone number if you need to check on me."

"Buzz have a last name?"

"Sharper."

"We'll need that phone number."

Zach thought a moment then rattled off a phone number for Buzz and one for Sydney Nicholson, another friend he'd been drinking with.

"Your father... do you know anyone who wasn't getting along with him?"

Zachary snorted. "No. But somebody wasn't. Obviously. Somebody didn't get along so much they killed him. Maybe some idiot is still pissed off about the gas station. Maybe somebody got tired of the sleigh, pissed because he painted it black this time. You know that Stones song... *Paint it Black?* Maybe my old man shouldn't've painted it black. Can't take the plane kit, huh? Can I take a picture?" He pointed to the array of framed photographs on the mantel. "Can I take one of those?"

"Did your father—" Randy stopped when Zachary held up a hand.

"Saw him at Christmas, I said. Talked to him on the phone at Thanksgiving. Bumped into him last July at the thing in the park." The tears started in earnest now, edging out slow, and Zachary blinked and ran his shirt sleeve across his eyes, not looking as tough as he had minutes ago. "That's all I got. The neighbors know him better than me. *Knew* him better. You should be talking to them, Chris and Joan Hagee across the street. Listen, I gotta be back to work tomorrow. I'm gonna put him at the funeral home in Rockport, the one on Main. Gotta go over there and make some arrangements, pick out a casket. Something nice that I can't afford. Order lots of flowers that I can't afford."

He rubbed at his eyes, composed himself, and looked from Randy to Oren and then to the floor. "I never figured I'd be burying my old man, you know. I figured as much drugs and shit as I was into that I'd OD in some vacant lot in Kentucky and he'd be the one planting me." He sucked in a deep breath and let it out slow. "Listen, I don't have the kind of money to pay for this, a funeral and all, the casket. The cemetery's gonna cost, too, opening a grave. Do you know how much all of this is gonna run? Shit. I should've stayed Christmas night. Shit."

Oren came closer. "Don't know whether your father had a will, Zachary, or what all is involved with it. Maybe you'll inherit money to cover the costs. Maybe he set aside money to handle his final expenses. You need to check with an attorney who handles probate."

"Shit. Prorate?" Zachary stood.

"Pro*bate*."

"Probate. What's probate?"

Oren knew better than to talk about the legalities. If Conrad Delaney had a will the attorney who'd prepared it would have a copy. No will, the estate would be divided up pursuant to statute, probably equally between the two brothers. Creditors could stake claims. It would take time, and Oren had no intention of explaining all of that to Zachary. Besides, it could be considered a misdemeanor for a sheriff's deputy to dispense legal advice. He could give Zachary a house key... but he decided that wasn't happening today.

Zachary reached for his coat. "Find an attorney, huh? Probate. How am I going to pay for a funeral? How am I gonna pay for an attorney? How the hell—" His hands shook and he stuffed them in his pockets. "I suppose I could poke through the Yellow Pages and—"

"Why don't you check with Harlan Cook?" Oren suggested. "Harlan's got an office right across from the courthouse and next to Rudy's Tap. Harlan handles probate."

"Harlan Cook." Zachary nodded. "Thanks, I appreciate that. Harlan Cook."

"Harlan's just down the street from the funeral home," Oren continued. "He's got a green awning over his door. You can't miss it. Harlan Cook."

Zachary sighed, the sound of dead leaves scudding across a sidewalk. "Thanks, really. I appreciate it. Harlan Cook. I'll stop in right now. Good luck catching whoever killed my old man. Harlan Cook."

Oren didn't budge until after Zachary left.

"Harlan Cook?" Randy shook his head. "Harlan *Crook* is the worst attorney in the county, maybe in all of Indiana."

"He is that, isn't he?" Oren suppressed a smile.

"Don't like Zach, do you?"

"I wanted to like him for Conrad's murder."

"Be nice if it was that easy." Randy chuckled. "Zach doesn't have the wherewithal."

Oren stared at the pictures on the fireplace mantel. "No, he does not. But some evil bastard had the wherewithal, and I intend to find out who."

FIVE

Piper hated how death looked. She hated the empty facial expression, the fishbelly white that a man's skin turned when the blood settled. She hated the smell, especially the blood and the rot, and the piss and shit that were expelled. She'd seen a lot of death in Iraq, and over there it was often accompanied by the stench of burned and bombed buildings, sometimes with acrid chemicals thrown in for the real hurl factor. Death was messy and ugly.

It depressed the hell out of her, but she'd learned to handle it; being stationed in Iran with Alpha Company, a lot of downrange assignments had given her an iron resolve. She wouldn't look away from a corpse, no matter how much of it was missing or how long it had been decomposing. She might have hated how bodies looked after life fled, but she respected enough that souls had occupied those shells, and so she would never turn away.

Conrad Delaney was the most pristine corpse she'd had to contend with.

She took the stairs to the hospital basement. The stairwell smelled fusty, like an old closet rather than like the bottle of antiseptic the rest of the building reeked of. She loitered outside the morgue, thinking about her father, who would be undergoing a chemo session right about now, and praying that this go-round would be effective. Forcing her father from her thoughts, she went inside.

The morgue was so much different from a war zone, where the dead were in the domain of the living. Here a wall-sized refrigerator with stainless steel doors dominated, and the living—she and the coroner, Dr. Annie Neufeld—were in the domain of the dead.

Piper saw a form in an open file folder on the counter, the coroner's report partially filled in with pencil. The finished form would be ink and duplicated with computer records. Conrad Reagan Delaney. Height, weight, date of birth, all had numbers. Under cause of death, Dr. Neufeld had listed: Strangulation, C.C.K. The time of death was blank.

Conrad lay on a stainless steel table. A half-sheet across his middle afforded the body some amount of modesty. The table was slightly tilted, and there were troughs on each side to catch fluids. She'd learned on her way over that they'd cranked up the heat in one of the basement rooms yesterday to help Conrad defrost. Maybe this room. It felt overly warm in here, and she slipped off her jacket and laid it on the counter next to the folder.

Dr. Neufeld spoke into a microphone attached to a headset, leaving her hands free. It looked like she was finishing the autopsy rather than just starting.

Piper checked her watch and gave the coroner a businesslike smile. "You're almost done. I thought you told me 10:30."

"I started early. Had trouble sleeping. Probably should have called you, eh?"

Piper figured the coroner was also a friend of Oren's and would have preferred that he'd won the election, would have probably waited on the autopsy... or at least called about the early start.

"Yeah, you should have called."

Dr. Neufeld was covered in scrubs head to foot. Piper could see her eyes well enough. No makeup, dark circles and age creases at the edges; gray-brown hair escaping the cap—much the way she looked yesterday, though her wrappings then had been winter clothing and a heavily-snagged long red scarf. Oren had said she'd retired as a pediatrician half a dozen years ago, citing rising malpractice insurance costs. She'd run for coroner and had held the office for four years, and had won reelection in the fall.

"Oren said you were friends with Mr. Delaney."

"Always hard to do an autopsy on a friend, Sheriff Blackwell. I could've passed this along to someone else here, but didn't want to give Conrad to a stranger." A pause. "Yeah. Conrad and me, we were close. Went to grade school and high school together, lived on the same street in Rockport growing up. He was two years older, but we hung out a lot, went fishing all over in the summer, sometimes Oren tagged along. I went with Conrad to his senior prom." Dr. Neufeld laughed. Piper thought it was a good laugh, sounding like crystal wind chimes. "That was back in the day when I tried very hard to be straight."

Piper had heard that Dr. Neufeld married her longtime companion in the fall of 2014 when the state's same sex marriage ban was struck down. Racy news for Spencer County. She probably wouldn't have been elected to coroner, as conservative as the county was, but apparently no one else wanted the job.

"Pattern bruising on his back. So whoever killed him—man or woman—held him down with a strong knee, enough force to break two ribs, looped a belt around his neck, and strangled him. It was Conrad's belt. The killer threaded it through the jeans afterward. Matches the pattern on the neck." She pointed to the corpse's throat; the marks were so deep they had broken the skin. "You wouldn't have seen the ligature marks last night with the sweater, as high-necked as it was. My guess is Conrad's killer dressed him after he was dead. Cleaned him up a little first, nothing to find under the fingernails. Absolutely nothing." She shook her head, more wisps of gray-brown hair coming lose. "Damn shows like CSI; in reruns for eternity it shows you how to not leave evidence."

Piper pointed at Conrad. "If he was strangled, why do—"

"—a complete autopsy? I don't do anything half-assed, sister. Conrad can talk to us with a complete autopsy. Problem is, his core temperature was twenty-six degrees. Same as the air outside. That means he'd been dead long enough to cool all the way down. It's going to make it tougher to give you a time of death. See, under normal circumstances, a body will lose heat a degree and a half an hour. But outside… winter… throws that out the window. Maybe a body loses three or four degrees, depends on the wind. Even Conrad's deep organs were frozen."

"So you can't give me a time of death."

"I can give you a range, a broader range than I like to hand out, but a helluva lot narrower than someone who didn't know Conrad would give you. Stomach contents were ravioli and green beans and more chocolate brownie than he should have eaten, all barely digested. That smacks of supper to me. So I'd say he was killed right after an evening meal, which he sometimes took as early as four and never later than seven. Without exception, Conrad always reserved his sweets for supper, that's helping me narrow it. Not killed the evening you found him because his core temperature wouldn't have been this low. So the evening before that, making my best guess that Conrad was killed twenty-eight to thirty-three hours before the Hagees spotted him sitting in the sleigh."

Piper took a step back from the table, mulling over why a man who supposedly had no enemies would end up strangled and trussed up amid his Christmas decorations. "Sending anything to the state lab?"

"Sure. But I'm having tox panels run here." Dr. Neufeld removed her headset. "You said you wanted the mug. It's bagged and in the other room." Dr. Neufeld tugged off her cap, and a shock of curly hair spilled down to her shoulders. "I want you to get the son of a bitch that did this. Conrad Delaney was a very nice man. You and Oren, get the son of a bitch that did this very sick thing to my very good friend."

"It is my every intention—" Piper's phone buzzed. She reached in her pocket, saw that it was her chief deputy, and answered it. "I'm in the middle of something, Oren, can't—" She listened for a few minutes. "Randy's riding over with you? Good. I'll meet you there. I'm with the coroner now, so you don't need to call her. I'll tell her. What's the address? In Grandview. Yeah, I can find it. I know where Grandview is. Yeah, Oren, I've got a GPS. I'll head back now. Should take me about fifty minutes, maybe an hour. The roads are all good." She replaced the phone. "We have another death, Dr. Neufeld."

The coroner's eyebrows rose.

"Oren says it's an elderly woman, Abigail Thornbridge. Oren's calling it murder, but he's not seen the body yet and—"

"Another murder? Thornbridge, hmmm, name's familiar. Was she a principal? A teacher?"

Piper shrugged.

"We go a few years without a murder, then you're elected sheriff and bodies drop back-to-back." Dr. Neufeld gave Piper a half-smile, maybe an attempt at humor, then glanced at Conrad's body. "I'm going to be a little bit here. Write down the address, will you? And before you go, let me show you something." Dr. Neufeld strode through a swinging door, pulling off her gloves as she went.

Piper followed, inwardly fuming at the "bodies drop back-to-back" comment. The office was cramped, the right hand wall cement block and all of it painted grade school green. There were two old metal desks—on the closest sat Conrad's red Merry Christmas mug in a plastic bag next to a small folded laptop. On the other desk was a big tower case computer with an out-of-date boxy monitor displaying a surfing turtle screensaver. The rest of the space was filled with file cabinets, a coat rack, and a book shelf overflowing with ring binders. Dr. Neufeld went to the far cabinet and pulled a hobo-style purse from the top drawer. She rummaged inside the purse and retrieved a red envelope, addressed to her, the return address label Conrad Delaney's.

"I'm Jewish, but Conrad sent me a Christmas card every year." She dangled the envelope in front of Piper and replaced the purse in the file drawer. "Open it. Go ahead, open it."

Piper pulled back the envelope flap and took out the card, which was an oversized picture postcard. "Oh my," she said.

The header read: Merry Merry Merry Christmas. The centered picture was of Conrad Delaney seated in his sleigh—wearing the same sweater, right next to St. Nick. The caption: Have a cup of cheer,

Conrad. On the back was a personal handwritten message: *Annie, I wish you and Bebe a warm and wonderful Hanukah, and let's get together at the country club for breakfast sometime. Been too long since I've had a decent Western omelet. I'll bring the booklet for the RC kit I bought. It's a replica WWI fighter, a Fokker DVII, came with a decal set. Found it on sale. I think I'll paint it red. Got some leftover red in the garage. Maybe we can all go "flying" together. Hugs, Conrad*

Except for the color of the sleigh, the Christmas card eerily matched the crime scene—the way Conrad was posed, the clothes, the Santa, but the mug was like one Piper had seen in his kitchen cabinet, not the one he'd been posed with. Whoever killed Conrad Delaney received one of these Christmas cards, or at the very least had seen it in order to arrange him so precisely.

"Can I take this? The Christmas card?"

"Of course. But I want it back. Last thing he sent me, you understand."

"I understand. I'll be careful with it."

"You get the son of a bitch." Dr. Neufeld handed Piper the bag with the mug in it. "You and Oren catch whatever sick son of a bitch would do that to my friend Conrad." She tapped her foot. "I'll tell Oren that myself when I go on your Thornbridge call."

Piper glanced again at the open file folder on the counter on her way out of the morgue. Under cause of death, Dr. Neufeld had listed: Strangulation, C.C.K. Piper figured the initials meant Christmas Card Killer.

SIX

Oren parked to block the end of the driveway and motioned for Randy to get out first. He eased out a moment later and locked the Explorer, glanced up at a battleship gray sky.

Oren usually didn't mind winter, thought it made the world look like a pretty postcard, and the Explorer drove through drifts like they were nonexistent. But this year there'd been way too much of the white stuff; it was making him feel his years.

"Let's take a look," he said. "Get it started. Get it over with. My wife's slow-cooking a pot roast for tonight."

Abigail Thornbridge's place was a Roosevelt Cottage, a term for the WWII-era homes that looked mostly the same—rectangular with a hipped roof and minimal eaves, a one-car attached garage, and a hood over the stoop at the front door. Hers was an olive green wood-frame, the paint so chipped in places it looked like patches of dried fish scales had been glued on. All of the houses on this street in the small town of Grandview were built in the late 30s or early 40s, likely by the same contractor, and most having only slight variations to Abigail's. About half of them still had Christmas decorations, icicle lights strung along the eaves, bows on mailboxes, wreaths, and one had an inflatable snowman that was listing.

Abigail's front door had a silver and red garland bell hooked to a nail.

"Good morning, Sheriff!" Directly across the street a woman with a broom stood in her driveway. She made a show of brushing away some snow, waved to Oren and called out again, "Something wrong at Abigail's, Sheriff?"

Oren didn't correct her on the sheriff part. "Can't talk about it right now, ma'am."

"I haven't seen Abby for a few days. I was starting to worry. I hope she's okay."

"*Kochleffl*," Oren muttered.

"Nosey Parker," Randy hushed. "A busybody, but not busy enough. You'd think if she hadn't seen her elderly neighbor that maybe she should have checked on her."

Grandview was on the southern edge of the county, overlooking the Ohio River, and so named because of its "grand view." It covered a tad less than a square mile and had roughly seven hundred and fifty residents. Oren considered it one of the county's younger towns, with only ten percent of the population sixty-five or older, and the women outnumbered the men by only a handful of percentage points. Abigail had fit into both of those categories.

Abigail's pastor had found "Sweet Abby T" a short while ago, dialed 9-1-1, and the dispatcher put it through to Oren. The pastor had said Abigail rotated with another woman playing the piano at the Baptist church, and that he'd stopped this morning to talk about his upcoming selection of hymns. When she didn't answer the door, he had a bad feeling because "she was getting on in years" and let himself in; it was unlocked.

Oren put on gloves and nudged open the door. One glance into the living room was enough; he agreed with the pastor's judgment that Abigail Thornbridge had been murdered. "After you, Randy."

"Gee, thanks." Randy started recording with the department's handheld video camera.

At first Oren thought Abigail's dog was dead, too. It was a pug, a black one with a mostly white face, suggesting it had some age to it. The dog hadn't moved, curled between Abigail's feet. Finally, he noticed it breathe. It was sound asleep, hadn't heard them come in.

Randy held his free hand over his nose and shuddered. "What's the difference between a serial killer and spree killer?"

Oren read all the law enforcement newsletters the department received, and the terms had been recently redefined. "Mass murderers kill four or more in one location, like Richard Speck or college shooters. Spree killers, they kill two or more, but not in the same spot. Serials, they're the ones who ice folks more methodically, select them, plan the killings in advance, and wait a while between the victims. That'd be your Ted Bundy types."

Randy whistled. "So I wonder what settled into sleepy Spencer County. A spree killer, or a serial?"

"One sick bastard," Oren said. "That's what settled."

Abigail was posed in a high-backed wooden rocking chair in front of her Christmas tree, lights still blinking and setting the silver tinsel to glimmer with motes of red, green, and yellow in a room that was otherwise dark because all the shades were drawn. Old-style ornaments—some made out of popsicle sticks, hung from the lower branches of the tree, while delicate crystal globes and frosted pears hung higher. The angel at the top was crooked and looked like it might topple at any moment; it had the head of a pug dog.

Oren stared at the tree before returning his gaze to the corpse. Where Conrad's body had appeared nearly perfect, Abigail hardly looked human. The hands were almost black, the eyes sunk into the skull, and her head and neck were tinged blue-green. There were large blisters on the exposed skin, and all over she looked swollen like a balloon ready to pop. Fluids had seeped from her mouth and ears, staining the red flannel nightgown that came down past her knees. Thin white curling ribbon held an overlarge red Merry Christmas mug tight in her hands and resting on her lap, accentuating the darkness of her fingers. The mug had liquid in it, tea judging by the teabag tag that dangled over the edge. More ribbons tied her ankles to the rocker's legs, and another length wrapped around and around her neck kept her head up against the back of the chair.

The mug matched the one found with Conrad.

Oren likened it to an image from a horror film. He went to a window, moved the drape, and levered it open, letting in a cold blast of air that he pulled to the bottom of his lungs. The direction the wind was blowing, he thankfully could smell the river and the smoke from a nearby chimney.

"Same guy," Randy said. "Same guy killed her as killed Conrad Delaney. Mug's a signature. Bloody hell."

"You think? I'm not the detective, but I could've told you it was the same guy."

"Was she first? Or was Conrad?"

"*Gornisht helfn.* You're the detective. Detect." Oren took another deep breath and eased back into the room. The pug dog picked up its head, snorted softly, and looked at him.

"And why kill either of them?" Randy continued recording. "Lived alone, Delaney did. Dispatcher said Thornbridge did, too, and according to the pastor she'd always lived alone." He headed toward the kitchen.

"Easier to kill that way," Oren said. "No one else in the house to contend with."

"Money? Robbery?"

Oren knew Randy wasn't really expecting an answer, that he often talked to himself on a scene. "Conrad, he was comfortable, nice house, had money from selling the gas station. But this woman, place rundown around the edges, furniture old. Unless she had a fortune in a mattress, it wasn't money the killer was after."

"Whoever did it thought kindly about the dog, didn't want it to die. Oren, come check this out."

Oren padded into the kitchen. A big casserole dish partially filled with water was on the floor near the sink. Next to it, a ten-pound bag of dog food was on its side, sliced open. That was in addition to small, but empty, plastic bowls on the floor on a blue velvet placemat embroidered with the word "Wrinkles."

"Didn't want the dog to starve," Randy said. "Had it in for the old lady, though. The guy really really really didn't like the old lady."

"Didn't like Conrad, either, but had put food and water out for the cats." Oren opened a window in the kitchen, noticed a few big flakes drifting down, and figured the busybody across the street might get something to sweep. "I'm going to get the kit—"

"—and my camera, please. When I'm done shooting video I'll need the camera for close in, the details."

Grisly details. "Yeah, I'll get your camera, and I'll radio Buck and Marsh and get them out here—"

"Shouldn't we wait to see what Sheriff Blackwell wants to—"

"Need more people, don't we? But not too many people, to process the scene, talk to the neighbors, don't we?"

Randy nodded.

"We don't need to wait on Sheriff Blackwell for that. And I've been doing this stuff for a lot more years than our sheriff has been alive." Oren stuck his head out the kitchen window and breathed deep. In the passing of a few moments the snowfall had increased. *Besides, she might only be sheriff until spring. She couldn't keep the office if she didn't pass the state tests come April. Dear God, don't let her pass the tests.* "I'll get the kit and make the radio call."

The *kochleffl* was still making a show of sweeping the same spot of driveway. In the yards to either side of her, children and their mothers had come out and were playing in the snow, school not resuming until next week. One of the women pulled a cell phone out of her pocket and held it to the side of her face. He smiled sadly as he retrieved the evidence kit from the back of his Explorer. He radioed dispatch and was put through to Buck Hannoh, and then Marsh Eberfield.

Randy was right. Protocol would have been to wait for the sheriff and let her give the orders—since Piper had said she was on her way. But she'd never handled a murder investigation, didn't know which deputies to call in for interviewing the neighbors, and beyond all of that she shouldn't be sheriff.

You should never wait on gathering the clues, he rationalized. Trace materials, fingerprints, fibers... there would be a wealth of them, sift through everything they'd collected, see if anything belonged to someone other than the victim.

Couldn't wait on the sheriff because every hour, every minute that passed, could degrade the value of evidence, more people traipsing through the scene touching things, examining things, possibly disturbing or ruining some crucial piece that would point a finger at—

"—a sick bastard," Oren said as he went back inside the house and caught another look at Sweet Abby T.

Hadn't seen any blood; that was always a good source for evidence. The killer stepping in it, touching it. No spent shell casings, either. Oren had worked a murder about fifteen years ago where a fingerprint on a shell casing led to a disgruntled farmhand who would be eligible for parole in another twenty.

Strangled, like Conrad, the old woman was. Oren wasn't going to look too closely into her sunken eyes to check for signs of petechial hemorrhage. And there was the Merry Christmas mug, a mirror image of the one tied to Conrad's frosty fingers. He placed the kit just inside the door, opened it, and motioned for Randy, who came down a stumpy hallway, closing the screen on the video camera.

"Snowing out, eh?"

Oren leaned out the front door and brushed the snow off his hat and shoulders, then came back in. "Yeah, it's snowing out. Again. Let's get to work."

"See how much we can process before Piper gets here?" Randy pulled out a dusting kit. "You don't like her much do you?"

"Do you?" Oren returned.

"I don't really know her." A handful of minutes later, he announced: "I hear a car."

Oren looked out the door. "Buck and Marsh. That was fast. I'll get them started."

Oren was grateful for the opportunity to go outside again. He stood on the stoop, under the hood, so he wouldn't gather more snow. He pointed to the woman with the broom, then the people in the adjacent yards. "And then get to everyone else in this block. Hit the gawkers first." He gave Buck and Marsh a quick briefing on the scene inside. Several minutes later he was back in the living room with Randy, stomaching the stench and concentrating first on the area around the corpse and the tree. The dog detachedly watched them, but stayed between Abigail's feet.

"The shelter's overcrowded," Randy said, catching Oren stare at the pug. "I rent, can't have pets."

"I have cats. Maybe Sweet Abby T has a church friend who'll take the dog. Maybe the sweeper across the street." Oren heard another car and figured it was either the new sheriff or Dr. Neufeld. He was an old friend of the coroner and hoped it was her. He'd like to talk to Annie before Piper showed up, maybe talk *about* Piper. At least the new sheriff hadn't taken his Explorer. She'd opted for a Taurus.

He growled softly as he looked out the front door. It was Piper, picking her way up the long drive and avoiding the thickest ice patches. "Dr. Neufeld coming?"

"In a little while."

"You might want to stay outside, Sheriff Blackwell. This one's a tummy-twister. Smells like rotten meat in here." Despite his warning, he figured she wouldn't stay out, especially because he'd suggested it. "If you're coming in, Sheriff Blackwell, ditch the snow."

Oren drew back into the house. He heard her brushing on the stoop and then watched as she came in the front door, wanting to catch her reaction to the body. It was rough on him… *Dear God let it be hell on her*; maybe she'd rethink the whole sheriff thing.

"Posed. Premeditated. Evil and sick." Piper's voice was flat. "Same guy that killed Mr. Delaney."

"We'd already figured that out, Sheriff Blackwell." Oren noticed that she breathed shallowly, and he waited for her to turn white, but that didn't happen. He also noticed she'd put on little booties; he had some in the Explorer, but hadn't thought about using them. Randy hadn't either.

"I see you have deputies going door to door."

"That'd be Marsh and Buck."

"Good."

"Randy and I started here, and—"

Randy interrupted. "I recorded the whole house first, Boss, did a walk-through, the inside. I'll get the outside when we're done with—"

"What can you tell me about her?"

Randy finished lifting fingerprints off a coffee table. "Abigail Marie Thornbridge, eighty-two, never married, worked as an elementary school teacher in Rockport, later a principal, retired at sixty-four and moved here. Apparently was looking to move again." He nodded at the coffee table, where a few retirement home brochures were fanned out. "Parents dead, of course, a sister in California older than her, a pair of nieces in Nevada. That's all we got so far from dispatch. She—"

"Was she a friend of Mr. Delaney's?" Piper edged past them and squatted in front of the rocking chair. The pug swiveled its head up and made a *wuffling* sound.

"Don't know that yet," Oren said. He was surprised she got that close to the corpse, had expected her to toss her cookies. "Need to process the scene first, and—"

"How good's your vet?" She stood and headed to the kitchen.

"Excuse me?" Oren watched her stop at the sliced open dog food bag.

"Definitely check that for fingerprints," she said, "and the water dish."

"My vet—" he prompted.

"Wrinkles," she pointed at the velvet placemat. "Wrinkles has some blood on his chin. Might be his blood. Maybe bit his tongue or something. Might be Miss Thornbridge's. Might be the killer's; maybe Wrinkles got a piece of him. The vet can check the dog's teeth, nails. Give him some evidence bags and stay until it's collected."

Oren hadn't noticed the blood on the dog, but he looked now and spotted it. "An old dog," he said. "Shelter's full, and ain't nobody going to adopt an old dog like this."

"Maybe one of the neighbors will take him." She returned to the living room with a leash she'd found on a hook by the back door. "There's dog poop in the kitchen corner."

"Three day's worth of poop, I'd guess. Maybe four." This from Randy. "A body in this condition... I'd say it's been sitting here that long."

"You're probably right," Piper admitted. She stepped to a low small curio cabinet. On top of it was a stack of Christmas cards tied with a length of white curling ribbon. Softer, "I wonder if I'm right."

Instantly curious, Oren watched Piper gently pull the ribbon off the stack and look through the cards.

"Our victims knew each other," she told him, holding up a picture card of Conrad in the sleigh, just like the one Dr. Neufeld had given her. "Oren sent these out in December." She read the note on the back. *"Abby T: I hope this winter finds you well and pleasantly busy. I really should drive over to your church and hear you play. Haven't been to church in quite a while. Your congregation would think the Nile had flowed backwards if I walked in. Maybe I could sit in the back and no one would notice. Hey! Thanks for recommending that roofer. He did a great job on my house, I even had him use the same color of shingles. A real jack-of-all trades, and great prices, he also put in a new kitchen floor for me. Small world, he used to go to high school with my boy Anthony. I thought he'd looked familiar. I kept his business card. Might have him upgrade the master bathroom this spring if he gives me a good quote. I'll do the painting, though. I like to paint. I'll try to be better about staying in touch. I should do more than this one-letter-a-year. Oh, and speaking of paint, I painted my sleigh black this Thanksgiving, just not in time for my Christmas card shot. It looks super sharp. But you'll see the black paint job on next year's card—already had the photo taken. Have a Merry Merry Merry Merry Christmas. Hugs, Conrad."*

Oren stared at the picture, Conrad in the sleigh, a near mirror image of the Delaney murder scene. "What the hell?" And why did Piper get to play connect the dots with a Christmas card? She didn't need to be poking into the investigation; he would have found the connection with the card. Why the hell didn't she spend her time writing traffic tickets? This was his investigation—his and Randy's.

"Randy, did you bag up the cards at Conrad's?"

His voice came from the kitchen. "No, Boss, hadn't seen a reason to. But I can."

"I'm going out to the Delaney house, so I'll get them." She looked at Oren. "After I stop and get some gas. When you're done here, and done at the vet's, meet me at the office. I had a whiteboard delivered, figured we needed one for our C.C.K."

"What the hell's a C.C.K.?" Oren asked.

"Ask your friend Annie Neufeld when she shows up," Piper returned as she headed for the front door. Oren watched her remove the booties, square her shoulders, and step outside. "Dr. Neufeld coined the term C.C.K. for the twisted soul playing some deadly game in my county."

Piper left and closed the door harder than necessary.

Oren hadn't liked the *my* county part.

"What'd the sheriff say?" Randy poked his head up.

"She said one very sick bastard has moved into sleepy Spencer County."

SEVEN

She'd picked the navy blue Taurus; it was too large for her liking, but it was smaller than the Explorers and the Crown Vics. She'd nearly taken Oren's Explorer though; she knew he coveted it and that it was a status symbol because it was the newest vehicle in the fleet. And it would spite him, might be that proverbial last straw that caused him to hand in his resignation. Would that be a bad thing? Better than her firing him. She didn't like working with him because of his verbal jabs and condescending glares, didn't like him period, but she needed him—at least until she was more familiar with the department and the county. And at least until this murder —*murders*—were solved.

So she'd picked the Taurus.

Piper didn't like big cars because the gas mileage was sad, they didn't maneuver as well, and it felt like too much metal, bringing to mind her days in Iran of riding in Hummers and LAVs, Light Armored Vehicles. Before leaving Fort Campbell, she bought an apple red Smart Fortwo, a "suggestion of a car" her dad called it. It was a three-cylinder turbo-charged five-speed manual with an oatmeal hued interior, and it registered every dip and rocky patch in the road. Piper didn't mind that it wasn't the smoothest of rides; it averaged thirty-five miles a gallon and was effortless to parallel park. The Taurus? She'd find out in a handful of minutes what kind of mileage she was getting. The car'd had a full tank when she headed to Evansville this morning, and though she didn't *have* to fill it up just yet, there was a gas station she needed to visit.

Piper pulled into Phan's Quick Stop in Fulda. There were four pumps under an aluminum canopy that provided limited shelter from the snow but did nothing to cut the wind. Two pumps offered regular and premium, the other two were diesel with nozzles set higher up, probably to accommodate farm vehicles. She flipped the pump for regular and held her breath while the gas flowed.

The snowfall had increased since she'd left Miss Thornbridge's house, and the dispatcher told her five inches were expected. Why did this winter have to break with Southern Indiana tradition? Why did it have to dump so much snow and threaten to rewrite the record books? Why did Oren have to be such an ass? Fort Campbell would be warmer, less snow probably, certainly, her life more comfortable there, and no Oren. Her life more comfortable even if she'd be spending it on another tour in the Middle East. Military life suited Piper, the routine of it, the rigorousness, and the friends she'd gained there. She'd seriously thought about making a career of it, knew she could climb the ranks. There was a routine to the Spencer Counter Sheriff's Department, too, and so far all of it involved tragedy.

"What the hell am I doing?" she said as she replaced the nozzle in the pump and screwed the gas cap tight. "What the holy hell am I doing here?" Piper didn't mean the gas station. She parked and went inside.

It was near to immaculate and pleasantly warm, and it was reminiscent of her favorite 7-Eleven right off the base. She walked up and down the four tight aisles offering snacks, bread, cereal, coffee, canned fruits and vegetables, and assorted home supplies. A display at the front was filled with ice scrapers, snow shovels, caps, gloves, and bagged salt; another held a scattering of holiday items marked After Christmas Sale. One wall consisted of a series of glass refrigerator doors, and behind them an assortment of soft drinks, juices, milk cartons, lunch meats, eggs, butter, and cheese. A smaller section was a freezer stocked with pizza, egg rolls, breakfast sausage, ice cream, and boxed chicken breasts. Piper considered it a good stock, reasonable prices from what she could see, and offering Fulda residents an alternative to driving to Rockport for groceries. But the choices were limited. Cheerios, but no corn flakes.

An area roughly a dozen feet square beyond the two restroom doors had three round tables, each with four chairs. A large, bright menu hung on the wall behind the small counter, and through a doorway behind the counter she spied a tiny kitchen. So a gas station/grocery/restaurant, all in roughly three thousand square feet. Piper stepped up and nodded to the man at the cash register. He was Asian, Vietnamese according to her dad.

"You must be Phan," Piper said, as she reached into her pocket for her wallet. "I'll need a receipt." The Taurus appeared to be getting twenty-three miles to a gallon.

"Nang," the man said, taking her credit card and running it through the machine. "Phan is my family name."

"Nice to meet you, Nang." Piper looked at the menu, twelve items on it plus a "today's special." It was well past lunch, but she hadn't eaten. And though she'd told Oren they'd compare notes at the department, she knew he wouldn't get there until later. She could spare the time to eat. The spices swirling in the air were making her mouth water.

"You hungry, Sheriff?" She noticed he had no trace of an accent, beyond the Midwestern one people in the area spewed.

"Yes, very."

Piper saw that everything was Vietnamese fare—except the drinks.

"I'll take the Crab Meat Sui Mai and Dan Dan Noodles Chen. That's for here. To go, and so I don't need that hot, I'd like... what is your Tears in Eyes?"

"Spicy mung bean noodle soup. It is good. I make everything fresh."

"A large cup of that and an order of pork dumplings in chili oil." Her father liked spicy food, and she intended to stop home and check on him before returning to the department, bring the food as a treat, hoping the chemo treatment left him with an appetite. "Oh, and a large cup of coffee, that's for here, too."

"Take a seat, please, and I will bring it to you."

Piper picked the table that afforded the best view of the store and the pumps outside. There were decorative cardstock placemats with a January calendar on one half and a picture of a striking pagoda-style temple on the other with big red flowers growing around it, making her wish for warmer days. A website was listed beneath the flowers, and she raised an eyebrow. "Maybe—"

A bell jangled and she looked up as a burly man in lightweight jacket came in, stomping snow off his shoes.

"Nang, I'm at the diesel," he announced. "Got my truck out today. This weather!"

Piper thought that an obvious statement, about the diesel, as his was the only vehicle she saw out the front window.

"Fifty-two," Nang returned.

The burly man chuckled. "Yeah, I always have to finesse the pump so I owe an even amount, don't like to keep coins in my pocket. They make holes." He pointed to a small display on the counter. "And give me eight dollars worth of scratch-offs, the ones with the bluebirds on them."

Piper watched the snow come down; a few minutes later noting another person come in for gas, a man in an oversized Indianapolis Colts jacket and stocking cap. He looked familiar, probably the Colts' fan that had been standing in Conrad's driveway, a Hagee New Year's Eve guest who lived around here. He looked her way and nodded, paid for his gas, and bought a lottery ticket.

Where's my lunch? She touched the cell phone in her pocket, could call Oren and see if he and Randy had found anything especially interesting at Miss Thornbridge's house, could call her dad and see how he was doing, could just watch the snow fall and wonder what she'd be doing if she'd stayed in the Army and how much longer she'd have to twiddle her thumbs until her meal arrived. *Where's my coffee?*

More to the point: *What the hell am I doing here?*

"Here you go." Nang carried a tray and sat it on the table, and then took off a plate brimming with crabmeat and noodles and placed it in front of her. He arranged the silverware—metal, not plastic—and retreated, coming back with a tall Styrofoam cup and pouring coffee in it. "Cream? Sugar?"

Piper raised an eyebrow. She was being treated as if this were a restaurant, not a gas station's convenience store. "Black's fine."

"I voted for you," he said after he returned to behind the counter. "Thought the county could use some new blood." He adjusted the display of lottery tickets, and then picked up a rag and wiped the counter.

"Thanks." Piper took a sip of the coffee, hot, not as good as her dad's, but passable. Better than the liquid sludge in the department office. She speared into a piece of crab and started eating. "This is very good."

"Everything I make is very good." Nang came back to the table with a cup of coffee for himself, pulled out the chair opposite her and sat without invitation. "Did you find out who killed Conrad Delaney?"

Piper swallowed hard. That was blunt. "No." She took a bite of the noodles, finding them also delicious. "In fact, I stopped in to talk to you about Mr. Delaney."

"Two other deputies talked to me yesterday."

"That's fine. But I wanted to talk to you, too." Another swallow of coffee. "If you have a few minutes."

"Sure." He rested his cup in the middle of the pagoda on his placemat, leaned forward, and steepled his fingers. "I bought this place from Conrad. It used to be called Conrad's Quick Stop and Go."

"You seem young to own a business."

"You seem young to be a sheriff," he countered.

"Touché. Were you born here, Nang?"

"In Owensboro. First generation American. My parents moved here from Vinh. My father was hired as the associate dean of electrical technology at the community college. He is still there, full dean now, but my parents are divorced."

"A lot of that going around," Piper said softly. "So Owensboro isn't all that big, but next to tiny Fulda—"

"The air smells good here, in Fulda. It is a place with history, dates to the 1840s I'd read, founded by German immigrants, and named for a city in Germany more than twelve hundred years old—where missionaries joined with Charlemagne's armies to spread the Christian word."

"I didn't know that about Fulda," Piper confessed. "And I don't know the history of most of the tiny towns around here."

"I like tiny towns, this one especially. Very quiet, clean, lots of trees, and most of the people are very friendly."

"But not all of the people," Piper said after another bite of crab. "Word is some were upset you bought this place."

"A few, I suppose. I think they got over it."

A bell rang announcing another customer. Nang got up but left his coffee cup. "Busy day," he said. "All this snow, people fill up their tanks."

The shopper was a stoop-shouldered man in a coat two sizes too big. He paid for gas and a snow shovel, turned around and fished in his pocket for a dollar and bought a scratch-off ticket. "For Mary," he said. "She likes to waste money on these things. Self-taxation at work, huh?"

Piper continued to eat, decided she would come back and try some of the other dishes, maybe bring her father.

Nang returned and sat. "A few people," he repeated. "Yes, a few people, I suppose, were upset I bought this business. One man who'd wanted this shop told Conrad he should not sell to a foreigner. But Conrad, he pointed out that I am an American. Then the man said it was because I was not local. But I am local now."

A silence settled between them for several minutes, Piper eating, the purr from the bank of refrigerators providing white noise, Nang sipping his own coffee.

"It was summer five years ago, and I was driving back from the winery near the Monastery," Nang said. "I had bought a case of peach wine for my mother, her birthday. She likes wine, maybe likes it too much. I needed gas and so I stopped here. There was a 'for sale' sign in the window. Mr. Delaney was behind the counter, and I paid him for the gas, bought a carton of chocolate milk to drink on the drive home. I lived in Owensboro then, with my mother. I also bought a lottery ticket." Nang paused and finished his coffee, got up and brought the pot to the table, pouring first for Piper, and then refilling his cup. He folded a towel and set the pot on it, careful not to let the heat mar the vinyl tabletop.

"I wasn't doing anything with my life," he continued. "Turned twenty-one, had just graduated from Owensboro Community College with an automotive technician degree, living at home. Hadn't found a real job yet, was flipping burgers, figuring out what I should do, where I should go."

Piper swallowed the last bite of crab and took a long drink of the coffee. "So you bought this place? Why? At twenty-one?"

Nang's smiled big. "That lottery ticket I bought. I won. A million and a half. I figured it was a sign, God telling me what to do with my life. Mr. Delaney wanted eight hundred and fifty thousand for this place, and that's what I had after taxes... and after I bought my mom a new couch and recliner and replaced her microwave. I figured my buying that ticket and winning was a sign."

Piper laughed.

"You shine," he said. "You have a good laugh."

"So you're twenty-six years old now, and you own a convenience store."

"A convenience store *and* a gas station." Nang tapped his coffee cup. "And I will add a big garage bay in the spring, where I will repair cars, use my degree."

"Twenty-six."

"And you are twenty-three, according to the older deputy who talked to me yesterday."

Piper *really* didn't like Oren. "So, like I said, word is some people around here weren't pleased you bought Mr. Delaney's station."

"Conrad, I am so sorry that good man is dead. Conrad, he was a friend. He said three people made him offers for this place, but said he would not take so little for something he put so much time and work in. I did not..." Nang paused as if looking for the word. "—haggle. I paid exactly what he asked."

"The mobile home back there—" Piper gestured behind her.

"—I bought that with a loan, and since paid it off. I live there. Maybe someday I will have a house built instead. But for now the mobile home is big enough."

She let out a low whistle. "Impressive, Nang."

"Conrad... Mr. Delaney... he would come here every week, order lunch, a different day every week because the specials changed, and he always got the special. I never charged him. He would argue with me about that, but I wouldn't take his money. He was a very nice man."

"Someone didn't like him," Piper said softly.

"You find out who killed Conrad Delaney."

And Abigail Thornbridge, Piper thought.

"I will bag your to-go order, Sheriff."

"Piper," she said.

"Piper," he returned. "A fun name. You shine."

She stood at the counter, staring out the window while he rang up her bill. *Five inches, wonderful*. It looked like it was snowing even harder now. She added a window scraper to her order, as the one in the Taurus had a short, cracked handle. Briefly, she thought about buying a lottery ticket, but dismissed that notion.

"So you were born in Kentucky, and in teeny tiny Fulda you serve only Vietnamese food. Not a hot dog on your menu."

"Hot dogs are bad for you." He smiled wide again. "I like Vietnamese food, and I have no competition. I am the only place in all of Spencer County that serves Vietnamese food. Sometimes I cater if I have enough notice. I also like Italian fare, but I limit my menu as it makes things more manageable."

"Sounds like you're not a fan of free time."

"I have two part-time employees, three in the summer. I want more time off then because I am restoring a car, and it is best to do that in good weather."

"So you fix cars, run a business, and cook."

"Of all those things, I probably cook the best. Why don't you come back and I will prepare Bún bò Huế and Bún Thịt Nướng, they go well with pear wine. I will make sure I have free time to do that."

"I have no idea what those things are, but they sound delicious."

"Everything I cook is delicious. Friday?"

Piper stared. Had he just asked her for a date? "This murder investigation keeps me busy—"

"But you have to eat."

"Friday. Sure." Had she just accepted?

"Six," he returned. "I don't like to eat late, have to get up early and open this."

"Six. Sure."

A white Volkswagen beetle pulled up as she was leaving. It looked like a rolling mound of snow. Piper brushed off the Taurus, cranked the heater, and headed to the Delaney house to pick up all of Conrad's Christmas cards and poke around one more time.

What the hell am I doing here?

EIGHT

Piper thought, perhaps, she'd found Conrad Delaney's Christmas card list. Not a list, actually, but the names of local folks he likely sent Christmas cards to. Searching through a desk drawer—again—and she kicked herself for not noticing this before, she saw that the county phonebook had post-it strip notes affixed to pages. The notes didn't extend outside the book, and so she understood why Randy hadn't noticed it either. The top margin of each note served as an underline to the name, address, and phone number above it. A. Neufeld had a bright lime green tab under it. Christopher P. Hagee had an electric orange tab. Carefully flipping through the book, she saw other post-its. Rough guess, forty names were tagged. There were other phonebooks—for Evansville, Owensboro, and Henderson, but those lacked post-it notes, or any notation for that matter.

She bagged the phone book, quite pleased with herself, called the department, and learned Oren and Randy were still at the Thornbridge house. So she spent another hour looking around, mostly trying to get a better feel for Conrad. A glance at her watch told her it was 5 p.m.

Gotta head back, check on Dad, bring him dinner. After a chemo session, he usually didn't have the energy to cook.

It looked later than that, the sky so full of clouds and dark like wood ashes. Looked like evening. Another glance at her watch: 5:05. She'd call her dad on the way, tell him not to fix anything, she had a treat. One more sweep through the house.

By the time she pulled out of the Delaney driveway the snow had worsened, becoming a veritable blizzard. The Christmas cards—she couldn't find the envelopes they'd come in, no doubt tossed by Conrad—were properly stored in evidence bags and resting on the seat beside her with the bagged phonebook. Five inches, the dispatcher initially had said of the forecast. Typically, Southern Indiana saw about a foot of snow total during winter, four or five inches of that coming over the course of January—not in one day. There were exceptions, this winter certainly—so far more than double the average—and Piper recalled a ten-inch overnight dump during January 2014. The record was twenty inches in one whollop a century back. Global warming? El Niño, or dumb luck? Her dumb luck.

"Teegan?" Piper contacted the dispatcher. "The forecast updated yet?"

Static, then, "Supposed to quit about eight or nine. They're calling for a foot now, Weight Watchers meetings, flyball, and Catholic bingo cancelled, and some more will come in. Maybe we can set a new record. Good thing schools haven't started back up, huh? Oh, and Randy and Oren radioed, said they're on the way. Randy anyway. Oren's going to some vet in Santa Claus who's staying open late. Buck's Vic slipped off the road and is getting towed."

"Wonderful. Hey, has anybody had any luck finding Anthony Delaney?"

"Nope. Nada. Zippo. Coroner's gonna release Conrad's body tomorrow to the Rockport funeral home. I guess his son Zachary has set something up." A pause. "Any suspects, Sheriff Blackwell?"

"Not yet. Talk to you later, Teegan."

So far, she and Oren had nada... zippo... on the suspect list, though maybe her chief deputy had some names and wasn't about to share them yet, keeping the investigation firmly in his age-spotted hands.

A glance at the bags of Christmas cards. Maybe she wouldn't have nada after she gave the cards a closer look—she'd found one from Abigail to Conrad, and it was unsettling. While she had the phonebook, and certainly that would help, what she really wanted was Conrad's Christmas card *list*, and no one had found such a beast at the Delaney house. He had to have a list, as precise as he'd been, as *Better Homes and Gardens* as his place was. Hadn't found those antique sleigh bells either. Maybe Randy had found a list at Abigail's.

A plow had been this way a while ago, but it should make another pass, Piper thought as she left Fulda, driving past Phan's Quick Mart and heading south on 545. She was the only soul on the road, everyone else wisely staying off it, at least around here. She'd pick up 66 near Troy, another dinkburg, and take it back into Grandview, stop by the Thornbridge house for another ogle, then keep going. Rockport was a straight shot out of Grandview where 45 led off 66, drop the food off and check on her dad, grab a change of clothes, and go back to the office. It might be an all-nighter.

Piper could smell the spicy takeout, nestled on the passenger side floorboard. Friday dinner at Nang's? She wondered if he meant his trailer or the Quick Stop, and she wondered if she'd actually take him up on it. Was it a date? Or was it just a friendly invitation to dinner? Easy to find an excuse to cancel in any event. But it could be a good way to learn more about Mr. Delaney; it seemed the two had become friends. Could also be a good way to gain tidbits about Fulda's residents, maybe find a suspect or two. *Was* it a date? Nang was good looking, clean-cut, polite, near her age, and—

The Taurus lurched and Piper grabbed the wheel and pumped the brake. She looked up into the rearview mirror and saw snow and the ghostly image of a big pickup, no lights on. When the truck struck the Taurus again, hard enough to make her swerve, she knew it wasn't an accident. The driver was trying to run her off the road. Some idiot with a hate for law enforcement, or maybe just some idiot playing in the snow. Couldn't get the license plate number; he was riding so close she couldn't see a plate.

Piper's throat tightened as she thumbed the radio and pressed on the gas. Not good conditions to drive fast, but the pickup outweighed her Taurus by at least a ton, and so she wanted to put some space between them, consider her options.

"Teegan... Teegan."

Static came back.

"Shit. Shit. Shit." Piper slammed the palm of her hand against the wheel and took option #1, flipped on the lights and siren; that might get the truck driver to call this quits. Again she focused on the rearview mirror, trying desperately to make out something... color of the truck, something about the driver... the license plate was a hopeless notion. Two pickup trucks had pulled into Phan's while she was there, a blue and a silver. But everything was gray and indistinct in the rearview, the snow coming so fast and angry that the world looked like an impressionist watercolor. Couldn't even tell if the driver was a man or a woman, just the vague shape of a head and shoulders.

Hard to keep the car straight, the road slick, the temperature hovering in that murky area to make the pavement icy.

"Teegan! Answer! Shit." Her cell was in her pocket. One hand on the wheel, she reached for it.

The cell phone flew out of her hand when the truck struck her a third time and she felt the front right tire drop off the road. Piper panicked and jerked the wheel too far to the left too fast, and though the Taurus came back up, it spun sideways, and the truck plowed into her, clipping the passenger side door panel and spinning her some more. A blur of maroon shot past, snow spraying up to cover her side windows. Maroon? The color of the truck? She pumped the brake as the car continued to turn, the right rear tire levering off the road this time. Now she was pointed in the opposite direction, back toward Fulda. A glance in the rearview mirror, the truck was on her, had somehow turned around.

Piper fought the panic. She'd been through worse, a far different clime, far away, riding in an LAV in Iran, heading out on a downrange mission, unexpected shelling. Dirt and sand flying, the vehicle quivering from a near-impact, a rocket-launched grenade passing too close overhead. She made it through that, and other close calls. Her adversary here was a lone nutso driver in a pickup truck, no mortars or landmines to contend with.

Easy, right? "Easy," she said, as she pressed the gas pedal down farther.

Just the awful snow to contend with... and someone hell-bent on sending her off the road. Trying to kill her? Why would someone try to kill her? She had no enemies here. No *real* enemies when she thought of Oren.

She slammed on the gas pedal, tires spinning, heard the engine grumble and a spray of gravel from the shoulder struck the wheel well. The Taurus surged forward, slipping, cutting across both lanes before she could even it out. Another strike and the car shimmied, starting to spin again, but Piper adjusted to keep it straight. If the roads were good, visibility good, she'd be the aggressor, would find a way to turn around and pursue whoever was—

Once more the truck slammed her. Warning lights blinked on the dash panel. She heard a *thunk,* and looking out the side mirror saw her rear bumper fall off, the pickup weaving to miss it. Thank God the airbag hadn't deployed, or she'd be even more screwed. Thank God she wasn't in her "suggestion of a car," as the Smart Fortwo would be squashed like a stomped soda can.

"Teegan! Teegan!"

Still static.

The pickup roared close and nudged her, trying to push her off the road near a telephone pole. And then what? If he got her off the road, then what? Would he drive away? Or would he come after her... provided she was still breathing?

This had to be related to the Delaney murder, she'd just come from the house.

What had she uncovered at the Delaney house that would cause this?

Piper pressed on the gas, and then the brake, turning the wheel and trying for a controlled spin, something that would take her in the opposite direction once more, let her be the antagonist even though the truck was bigger. She wasn't going to lose to the madman! She wanted him... to know who he was, why he was doing this, wanted to shove his wrists into a set of handcuffs and push him into the back-seat of her wounded Taurus, get the hell back to Rockport and throw his nasty ass in a cell.

He could well be Conrad Delaney's murderer.

But the slippery road and the Taurus disagreed with her plan, and she instead headed across the other lane and toward what she guessed was likely a pretty steep ditch. There was a deep drop off all along this section of road, she just couldn't see it—couldn't see hardly anything —because of the damnable snow. The few lights she saw ahead and off to the side were probably houses or farms, and they looked ethereal and ghostly, fireflies in the mist. She somehow managed to coax the Taurus the other way, straighten it again, but it fought her, like the wheels were out of alignment. *Should've taken Oren's Explorer, a better match for dealing with the pickup and this snowy morass.*

"Holy—"

The pickup was full-sized and then some. She could tell that now because it had finally turned its lights on. It rammed her again, and through the rearview she saw her Taurus' trunk pop up, so now that mirror was useless and she couldn't see her attacker. She pressed on the gas, the Taurus punching through a drift of snow, dropping off past the shoulder and then coming all the way back on the road, gaining a few lengths on the pickup, according to a glance out the side mirror. At least she could see a piece of the truck that way. Couldn't see any details, everything still gray. The pickup looked gray. She'd try the radio again.

"Teegan! Teegan!"

"I'm back, Sheriff, what do—"

"I need backup, Teegan! I'm on 545 somewhere south of—" This time the truck hit her with so much force both vehicles went off the road. She briefly had the sensation of flying and then all the sound in the world went away.

Maybe this was death, an absolute nothingness, swirls of gray and white.

But the sound returned with a roar of protesting engine and crumpling metal, the Taurus' siren still wailing. The landing was rough.

Piper had been right; it was a long, deep ditch. And everything seemed to happen at once. She had the sensation of the car barreling down the embankment, though her feet were pressed on the brake. Then it listed and she had the image of a pinball caroming along the slope, the brakes worthless, steering impossible, vision a solid sheet of gray-white with flashes of blue from her lights reflecting. A crack and a snap, the car had hit something and she bit her tongue. The airbag popped—she was surprised it hadn't before now—and pressed her against the seat, smothering her. It felt like she was in a carnival ride from hell. The Taurus flipped. Once, twice, landing on its roof. The dome light came on, her siren's wail died, and the car made a chugging sound, gasping its last.

Don't panic! Don't ever panic! The military had taught her resolve and patience and how to swallow her fear.

Upside down, Piper fumbled in her coat pocket, gloved fingers finding a pocketknife, pulling it out. Couldn't open the blade, the material of the gloves too thick to find the latch. It took some maneuvering, getting her hand between the airbag and her face, all the while listening. The Taurus made popping and wheezing sounds, the radio crackled. Faintly, she heard, "Sheriff? Sheriff Blackwell?"

She bit the glove and wiggled her hand until it was free, then fumbled around near her face until she felt the trapped pocketknife. A little more wiggling and she had the knife, the blade open and punching at the airbag. It should have deflated on its own, but that mechanism had failed. Piper closed her eyes and turned her head to the side. She smelled something chemical, some spew from the airbag, and there was the strong odor of Vietnamese soup and chili oil, the takeout splattered over the evidence bags, which were now resting against the roof below her. She snaked an arm out and turned off the car.

"Sherriff Blackwell?"

Nothing felt broken, but everything felt sore. Her head pounded.

The seatbelt was jammed, so she used the knife to cut the strap, bracing herself with her free arm and her legs so she wouldn't drop on her head. A little twisting and she crouched on the roof, thumbing the radio.

"Teegan, I really need that backup." She recited a short version while she grabbed up the evidence bags and despite the chili oil, shoved them inside her coat. Couldn't find her cell phone, and wasn't going to waste time looking for it. For once Piper was glad she was short. Cramped under the driver's seat, she worked the knife to lever the window open and crawl out.

The Taurus' headlights were still on, stabbing crooked beams across an uneven field where cornstalk remnants poked up stubbornly through low drifts.

The snow came sideways, like looking out the viewport of the *Millennium Falcon* when Solo put it into hyperspace in *Star Wars*. Piper couldn't see the pickup, but she barely saw tracks indicating the driver had managed to pull back onto the road and avoid her fate.

She snaked back through the window and thumbed the radio. "Put a BOLO out on a big pickup, possibly maroon, maybe gray with maroon trim, front end damage."

"Sheriff Blackwell, are you all right? Do you want an ambulance?"

"No." Piper meant that on both counts. "No ambulance."

She crawled back outside and pulled herself up by grabbing a door handle She tasted blood; her lip was split, and when her fingers brushed her nose they came away bloody. She'd been injured worse, took a bullet in the shoulder on her first tour, but she didn't recall that hurting as badly as this. Nothing broken, she worked her arms and legs to be certain. Well, maybe her nose; that was probably broken.

The radio crackled, Teegan saying she'd found Piper by pinging her cell phone, was directing a deputy there, said that maybe the department Taurus should have GPS to make things easier. Again Teegan asked if Piper wanted an ambulance.

Piper wasn't going to crawl back into the car to answer. Instead, she slowly trudged up the embankment, slipping and falling, getting up, falling, and clawing her way until she felt gravel beneath her knees and the ground leveled out. She'd found the shoulder. Crawling was easier, getting back on her feet was a serious chore. When she managed it, she spread her legs for balance as a wave of dizziness hit.

So cold.

So pissed.

Piper had a murder suspect now, someone who drove a big pickup, maybe maroon, maybe gray. It would be damaged. They'd check all the area body shops. Maybe Nang knew who drove a big pickup with those colors.

"You get the son of a bitch," Dr. Neufeld had told Piper this morning. "You and Oren catch whatever sick son of a bitch would do that to my friend Conrad."

And had also tried to kill her.

NINE

The sweatshirt was too large, but she pushed the cuffs up past her elbows. It was royal blue, faded in places, and had a vinyl Superman "S" on the chest that was shot through with spidery cracks like the face of an antique porcelain doll. The sweatpants were a different shade of blue and also voluminous; she'd used shoe strings tied above her knees to gather the legs so she wouldn't trip. But the borrowed outfit was warm and dry and did not smell like chili oil. She was thankful Randy'd had it in his locker and loaned it to her.

She sat at her desk, turned to the side, and Randy hovered with a first aid kit. He'd been the deputy who picked her up and said he was taking her to the hospital across the river in Owensboro. She'd declined. Too much to do, not hurt all that bad, nothing broken except her pride and her nose, the latter of which he'd set with a painful jerk —he'd clearly performed that trick before. She'd washed up in the restroom.

"No concussion, Boss," Randy pronounced after shining a flashlight in her eyes. "But I really think—"

"I'll go to a doctor tomorrow if I need to." While Spencer County lacked hospitals, there were several physicians in Rockport and Santa

Claus, including a cheery-looking place called Santa's Med Center. "But now I need to work."

"And call your father." This came from Teegan, who poked her head around the corner. Teegan was a dispatcher/secretary who resembled Morticia Addams because of her pale complexion, straight black hair, and heavy eyeliner. "Paul called twice, was listening to the scanner and—"

Piper groaned.

"I told him you were okay. You are okay, aren't you, Sheriff Blackwell?"

"Fine. I'm fine, Teegan." But she didn't feel fine. She felt like an old tennis shoe clunking around inside a clothes dryer. She felt pretty awful, and she was getting a hell of a bruise from where the shoulder strap of the seatbelt had held her.

Piper closed her eyes while Randy cleaned up her face and lip, wiped the dried blood from under her nose. On the drive here he'd given her a rundown on the evidence collected from Abigail Thornbridge's house, what they would send to the state lab, and the Christmas cards and address book that was bagged and in the other room.

"Oren's going home after he's done at the vet's, probably done by now, actually. He'll be in early tomorrow. Dr. Neufeld is scheduling the Thornbridge autopsy, but doesn't have a time yet." Randy stood back and nodded. "Better."

"Thanks. How 'bout you go home, too," Piper suggested. "It's almost seven, been a long day."

"I'll give you a ride."

"I'm gonna be here a while." She shook her head and winced as she felt a stab of pain behind her eyes. "Really, there are some things I want to look through, think about, peek at the budget and figure out what to do about a car because—"

"—that Taurus is history, and any body shop around here'll agree. We don't have an extra floating around, not in the budget. So we have a few dealerships on a list to bid on replacing vehicles. Ford dealer in Evansville usually wins. Insurance should cover most of it." Randy closed up the first aid kit. "But that'll take days, and there's a report to file first, county board requires it, and—"

"I have a lot to learn," Piper admitted. "About paperwork." It was something she wouldn't have said to Oren or her father or—

"There's a used car dealer in town we've rented from before... when something's been out of service or otherwise wrecked. Good prices 'cause she likes us. Her grandfather used to be in the department. We'll call her in the morning. And we'll have to rent two because of Buck's slippy-slide."

Piper nodded and waggled her fingers. "Go home, and drive carefully. Get some rest."

"And how will you get home, Boss?"

She shrugged, setting her shoulders to throbbing. "I'll get someone tomorrow to drop me by my apartment."

Randy leaned against the doorway and yawned. "I thought you lived with Paul... your dad."

"Not exactly. There's an apartment above his big garage. Once upon a time he rented it out. Now it's mine. I need my own space. He needs his own space."

Randy stared at a spot on her desk. "How's he doing? Your dad?"

She shrugged again; it didn't hurt quite as much this time. "I'd like to say well, but I don't know, really. He's got six more treatments before he gets another scan. I'd like to be optimistic, but..."

"I should stop in and see him soon, have some coffee. He brews a great coffee. He's a good man, your dad. It was good you came back for him." Randy stood there, like he was going to say something else. Finally, he turned away.

Piper wondered if Randy was going to say good she came back, bad that she won the sheriff's race.

Her desk was empty, save for the laptop and an ancient-looking phone. She intended to bring in a few things, personalize it, a group shot of the guys from Fort Campbell, a paperweight she'd bought at a market in Egypt when she was on leave, maybe have a photo framed— one of her dad in front of his beloved Christmas tree. But she'd been plunged into the job, not eased into it like expected.

The department building was reasonably new, as in built within the past dozen years or so. Piper remembered that the previous building was old, like much of the downtown, had leaks, everything outdated. A glance at the phone... some things still were outdated. This building was something to be proud of, though, with an attached jail, brick exterior, white walls inside. Pictures on the walls, including in her office, of past sheriffs and different angles of the courthouse. She'd see about painting her office beige or gray or "potter's wheel," a shade she noticed in the hardware store when ogling colors for the apartment.

She opened her laptop and turned it on, sat back in the chair, and then reached for the handset. It had a cord; at least it had push buttons rather than a dial. She'd spotted one phone in the office that was rotary. She held the handset for a moment, it seeming to weigh a ton because it might impart bad news.

"Get it over with." She'd call her dad, see how he was doing, tell him she was fine though she ached all over, tell him she would be here through the night. Lord knew he'd pulled plenty of all nighters. Besides, Piper wouldn't be able to sleep anyway, as uncomfortable as she was, and all these things whirling in her head.

Somebody had tried to kill her.

Teegan poked her head back in, hair dangling down. Piper wondered if the woman ironed it. She spotted blue at the tips, not quite matching the pantsuit. Teegan was forty-something, not a single gray hair—of course from the unnatural inky color she displayed it was obvious she relied on dye.

"Yes, Teegan?"

"Nothing on that gray or maroon pickup yet, Sheriff Blackwell. The BOLO's out with city police, Vanderburgh County Sheriff, Evansville, Owensboro, got it on the wire and—"

"Thanks, Teegan."

"Somebody really tried to kill you, huh? Not some road rage nutball 'cause you cut somebody off?"

"I didn't cut anyone off."

"Not some slippy-slide 'cause the roads were icing over?"

"Someone really tried to kill me, Teegan."

"It was the murderer then, right, whoever gacked Conrad Delaney?"

"And Abigail Thornbridge," Piper said. "Yeah, I think so."

"Because you're on to him... or her." Teegan shuddered. "Wow. How about some coffee, Sheriff?"

"That'd be lovely. Black."

"That's how your father drinks it, too. How's he doing, by the way? You should call him, you know." Teegan pointed at the handset and disappeared without waiting for an answer. "Call him," she hollered from the other room.

Piper called and gave him an abbreviated version of her day's events. When she asked how he was feeling, he said he had to go, that his show was coming on. "So he's feeling lousy," she translated. Piper stared at the laptop; the screensaver image was a shot of the courthouse in the spring, dogwoods in full bloom, matching one of the pictures on her wall.

Teegan came in soundlessly and set a steaming mug on the corner of the desk. "You ever need to talk, Sheriff, I'm here." The phone buzzed in the other room and Teegan hurried away. "Probably another slippy-slide into a ditch!"

The screen image shifted to a picture of the bridge that crossed over to Kentucky, so not a static screensaver, but a slideshow. Piper watched it a few minutes while she sipped at the too-hot and not-as-good-as-Nang's coffee. Other images played across—a rusting tractor in front of a closed mechanic's shop, an antique store with a wedding dress hanging in the window, children on a slide at the Santa Claus water park.

"Four hundred square miles," she said. That was the size of sleepy Spencer County. Four hundred and ten, actually, but a dozen of it was water. There were seven hundred and thirty-eight miles of county roads, one hundred and forty-seven highway miles. A lot of department time taken up in driving because calls might be fifty miles away. Fourteen deputies to cover it in three shifts working four days on, two off, rotating shifts so no one was stuck on the night tour forever. The youngest deputy was a year older than her, the oldest was Oren, three were in their fifties, only one other woman... Jeri Jones, or JJ as everyone called her, ten years with the department, married to the athletic director of the high school. There'd been three murders in the past ten years, JJ had told her.

There was no diversity in the department in Piper's eyes. One woman... one *other* woman, all but one of the deputies white; the twenty-four-year old, in his first year with the department, was a very fair-skinned Hispanic with an associate degree in law enforcement. She'd told her father that bothered her, the lack of diversity, said that a department should be a slice of the society it sat in. He laughed and pointed out that judging by the last census, only fifty or so of the county's whopping twenty-thousand people were Hispanic, and less than two dozen folks were black.

"You should've remembered that from when you lived here," he'd said. "You want diversity, go to Evansville."

Or Owensboro just across the river, she thought. Piper had left right after high school graduation, enlisted in the Army, and trained at Fort Campbell. She'd not thought about diversity growing up here, but the Army had opened her eyes. When it came time to add another deputy here, she'd address it, census figures or no.

JJ had been the most helpful—and friendly—of her current deputies, meeting Piper and her father for dinner at the country club before Christmas, rattling off statistics. Piper had tried her best to commit them to memory. DUIs were the number one offense in the county—as Oren had pointed out to people gawking on Mr. Delaney's driveway—then theft, followed by public intoxication, minors drinking, battery, manufacturing meth, marijuana and drug paraphernalia possession, domestic violence calls, and vandalism. Deputies had found twenty meth labs the previous year, a record, all of them apparently run by single individuals who did most of their dealing in Owensboro. Her dad had said the county being so rural made it inviting for the manufacturers to move in, thinking they'd have less chance of being discovered. How many meth labs were operating here that hadn't been discovered?

Piper intended to delve into the meth problem after the murders. Sleepy Spencer County apparently wasn't so sleepy after all. Maybe she'd stay too busy to miss Army life.

Probably not.

The laptop screen was back to the image of the courthouse. Piper clicked a few keys and started her Google search. It was the placemat in Nang's tiny restaurant that gave her the idea, the picture of the pagoda with the website for a Buddhist temple underneath it. That website hadn't been the correct one; she hadn't expected to find the needle on her first exploration of the Internet haystack. But it had a link to the World Fellowship of Buddhists in Bangkok. From there, she found a list of monasteries in Thailand, some phone numbers, and after two calls that certainly would have her worried come budget time, she found where Anthony Delaney lived. She left a message for him, finished her coffee, and then levered herself up. Her aches had aches.

Time to take a look at those Christmas cards.

TEN

Piper spotted the Christmas cards in the break room, which also served as the conference room, actually a large all-purpose space that according to her father was the site of the department's annual potluck and chili contest. She leaned in the doorway. Randy had spread the cards out on two long tables. He was bent over the one with more cards, those taken from Abigail Thornbridge's house.

"Randy, I thought you were going home?"

He tapped a card in the center of the table, the photo card from Conrad to Abigail.

"Delaney ordered fifty of these sleigh cards from an online company. I found the receipt in his desk, along with five unused cards. So I'd wager he sent out forty-five." He stood straight and faced her. "In the same drawer I found five unused cards from the year before, and another five from the year before that, all with him and the sleigh, though from different angles and him in different sweaters. Two years ago he wore a reindeer antler ball cap in the shot and had stuck a red ball on his nose. A good bet he's been mailing out the same number of cards for a while. Chris Hagee said he never knew Conrad to send anything but photo Christmas cards."

"So we have forty-five suspects," Piper mused.

"Forty-four," he corrected with a grin. "One of those recipients was Abigail Thornbridge, and she certainly didn't kill Delaney. But I'm thinking she was killed on the same day."

Piper came all the way into the room; the floor was slick and she nearly slipped. Recently polished, the place smelled strongly of pine cleaner. She slumped into the chair across from Randy. "And you know they were killed on the same day because—" Piper guessed that Abigail had been dead about four days or so judging by the ugly condition of the body. This morning Dr. Neufeld had said, "My best guess is that Conrad was killed twenty-eight to thirty-three hours before the Hagees spotted him sitting in the sleigh." That didn't equal about the same time; it was off by more than a day.

Randy crossed his arms and let out a slow breath. "Okay, the coroner thinks Conrad was killed sometime on the thirtieth. With me?"

Piper nodded, hoping this wasn't going to turn into something like a petechial hemorrhage lecture.

"And Sweet Abby T was likely killed on the twenty-ninth, maybe late on the twenty-eighth. I've seen enough bodies. Had to be the twenty-ninth or twenty-eighth."

"Sure, a day apart, killed close, but not the same—"

"Yeah. The same day," Randy said. "Had to be the same day." His eyes twinkled and his expression said, *c'mon, ask me,* but Piper just waited.

"Arnold Washington."

Piper leaned back as much as the chair allowed and looked up into his face. She noticed a scar along his jaw line, faint, so an old one. Again, she waited.

He seemed disappointed that she wasn't coaxing the tidbits out of him. "Arnold Washington... Arnie... lives a few doors down from the Delaney's, in a saltbox he inherited from his mother. He only lives on the first floor."

She waited some more.

"He's thirty-two, disabled from a motorcycle accident a couple of years back, stuck in a wheelchair. Doesn't get out much, but on December twenty-ninth a cousin took him grocery shopping in Rockport and to hit what was left of the after-Christmas sale at the pharmacy. They drove by Delaney's, and Arnie swore he saw Conrad sitting in the sleigh with a mug in his hand. This was in the morning, about eight."

"So Conrad sat in the sleigh for three days and no one stopped? No one noticed?" If that was true, Piper thought it very sad.

"Either they didn't notice him or they just figured he was sitting out there for a brief time. Evidently the partiers across the street hadn't paid any attention until Mrs. Hagee suggested her husband invite Conrad over. Really, a person only notices stuff when they pay attention."

"And you talked to Arnie when?"

"I stopped this morning, after I chatted with Zachary Delaney, and right before we got the Thornbridge call. Zachary had mentioned he'd been at Arnie's, and so I went to Arnie's, too."

"And you didn't tell me this when I saw you at Miss Thornbridge's because—"

He frowned, the scar showing a little more pronounced. "Because I was so wrapped up in the Thornbridge crime scene." Randy took a step back from the table. "In the past ten years, we've had three murders. Now in the past few days, two."

The comment Dr. Neufeld made about the bodies dropping back-to-back after Piper took office sprang to mind.

"So I just didn't think about it then to be honest," he continued. "Not then, but it was in my notes."

"No worries." Piper looked at the Christmas cards; from the side of the table she'd selected they were all upside down. "But good to know. One more thing they had in common. Killed the same day. Probably." She rose and walked past the tables to a whiteboard she'd set up before driving to Evansville this morning. It was blank.

She made three headers:

Commonalities Conrad Delaney Abigail Thornbridge

She wrote under the Commonalities column:

- Victims seniors, knew each other
- Murdered December 28th or 29th
- Strangled
- Killer posed victims to match Christmas cards they'd sent
- Pets unharmed/killer likes animals?
- Killer drives a big maroon and/or gray pickup?

Piper returned to the Thornbridge Christmas card table.

"She got seventy-two cards," Randy said. "Her address book has at least three times that many names in it."

"She was a school teacher and principal for a ton of years, knew a lot of people," Piper put in. "She probably sent out a lot of cards. Elderly, probably didn't go out much, stayed home and wrote Christmas cards. Probably sent more cards than she received."

"Yeah, haven't had time yet to match names in these cards to her address book. Figure I'll start that now. I found boxes of unused Christmas cards in a hall closet, like she was hoarding them, sale price stickers over the top of the original prices… cheap… like she bought them at after Christmas sales. Wrapping paper and ribbon, too, all with sale prices. Santa plates and napkins still in cellophane, sale prices. All of it, according to the stickers, from the big shop in Santa Claus. She had a closet full of half-price Christmas. Maybe enough to open her own store." He pointed to Conrad's table. "The card she sent him, that one there—"

Piper looked at it. She'd seen it hanging on the yarn line in Mr. Delaney's den, had taken a picture of it. Mrs. Santa sat in a rocking chair directly in front of a Christmas tree that was loaded with ornaments and silvery tinsel and topped with an angel. She wore a long red dress and slippers and had a cup in her hands, a swirl of glitter rising from it. There was more glitter on the tree. Abigail had been posed closely to resemble it.

"Abigail must have liked that design," Randy said. "There were two more unopened boxes of it, and one with a few cards left. Like I said, we don't know how many cards she sent out."

"Just need to find Conrad's list of forty-five and cross-reference it with hers. Our suspect list is the names that match. She went back to the board and added:

• Victims sent cards to the killer, knew him or her

"I think that's a good bet, the way I'm leaning. But maybe the guy just *saw* the cards," Randy said. "We have to account for that possibility, for every possibility. He might not actually have been on their card list."

"The killer didn't sell them the cards. Miss Thornbridge bought hers at a store in Santa Claus, Mr. Delaney ordered his online." Piper underlined it.

• <u>Victims sent cards to the killer, knew him or her</u>

"No, Randy, it's not likely the guy—or the woman—simply *saw* the cards," Piper said. "And it's not a coincidence that the victims were posed to look like the cards. Conrad Delaney, Abigail Thornbridge, they sent their killer Christmas cards. They *knew* the killer, had done something to piss him or her off. And, yeah, I'll concede that the killer is probably a man. Not many women could lift Conrad into that sleigh." But she could have. Piper had carried a two hundred and forty pound man out of a burning building on one of her downrange assignments. Her shoulders let her know it was a bad idea, but as small as she was she'd managed it.

She went to the Delaney table and picked up the card that Sweet Abby T had sent Conrad, the one the old woman had been posed to eerily resemble. There were only a few differences between the card and the crime scene. Mrs. Santa was in a long red dress, while Abigail had been wearing a lengthy red flannel nightgown. Mrs. Santa had a cap, and Abigail did not. Mrs. Santa's mug was green and white striped, Abigail's was red… just like the one in Conrad's hands, price sticker on the bottom, from the Santa Shop in Santa Claus. But Abigail was posed in the *same* manner as the Mrs. Santa image, head back, arms on the rocker, hands clasping the mug.

"One very sick S.O.B." Piper let out a long breath and came back to the Abigail table, sat facing the cards this time, and resting her elbows on the edge. She gazed at the cards and realized Randy had arranged them by type of image, not size.

To her left were the "word" cards: Merry Christmas, Season's Greetings, Happy Holidays, Peace, Peace on Earth, *Joyeux Noël, Feliz Navidad*, Let it Snow Let it Snow, Joy to the World, and Jesus is the Reason for the Season. There were no images on these cards, just the words in card-covering big fancy script, some metallic, the Let it Snow Let it Snow card in a glittery white against a foil blue, likely one of the more expensive cards on display. *Let it stop snowing,* Piper thought.

Next, the religious-themed set: A trio of angels with trumpets, more than a dozen manger scenes, a little drummer boy, wise men under a star, and a variety of churches at night with snow spreading away. Some were large and beautiful on embossed cardstock. Others were about four inches square, flimsy, and looking like they came from one of those discount boxes you'd find at the Dollar Store.

There were four picture postcards, Conrad's and the sleigh; a man and woman sitting in front of a fireplace with three dogs at their feet; a massive Christmas tree in front of some government building; and a Santa on a throne holding a baby, a toddler standing nearby, probably taken at some shopping mall. She intended to read every card, after she got a notebook out of her office, jot down names, any sentiments that didn't sit right. To get so many cards... Abigail must have had a lot of friends.

And among them one enemy.

Finally came a collection of carolers, Santas, decked-out trees, snowmen, ice skaters, reindeer, poinsettias, wreaths, stockings in front of fireplaces—one with Santa's boots hanging down like he was just sliding in to deliver presents—penguins in hats and scarves, and bright red birds sitting on snowy fence railings. There was a large one with a pug snoozing in a red blanket. Piper opened it to read the message: Hope you'll be snug as a pug in a rug this Christmas. *My love to you and Wrinkles, xoxoxo Betty B.*

"Poor Wrinkles," she said, thinking of Miss Thornbridge's aged pug. "Maybe Oren can find someone to take him."

"Probably," Randy said. "He's got a soft spot for animals."

"So does the killer, apparently."

"MP right? You were in the military police? My sister was in the Army, eight years, but she was stationed out of Fort Benning, Georgia. They trained her as a dental technician. She joined the Army to see the world, but they never sent her out of the South. All she saw was the inside of a lot of people's mouths. She was gonna go for twenty, get that sweet military pension." He paused. "But she met a guy, married him, and moved to Ohio."

Piper fixed her eyes on the picture of Conrad in the sleigh. "I joined to see the world, too. That and because I didn't want to go to college." Actually, she hadn't known what she wanted to do with her life... other than get out of Spencer County. She sounded a bit like Nang, listless until he got the lottery ticket. She'd seen a billboard with a woman in Army combat gear and thought, why not? Why not "be all she could be" as the saying went.

"Why the MP?"

Randy was nosy... no wonder he supposedly was a good detective, even though he'd missed Conrad's county phonebook.

"The MP field's wide open for women, a good choice, really. Because my dad was with this department for so long, brought the job home with him, I guess I was interested in law enforcement. So I told the recruiter to sign me up for the MP track."

Randy's pacing took him to the opposite side of the table. She looked up; he was studying her face. His expression asked her to continue.

"In boot camp I took OSUT, One Station Unit Training, as part of the MP division. My MOS was 31 Bravo. Became a crack shot. For whatever reason, I aced all my training, even won a few awards."

"MOS?"

"Military Occupational Specialty. They made me part of the Third BCT... Brigade Combat Team. The Rakkasans." A hint of pride crept into her voice, the words coming sweeter. "It's a Japanese word. In World War II, when the 101st out of Fort Campbell deployed, the Japanese saw the parachutes and called them rakkasan, 'umbrella men.' It's a very storied unit."

"So did you jump?"

"Parachutes?" She shivered at the memory. *Why should I jump out of a perfectly good plane?* she'd asked her instructor just before he gave her a push. "Yeah, I jumped and jumped and jumped."

"Cool."

"I didn't stay at Fort Campbell long. And when I was there, I was in a cruiser, watching for speeders, traffic violations, some ER calls on the base. Then I got deployed."

"Where?" Randy seemed genuinely interested. She figured he hadn't read any of the newspaper articles about her during the campaign.

"Iran, in the Alpha Company Brigade, part of an MP Battalion. I had a lot of 'downrange' assignments. It was dangerous as all-crap, IED exposure, household searches, Taliban threats. Shot during one household search. Same night I pulled out a miracle, saved my commanding officer and four other soldiers by routing an ambush and killing a group of insurgents."

"On your own?"

"Yeah," she admitted, the memory and the Purple Heart crystal clear in her mind. "Yeah, on my own. I was scouting. Hell yeah. I made sergeant in two and a half years, got some medals. My commanding officer called me a 'hot runner,' said I'd go far." She paused and traced the outside of Conrad's card. "I was up for another promotion and had a choice of assignments."

"But you found out about your dad."

She nodded.

"Good that you came back for him," Randy said.

"These cards aren't going anywhere. They'll be here in the morning. Go home, Randy, get some sleep."

"Okay, Boss."

ELEVEN

The sheriff was a little spit of a thing, not much more than five feet tall, and not particularly pretty, he'd thought the first time he spotted her. Thought the same thing when he'd seen her in the quick stop in Fulda a little while ago. She'd looked right at him when he was buying gas, sent goose bumps down his back. She'd looked at him a mite too long for comfort when she was sitting there eating that drippy oriental food.

He didn't like her looking at him.

Did she know something?

Had he left something behind inside the house? His gloves? He'd misplaced a pair of gloves recently. Had he left them there? No, he couldn't have. He'd been so very careful.

This new blood in the sheriff's department was a bad thing. Someone so young, fresh out of the military, she'd have lots of energy, might dig in and really try to solve the murders, like she had something to prove. Women were always trying to prove something, weren't they? Oh, not that the Jew deputy wouldn't be trying, but he was old and was probably more interested in retirement plans. He wouldn't try as hard as the woman. That new blood? That was bad bad bad news. Thinking about her had sent more goose bumps.

He'd paid cash for his gas, pulled out of the station that the slant-eyed guy shouldn't have bought, and then he waited in a nearby driveway to see where the little sheriff was going. Years back, you used to be able to order corndogs and pretzels at that quick stop, good old American fare. Tasty food you could eat on the road while you were driving, one hand on the wheel, the other holding your lunch. Not that garbage you had to sit at a table to eat because of the rice and noodles and drippy sauces. Couldn't eat that in your ride without making a mess.

He'd had to wait longer than expected, but eventually she came out, scraped off her car, and pulled away. She hadn't noticed him following; he'd stayed pretty far back, watched her park in the Delaney driveway and go right into the house like she owned the place. What was she looking for? Hadn't they been through the house enough, all those deputies? Hadn't they been to all the neighbors' houses, too? He'd driven up and down the county road, wasting his gas, sometimes stopping in the driveways, backing in so he could watch the Delaney place. The little sheriff had spent more than an hour in there this time.

Must have found something.

Maybe knows something.

New blood is bad blood. *Bad to the Bone*, George Thorogood; *Bad Love*, Eric Clapton; *Bad Company* by the band with the same name; *Bad Reputation*, Joan Jett—he really liked that one; *Born Under a Bad Sign*, Cream; *Bad Moon Rising*, Creedence Clearwater Revival—his favorite but way too old, really. He kept up the song-name game in his head for a while.

"Fuckin' *Bad Blood*, Taylor Swift," he said. The sheriff was younger than Taylor Swift. "Dead blood."

She'd finally come out, so he followed her again; she headed out of town, not that there was much to the town. Fulda was a blink-and-you'll-miss-it bulge along the road. That gave him the notion—make her a spot along the road. Kill the little sheriff, and kill whatever ideas and determination were filling up her little brain, destroy whatever pointed the finger at him. Make it look like an accident. After the first two, killing had come easy. This weather... it'd help.

It was snowing fiercely.

Wasn't supposed to snow this hard in Southern Indiana, was it? He'd remembered winters with only traces of snow, it all so thin you could see dead grass poking through. But the snow was working to his advantage, and so he didn't complain much. It covered the metal on his truck, disguising it, iced things up, and he didn't turn on his headlights; lights would have made it all seem less creepy. He liked the notion that he was being creepy, like some perverted dude in a thriller movie. All he had to do was focus on her glowing red taillights, shining all pretty through the snow like Rudolf's nose... noses. The image of two reindeers sprung into his head and he tamped down the Christmas song that threatened to come out. No Christmas songs after Christmas.

She was easy to follow with her pretty little Rudolf noses glowing through the snow. He'd kept a good distance back until she was well past the last house in Fulda, was in an area of fields and barns and snowdrifts, it all looking as dark as night.

He'd made a game of it at first, bumping her car, easing back, watching that Taurus shimmy clumsily like one of those overweight dancers at the nudie bar he frequented. He'd wondered if he'd scared her... hoped he'd scared her. He'd wished he could have seen her eyes; then he'd know if she was really frightened. But another one of those blink-and-you'll-miss-it-towns was coming up, and he hadn't wanted her to get that far. So he'd rammed her car hard and watched the trunk pop. Rammed her again and saw the shimmy, spun her 'round and came at her again, pushed her a little bit back toward Fulda. His stomach had rumbled then and made him think about dinner. He'd grab a couple of burgers somewhere, no ketchup or mustard. He liked them plain.

Another nudge and he nearly had her off the road.

That's it, he'd decided. Played too long. Finish her and get some dinner. Maybe she'd radioed for help, not that any was going to come in time to save her.

Pressed the gas pedal again and banged into her car so hard that he shot off the road, too. But he was able to muscle the wheel just in time and keep the truck from going all the way down into the ditch. Saw her flip over and over and land out in the field, headlights all crooked. At least the siren had quit. He'd pulled back onto the road and thought about parking on the side, walking down there to make sure the little sheriff was dead, finishing her if she wasn't.

But it was cold and snowing like hell, and there was someplace else he'd needed to be, and she might have radioed for help, and help might be coming despite the shit weather. Couldn't risk getting caught.

She was dead, he'd been sure of it, a little thing like that would be crushed, flipping over and over.

Dead dead dead. *I Love the Dead*, Alice Cooper; *Living Dead Girl*, Rob Zombie; *Dead Flowers*, the Stones; *Dead Souls*, Nine Inch Nails—that was a favorite.

But if she wasn't... just in case she wasn't, he'd get her later. Wouldn't be all that hard to figure out where she lived. Public records and all.

So he'd kept going. All this snow... had to take advantage of it. People would be staying off the road, holed up all nice and cozy in their houses, wouldn't notice him.

He'd turned back around at a wide spot in the road and headed to the next blink-and-you'll-miss-it-town. Had somebody there he needed to visit.

Somebody who'd sent him a Christmas card.

TWELVE

N ew Boston, or Huff as some of the locals called it, boasted two churches, a gas station that did not sell food other than peanuts and Twinkies, and a tavern that he stopped at, ordered two plain burgers to go, and downed an Uncle Jacob's Stout.

He ate the burgers in his truck while he let the engine run, keeping the defroster going so the snow wouldn't cover the windshield... not wanting to get out and scrape again. It didn't take him long; he was hungry and the burgers were tasty and had just the right amount of grease.

The county road stretched down the middle of the bittyburg, and no one else was on it tonight. Some people still had their Christmas lights on, dimmed because of the snow, looking oh-so-pretty. He scouted for the last house on the right; it had lights on too, those icicle ones dripping down from the eaves, more lights twisting up a few of the trees. Magical like maybe Harry Potter lived there. Three snowmen in the front yard, a big one flanked by two small ones, hats and scarves on them, sticks for arms with mittens on the ends—he could see them easily because the front porch light was on, could tell they were *real* snowmen, not like the inflatable one in old woman

Thornbridge's neighborhood. Sammy'd gone all out decorating this go-round.

He pulled in the driveway, all the way up to the garage at the back of the property, and went to the kitchen door. He knew it'd be open. Sammy never locked his doors. Who would in this itty bittyburg?

"Saw you pull up!" Sammy was at the kitchen table, a stack of seed catalogs in front of him, one opened and a few items circled on a page. "Is your truck messed up? You get in an accident?" Radio was playing, an oldies station that sounded sweet.

He loved music, but it was easy to get a song stuck in his head, started thinking about *Rudolph the Red-Nosed Reindeer* again. *Christmas is over, get a different tune,* he thought. *Sam*, Olivia Newton John; *Sam You Made the Pants Too Long*, Barbra Streisand.

"How ya' doing, Sammy? Sam-I-am?"

"I'm doing."

Sammy was short, about five and a half feet tall. He had curly black hair like an Italian ought to have, though Sammy was Polish. His wide, long nose didn't seem to fit the egg-shaped face, and he had attracted only a few girlfriends when they were in school together—probably because of his less-than-average looks and him being so godawful short. But Sammy'd had one girl that'd stuck around for a while, married her. She'd been good at hemming his pants 'cause otherwise they'd be like the Barbra Streisand song.

He'd went to Sammy's wedding, bought the happy couple a blender. But the wife didn't stick around for many years, probably took the blender with her.

"I was passing by, Sammy Sammy Sammy, saw your lights on so I thought I'd stop."

Sammy pushed the seed catalog away. "What the hell are you doin' out in this weather, man? You nuts? You could get yourself killed."

"Not likely." He pulled out a chair and sat. The chair made a wincing sound; Sammy had junk furniture, needed some new stuff.

"You're getting' snow all over my floor." Sammy paused. "Want a beer?"

He nodded, glancing through the open doorway off the kitchen and into the living room. Sammy had his little Christmas tree still up, but the lights weren't on, probably only plugged them in when he was in the room and could enjoy it. A train set circled the skirt, but it wasn't on either.

"You decorated," he said, nodding in the direction of the living room.

"I did indeed. A lot 'cause I had the twins. It was my turn to have them for the holidays. Six years old, the age when they're still playing with toys. Bought 'em dolls and shit like that, no clothes. They wanted toys. Spent too much money, but it was awesome. Made some snowmen in the yard to match the Christmas cards I sent out. You probably saw them out front, the snowmen. I took pictures."

"The kids sleeping?"

Sammy shook his head. "Gone. But they left some stuff, some sweaters, and they forgot a couple of toys. I could've said something before they bopped out the front door, but I figured it'd give 'em a reason to come back, for the sweaters."

"Too bad. I would have liked to say 'hello,' at least to little Samantha. Your ex? Did she stay with you, too? For the holidays?"

"Oh, hell no. She came and got 'em yesterday, 'cause I only had 'em a week. Her shop was closed yesterday, so it was easy for her. Took 'em back to Louisville." Louisville came out 'Loo-a-vool,' like a native would say it. "Good thing, 'cause she wouldn't be caught dead driving in this shit today, and I couldn't keep the kids any longer anyway. And I sure as hell wouldn't have wanted her to spend the night. Gotta be back to work tomorrow."

"Still on the three-to-eleven at the power plant?"

"Sure. Where else am I gonna work? Don't have enough acres just to farm. You know that." Sammy looked under the table and scowled. "Melted all over my floor, the snow. Couldn't've stomped it off, could you?"

"Sorry."

"I'd cleaned the place up 'cause of the kids and 'cause I didn't want Nicky to think I was some bum. The last few months we were together, she called me a bum all the time. All over my floor, that slop."

"Sorry 'bout that, I said." But he wasn't sorry. And it didn't matter anyway; Sammy wouldn't have to clean it up. He'd clean it all up nice and tidy himself before leaving. He had to admit the place smelled good, like cinnamon and cranberries, air fresheners or candles. Sammy was a real domestic. "Where's that beer you mentioned? I could sure do with one."

"Oh, yeah. Okay. Only got one kind. Where you working?" Sammy got up and went to the fridge, tugged it open with one hand and reached in with the other, pulled out two cans, and shut the door with a hip check. "Budweiser. Good stuff. Good stuff for a good friend." Sammy popped the top on his and started drinking, setting the other one on the table, and with his now-free hand folded the seed catalog and added it to the stack. "Soybeans this year. Can't do corn every year, messes with the ground. So I'm gonna do soybeans. They're easy. Gonna order me some peach trees, too, little ones, but I'll put in a line of 'em and some will take. Figure I'll let the twins help me plant them. They'd like that, dontcha think? Aren't you gonna take your gloves off? It's not cold in here."

"You still got that old spaniel?"

Sammy shook his head. "Died over the summer. Cancer. I'm gonna get me another dog, though, come spring. Probably go to the shelter this time, rescue a mutt. Try something different than a purebred. Jake... remember Jake? He helped me fix the roof on my barn last summer and put in some kitchen cabinets. He works with some beagle rescue group hooked to the shelter, said he'd fix me up with one already housebroke. They get in beagle mixes mostly. But I told him I had to wait for the spring, and I might want a little bigger dog this time."

No you won't be getting a bigger dog, he thought. *Too bad about the spaniel, especially dying to cancer. Dogs shouldn't die to cancer.* But at least he wouldn't have to worry about setting out extra food and water for it... in case Sammy went undiscovered for a while.

"It's not cold in here, really. Got the thermostat set at sixty-eight.

Dad had put in a new furnace the year before he hightailed it to Florida. It heats all nice and even. So take your gloves off and stay a while. I got some DVDs for Christmas. We could watch one."

He grunted and fumbled with the can tab, almost impossible to open with gloves on, but he managed, tipped his head back and let half of the Bud slide down his throat in one swallow. Not as good as the Uncle Jacob's he'd ordered at the bar, but it was cold and hit the spot and gave him the hint of a buzz. The burgers had made him thirsty. He'd sprinkled too much salt on them, probably had upped his blood pressure some points.

"Didn't get a Christmas card from you this year," Sammy said. "Wondered if maybe you'd moved."

"Or died?"

Sammy laughed. "You and me are too young for bucket kicking."

"That's half true." He finished the beer, got up and went behind Sammy, moving fast and reaching around his neck, squeezing hard. Sammy was strong, working at the power plant and in the field, not as easy a mark as the others, and put up a fight. Sammy tried to rise.

He threw all his weight into keeping his friend in the chair, pressing his fingers in deeper, clenching his teeth as Sammy kicked out, striking the table leg and sending the seed catalogs flying. More stuff he'd have to tidy up.

Sammy flailed back with his elbows, landing a blow, then his arms flapping, grabbing and punching, but not accomplishing much, probably not believing an old buddy would do this. Sammy tried to talk, but only beer spittle came out, coupled with a heaving sound that reminded him of a generator trying to fire up. Shit, he'd have to clean up the spittle, too. He strangled people because it was cleaner, no blood spray to contend with. This wasn't going to be too tidy.

"Just quit," he told Sammy. "I'm making this quick, don't want to hurt you, understand." *Just kill you.* "And it's your own fault, really. It's your fault you're getting a Christmas mug."

Sammy's struggles were feeble now, followed by a spasmodic jerking like had happened with old woman Thornbridge. Sammy hadn't been a third her age, and it had taken longer to kill him, maybe because he had a thick neck or because his lungs were younger.

He wondered if that young sheriff's body had been found. Running her off the road, her car flipping over and over, had put him in the mood to ice Sammy. If he hadn't been all jacked up over the sheriff, Sammy'd still be breathing.

And if it hadn't been snowing so hard.

Now it was going to take a good bit of work to set Sammy up just right, to match the Christmas card. Good thing this was the perfect night for it, the snow still coming down, people staying indoors. No house directly across from this one. Hell, if he hadn't gotten all riled about the sheriff, and if it hadn't been snowing like this, if the winter hadn't been so... significant... Sammy would have lived through it.

But this snow... perfect.

And the snowmen... aces. Just the right number.

It was like fate was saying, "Do Sammy in tonight, this year. Do it! Don't wait until next Christmas rolls around."

Leaving Sammy slumped over the table, he took off his heavy shoes and set them at the back door, padding through the house, listening to the gentle wheezing of the floorboards—old house. Investigating, turning on lights here and there, glancing sadly in the spare bedroom with bunk beds and stuffed animals, and keeping his gloves on, he was having a good time.

He'd seen the twins shortly after they were born. Six years old now? Wow, time had slipped by like lightning. Good thing Nicky had picked them up yesterday; he would've hated to strangle kids.

In the master bedroom he poked through the underwear drawer and found a little bank envelope with $120 in it. He'd read somewhere that people stashed cash in their underwear drawers—old woman Thornbridge certainly had, maybe had an issue with banks. He carefully replaced the socks, and shoved the money envelope in his back pocket. Not that he needed money anymore, but Sammy didn't need it. There was a fine-looking watch on the dresser, and he needed a new watch, but he didn't dare touch it. Didn't want the deputies to think this was a robbery. It wasn't. Well, not much of a robbery, and he certainly wasn't about to take a piece of jewelry that might get recognized. He'd watched enough cop shows, *CSI* being his favorite, that he knew what not to do. But underwear drawer money... that was fine to take because no one would know it was there to begin with so it *couldn't* be missed.

In the living room, he plugged in the tree and stood back to admire it. He liked Christmas trees, all the colored lights—didn't care for the lights that were all white and artsy looking. After a few moments, enough to heat them up, they started blinking. He didn't much care for blinkers, too distracting if you were trying to watch TV. But it wasn't his tree. The ornaments were generic, glass balls mostly, but a couple of Hallmarks—an Elvis Presley singing into an old-style microphone, and a red Mustang convertible. He almost took the Mustang, but stopped himself; his willpower was strong. Next he turned on the train. It was an old one, probably worth something, maybe was given to Sammy when he was a kid, probably twice as old as Sammy. Well, one of the twins would get it now.

A small desk had a laptop on it. Everyone had a laptop, didn't they? Except old woman Thornbridge. He unplugged the laptop and pawed through the desk, not easy because of the gloves, found an address book and set it on top of the laptop—both were leaving with him. Might have his name in them. He'd forgot to take the address book at Thornbridge's. That's why he didn't send Christmas cards this year, didn't want his name floating around someone's house. Didn't want to get caught.

He went into the bathroom and picked an old ragged towel out of the cabinet. He used it to clean up the kitchen, never taking his gloves off, taking the beer can he'd drank out of, crushing it and sticking it in his coat pocket. Couldn't leave that, DNA and all.

Now to set the scene. He took the Christmas card out, the one Sammy had sent two weeks prior to Christmas. It was folded and had been riding around in his shirt pocket. He smoothed it and set it on the table. Was going to take some effort to do this just right. Was going to be a long night.

But it would be worth it. Payback. Send a message. And money found in the underwear drawer was just icing; it was all good. And Sammy's computer might have some games on it... that would be a bonus.

And good thing he'd remembered to put one of those red mugs in his truck so he could add his signature, so to speak, to the scene. Gotta leave a calling card. In the movies, on the TV, killers worth their salt left calling cards.

His truck.

"Damn it all to hell and back." It had some front-end damage because of messing with the younger-than-Taylor-Swift sheriff, and he sure couldn't have it fixed around here. Couldn't have it fixed at all. He'd had the door fixed, replaced with a maroon one last month from the junkyard. Maybe it wasn't bad that he'd have to dump it, leave it with his sweetie. He could get a ride all one color. She'd watch it for him and keep it safe. He'd buy another ride, the Thornbridge under-wear drawer money would help. Maybe he'd get something more economical, a hybrid. Used. He liked used cars, more value for the money.

Money? He reached in Sammy's pocket and pulled out a worn, brown wallet. Eighty bucks inside. He took fifty and replaced it. If he left the wallet empty, some deputy might call it a robbery. This wasn't really a robbery. But he was walking away with one hundred and seventy dollars. A pittance next to what old woman Thornbridge had stashed under her bloomers. She probably gifted him enough to cover a whole car.

A glance out the window. Still snowing.

Good.

Perfect.

Time to get to work.

He smiled. "At least you had a Merry Christmas Sammy Sammy Sammy-my-pal, *Sam You Made the Pants Too Long*. Kids and snowmen. Bet you had hot cocoa, too. Ho. Ho. Ho."

THIRTEEN

Piper flipped the card over that Conrad had sent Abigail. She read it once again, hoping to find… what was she hoping to find?

Abby T: I hope this winter finds you well and pleasantly busy. I really should drive over to your church and hear you play. Haven't been to church in quite a while. Your congregation would think the Nile had flowed backwards if I walked in. Maybe I could sit in the back and no one would notice. Hey! Thanks for recommending that roofer. He did a great job on my house, I even had him use the same color of shingles. A real jack-of-all trades, and great prices, he also put in a new kitchen floor for me. Small world, he used to go to high school with my boy Anthony. I thought he'd looked familiar. I kept his business card....

Piper made a note to find the name of the roofer, something Abigail and Conrad had in common. Had Randy collected business cards from the Delaney place? And who took Conrad's picture in the painted-black sleigh? The pic he intended to use on his next-year card? Did Conrad have a camera lying around the house? She hadn't seen one when she explored, nor did she see one in the evidence boxes. Had Randy sent a camera to the lab? Piper scrawled: *ask Randy about any cameras found at the Delaney's. I want to see what's on his camera. And business cards. The jack-of-all trades.*

First day on the job: Mr. Delaney is found murdered. Second day: Miss Thornbridge turns up dead and she could have died too, her department vehicle totaled. Third day... what awful thing would tomorrow bring? She'd certainly have something to write to the Rakkasans about.

Piper usually sent out about a dozen Christmas cards each year. She got away with buying just one box, and she'd never bought extras like Miss Thornbridge had. Military life taught her to keep possessions to a minimum, no stockpiling of anything. This past December she'd broke with tradition and bought four boxes, sent out a bunch of cards, nearly all to the Rakkasans she'd left behind, some to folks who'd vocally supported her in the election. She'd even written one of those "Hi Y'all" newsletters that had a picture of her in front of an "Elect Blackwell for Sheriff" placard, and she'd added a personal note to each card. Stuffed the envelopes and sealed them during the half-time sessions of NFL games she watched with her dad. She'd figured if she was spending the money for postage and fancy Hallmark cards —a gold foil partridge in a green foil tree—She might as well go the distance and add a note. And stickers on the back, as she'd donated to the American Lung Association during its Christmas drive, and had been rewarded with a sheet of snowflakes.

She got a lot of cards in return, but not as many as she'd sent... some of the Rakkasans were awful about writing. Piper shared the cards with her father, who'd displayed his own on the fireplace mantel and bookshelves in his living room. Christmas—and Christmas cards —had always been a much bigger deal for Paul Blackwell. Had he stockpiled cards like Abigail? Did he have a stash of sale-priced wrapping paper and holiday whatnots? She seemed to remember seeing boxes of them in the hallway closet during her childhood. Again she thought about rides through the county to take in the lights, better times; back when she was a kid and Non-Hodgkin's lymphoma was not in her vocabulary.

Gazing across to the other table, the one with Conrad's cards, Piper saw some of the same designs as on Abigail's. Didn't surprise her. A county as small as Spencer, with a population of less than the city of Henderson, Kentucky, and well less than half the population of Owensboro... lots of people knew each other and would send each other cards. But Abigail was almost twenty years older than Conrad, had maybe been one of his teachers or the principal of the school he'd attended, or his kids had attended. Maybe Abigail had been a friend of Conrad's wife, perhaps through a church group, and that was the connection.

"The connection's important," Piper mused.

She got up, went to the whiteboard, and added:

• Used the same roofer/who is roofer?

Back in the chair, she tapped her notebook with the end of her pen. She'd start by jotting down the names of people who sent cards both to Conrad and Abigail. Would her suspect be one of those souls? Or had the killer not bothered to send Christmas cards this year?

"Who the hell would kill a couple of old people?" And try to kill her for that matter. During the holidays. And setting them up to look like the Christmas cards they'd sent. Macabre, and the fodder for a Stephen King knockoff.

"Sheriff Blackwell!" Teegan called from the other room. Her heels clicked against the polished tile, and she poked her head in. "Oh, there you are. My, look at all the Christmas cards. I've never gotten that many. Some of them look expensive, don't they? I suppose geezers send each other a lot of cards." She glanced at the whiteboard and shuddered. "You got a call, Sheriff. Long distance. Some guy from Thailand."

Piper pushed herself to her feet and discovered a few new jabs of pain.

"Calls himself Bee-koo Delaney. Maybe a relation to Conrad, you think?"

"Put it through to my office, Teegan." Piper suspected the dispatcher would listen in.

Bee-koo Delaney was Bhikkhu Anthony Delaney, an ordained monk.

"I'm sorry to deliver the bad news," she began.

FOURTEEN

WEDNESDAY, JANUARY 3RD

"I gave Oren a choice, you know." Piper drove the rented Subaru Outback along 231, big farms on either side, gentle hills, not much flat ground in this area. It was all slopes and tilts with stands of birch trees rising up—a postcard vista, she thought, especially with the snow coating. "He said he'd take Evansville and the autopsy." She passed a sign that read: SANTA CLAUS, Birthplace of Jay Cutler, NFL Quarterback. The small industrial park and the American Legion Post were ahead. Above it all stood a water tower that said "Holiday World."

"Of course Oren took the autopsy—no matter how bad the body looked." Piper's father was in the passenger seat of the rented car. When he'd learned she was coming here to pursue the Merry Christmas mugs, he'd asked to go along.

She was reluctant for his company at first—not that she'd told him that. Almost told him no, that she had other places to go afterwards—which she did—and had mulled over more reasons, all valid ones. It wasn't the lymphoma, or fearing he was too weak. *Don't baby him ever!* It was a worry that if any of the deputies caught wind of it, they'd think she was relying on the longtime sheriff for his expertise, that she couldn't handle this investigation on her own.

As if he'd sensed her apprehension, he'd said, "Our secret, my coming. I want to look at the ornament sales. Haven't bought a new one in a while."

That statement had buoyed Piper's heart; her dad was planning on *next* Christmas, thinking he might beat this stinking cancer, put up a tree again, add a new ornament or two. It also made her think about Miss Thornbridge with her boxes and boxes of Christmas cards and dozens of rolls of unopened wrapping paper, napkins, and decorative paper plates. Mrs. Thornbridge probably would have been shopping the sales, likely would have gone out the day after Christmas before things started getting picked over.

"Because he's Jewish, right? He took the autopsy because this Christmas store—"

"Seriously? It's because he's friends with Dr. Neufeld, Punkin. Because they can chatter like hens about you to their grizzly hearts' content. Because he might gain some interesting tidbit about the body, some clue he can covet for just a little while. Your chief deputy is going to work this case hard. He'll want to solve it on his own. Prove he should have been the one elected sheriff." He laughed good-naturedly. "Oren's a good man, Punkin. Really, he—"

She shrugged. "He lives in Santa Claus. This would have been easy for him." Her hands tightened on the steering wheel.

"And why did you give him a choice anyway? You're the boss and the sheriff's department isn't a democracy. If you wanted to attend the autopsy, you should have sent him here. Or sent Randy here. Randy's a damn fine detective and—"

Piper grumbled.

"What? I didn't hear you."

"Randy said there were a couple of people at the Hagee party he wanted to chat with again, didn't have a good feel for them. And he went out early to where I was rammed off the road, getting paint samples, seeing if anyone saw something… the pickup, the driver. But I know they didn't see anything. Nobody was out. It was just me and —me and the pickup on that road." And hopefully Randy could find her cell phone in the wreckage; she didn't want to buy another one and deal with loading it up with apps and phone numbers. Dear God, she still ached all over. Maybe a doctor visit would have been a good idea.

Piper had spent the night at the station, looking through the Christmas cards, making a few notes, talking to Bhikkhu Anthony Delaney long-distance, falling asleep at the table, waking up and giving in and napping on a downstairs cot until Randy came back the next morning. He'd given her a ride to her apartment, where she'd changed into her uniform, put the borrowed sweats in a clothes basket, stuck a bottle of aspirin in her back pocket, and checked on her father, who handed her a cup of coffee and a cheese omelet. Wrinkles was curled on a pillow in the kitchen. Sometime last night Oren apparently found a home for the aging pug.

"Oren's a good man," her dad had said then, too. Because he'd gifted her father with a scrunchy-faced, arthritic dog rather than dumping it at the shelter? Because he took in Mr. Delaney's cats?

"Oren and Annie are probably chatting about you right now." Paul tipped his head back and closed his eyes. "I miss the department gossip, going to work every day. It's been a little lonely, I hate to say. In the house I mean. But I have a dog now. I shouldn't have gone so long without one."

She'd given Oren a choice between the store and the autopsy because she thought it might improve the itchy working conditions, give him a *choice* rather than orders. And she'd hoped he would take the autopsy.

"Actually, I didn't want to attend the autopsy," Piper confessed. "Miss Thornbridge looked... awful. I could have stomached it. I really could have. I've seen a whole lot worse. You don't want to know just how much worse. I really just didn't—not today, I didn't want to deal with Dr. Neufeld and—"

"Two autopsies in two days? I wouldn't have wanted that either. But I wouldn't have given Oren the choice. I would have just sent him to Evansville and been done with it, had it be your idea."

"I bet the coroner started on time for him."

Paul raised an eyebrow.

"Nothing," she said. "It's nothing. Nothing." She pulled into the parking lot of what looked like a small strip mall but was basically one long cheerful-looking store, turned off the engine, stuck her gloves in her jacket pocket, and got out. Softer: "Nothing."

A banner read: Cheeriest Store in the World—Every Day is a Very Merry Christmas.

The air felt brittle, cold, and clean, the breeze nonexistent and the sky cloudless and bright baby blue. A big contrast to last night's snow, which had kept plowing crews busy until the early-morning hours. The snow along the edges of the sidewalk and on the roof, coupled with the splashes of red on the exterior made the store seem too happy. Piper thought that most of Santa Claus looked too happy. It was one of Spencer County's biggest towns, with a population chasing twenty-five hundred.

"Merry Christmas," her dad said, his gaze sweeping across the long building. "Gotta love a town called Santa Claus. And gotta love a store devoted to Christmas."

Piper didn't have to love it.

"So much history here, Punkin."

She knew the history. He'd spooned it in her during her childhood. Santa Claus was founded about a hundred and sixty years ago, called Santa Fe then, and had sixty-some residents. The US Postal Service refused the first post office application because there was another Santa Fe. "Pick another name," some official had told them. After a handful of town meetings, Santa Claus was etched in the record books. The town survived by attracting tourists—the bulk of them from the Midwest. But even international travelers stopped at the Santa Claus Holiday Store or at the post office to have mail hand cancelled with a special Christmas postmark—a different postmark each year—and to buy an ornament.

Piper had campaigned door-to-door in the town, but she hadn't come to this store... hadn't been to this store since high school—and that trip had been to buy her father an ornament, a moose in a sheriff's uniform. She thought the whole Christmassy town cheesy then, and her opinion hadn't changed much.

She opened the door and gestured for her dad to go first.

Christmas music still played inside.

Christmas music *always* played in the store, even at the height of summer.

It was crowded with bargain hunters.

And it was a feast for the senses.

Piper swallowed her sour mood and allowed herself be overwhelmed for a few moments while her father grabbed up a shopping basket and ambled toward the closest row of sale ornaments.

FIFTEEN

*J*olly old St. Nicholas, lean your ear this way!
    Don't you tell a single soul, what I'm going to say...
    Piper wished the stuffed Santa Claus on Conrad's sleigh would have "said" something, pointed a clue to the killer, but so far nothing—though test results wouldn't be back from the state lab for some time. The music flowed from speakers and mingled with the chatter of the shoppers that she threaded her way through. Cinnamon and peppermint were thick in the air.

Christmas Eve is coming soon, now you dear old man
Whisper what you'll bring to me. Tell me if you can.

"Tell *me* something," Piper said. Tell me why some sick S.O.B. would kill two elderly people who supposedly had no enemies. Sick *and* twisted S.O.B., Piper mentally corrected, maybe one who hated Christmas as much as his victims seemed to love it.

When the clock is striking twelve, when I'm fast asleep
Down the chimney, broad and black, with your pack you'll creep.

Did the killer come upon Abigail when she was sleeping? When Conrad slept?

All the stockings you will find hanging in a row,
Mine will be the shortest one, you'll be sure to know.

And why leave the signature of a Merry Christmas mug with a price sticker on the bottom, clearly indicating it came from this very store?

Johnny wants a pair of skates, Susie wants a sled
Nellie wants a picture book, yellow, blue, and red

A *red* mug, all bright and shiny and noticeable, a signature that stands out. Was he wishing his victims a belated Merry Christmas? Had they done something at Christmas to piss him off? Could she find a similar mug in this store today?

Now I think I'll leave to you
What to give the rest
Choose for me dear Santa Claus
What you think is best.

"Is she looking for shoplifters?" A boy nudged a woman that was likely his grandmother and pointed at Piper.

"Maybe she's shopping like us. Don't point. It's not polite."

Go Tell it on the Mountain came through the speakers as Piper strolled along the far wall filled with nutcrackers. They ranged from beautiful hand-carved wood designs painted in pastels that could be displayed proudly in china cabinets to man-high nutcrackers in bright blue, red, and white. One of the largest had eyes that sent a shiver down her back. It looked disturbing, and she thought it could be featured in a SyFy channel horror flick. Mrs. Thornbridge had a nutcracker with a pug dog head on an end table near the Christmas tree.

She passed by an assortment of holiday-themed wine bottle holders and delicate crystal knickknacks. A shelf full of scented candles added to the bouquet; she caught a pleasant whiff of vanilla. People obviously bought this stuff—otherwise it wouldn't be offered in quantity. But why fill your life and house with all the clutter? *A waste of money*, she thought. Or maybe Army life had made her too minimalistic. The candles, okay, she understood—you lit them, they looked pretty, smelled nice, and then they were gone and took up no space.

Maybe it was all some obsession. Her father's ornament collection certainly was.

A bevy of glass and ceramic dinosaurs in natural and unnatural colors hung from a tree covered in pinpoint white lights. She hadn't seen dinosaur ornaments before, and if she wasn't here for business, she might have picked up the purple tyrannosaurus for her father. Next was a display of spaceships and aliens hanging from every branch of a midnight blue fake fir. Piper had to nudge herself along, the child deep inside encouraging her to pick up the spangled flying saucer... at least for a close look.

Dog breed ornaments were on a larger tree, which brought her back to Miss Thornbridge. Abigail would have picked a pug ornament, maybe more than one. Piper had noticed a couple of pug decorations on the old woman's tree, in addition to the angel with the pug head. There might have been more pug Christmas trinkets, but she hadn't stayed at the scene all that long because Randy and Oren had it well in hand. A black pug sitting in a high-backed red chair, a brindle pug curled in a bed, a pug in a Santa suit, a pug head with a candy cane in its mouth dangled from branches.

"Oh, look at that one!" Piper hadn't noticed her dad approach. He gently removed the black pug in the chair and put it in his basket next to a few other ornaments he'd selected. "It's not on sale, but it looks like Wrinkles. Might have it personalized. See, there's a space right here. Whatcha think, Punkin? Wrinkles? Or Mr. Wrinkles?" Before she could answer, he wandered away, acting like a giddy twelve-year-old.

Had Mrs. Thornbridge been like that when she visited the shop, youth thrust upon her as she ogled the pug ornaments? How often had she come here? How often had the killer?

"Meemaw, is she gonna arrest somebody?" The boy, pointing again.

Piper wandered toward the cards, which Miss Thornbridge clearly visited, and she zeroed in on the SALE section. Boxes and boxes of cards on display, and after some looking she found one matching the design that Abigail had sent Conrad... that Sweet Abby T had been posed to resemble. Piper cradled the box under her arm and kept looking. Wrapping paper, bows, tags, and rows of trees, much of it on discount.

She stared at the lighted trees in another area, most in shades of green, but there was a pastel pink one with flickering white lights, a purple tree, and at the far back a baby blue that she had to concede was pretty. Some tabletop size, some towering at nine or ten feet with branches frosted and looking so real.

Deck the Halls started blaring, one of her father's favorite tunes. A thickset middle-aged woman in front of Piper started singing along... others joined in.

The store was altogether massive, especially for such a small town, had been several smaller stores at one time, she guessed, with doorways cut in the walls to link them. There was a room where an artist sat at a table personalizing ornaments—she saw her father in there—the tree room, the card and paper room. The largest room was a showcase of everything—trees and ornaments and cabinets filled with beautiful Christmas-themed dust catchers. Had Miss Thornbridge walked through all of it on every visit?

And the killer?

Piper went through another doorway into a smaller section; this room had been her favorite as a child. More than a dozen different kinds of fudge and cookies were displayed in a bakery case. However, not much was left of any variety; like the sale ornaments, the goodies had been picked over. A small sign said: everything must go today. The prices were so good that Piper caved and came away with six pieces of walnut fudge and nine of chocolate-mint. For her dad, she told herself, but they were large chunks, and she'd picked out so many that some would come her way. She added a dozen assorted cookies and a pound of chocolate covered almonds, and the clerk put everything in a large bag. The thought of buying the purple tyrannosaurus crept into her head.

"You'll have to pay for those Christmas cards in the main room."

Piper nodded. There were only a few people behind her.

"Did you know an Abigail Thornbridge?"

The clerk dipped her chin and shrugged, looked around Piper as if wanting her to move along so she could wait on the next shopper. Piper did a juggling act, and with a now-free hand reached into her pocket and pulled out a computer printed photo of Miss Thornbridge.

"Sure," the clerk said. "That's Sweet Abby T, right?"

"Yeah, I heard she was called that."

"A regular... an after Christmas regular mostly, looking for bargains. Always goes for the plain fudge, a four-piece box. We're out of the plain fudge. Just about out of everything."

"Did she shop here alone?"

"Usually." The clerk's brow knitted. "Something happen to her?"

The county paper was a weekly so the news story and obituary wouldn't have appeared yet. Piper said, "Thanks," and moved along.

Normally Santa Clause—a man dressed as Santa—sat at a table in the sweets room in a throne-like chair that today was empty. Kids could sit and chat or have their picture taken with him. A sign on the table said: Returned to the North Pole, see you again this May.

In Miss Thornbridge's living room there had been a small framed picture on the shelf of Abigail, Santa, and an unknown elderly woman. Judging by the throne-like chair it was shot here. So Miss Thornbridge had indulged in a little childhood frivolity.

Piper carried her prized treats into the next room, where her legs locked. Across from her a SALE banner stretched above a long, many-tiered display. Most of the shelves had been heavily picked over, and the remaining goods included twists of silvery garland and lengths of colorful beads, candy cane-shaped soap dispensers, artificial floral arrangements, reindeer figurines, and on the top shelf a half-dozen mugs.

Including a bright red one with Merry Christmas scrawled on it.

Piper's throat tightened. There were shoppers in front of the shelves, moving around the packages of garland. A young woman with broad shoulders and wearing an ankle-length quilted coat held up a snowman-shaped peppermill and giggled with delight.

"Only two dollars. Midgey! Midgey! Look what I found! It's almost like the one I broke."

Piper pressed herself against a gap between man-high plastic peppermint sticks and waited for an opening in the browsers.

Had the killer seen Miss Thornbridge shopping here? Mr. Delaney? Is that why the killer bought the Merry Christmas mugs and left them as a signature, because they visited the store? Looked at the mugs?

"Move it, sister," said a hawk-nosed woman with tight white curls. She nudged the broad-shouldered woman aside and reached for a package of gold and red garland. "Other people are shopping here, too."

"Happy New Year, bitch," returned the broad-shouldered woman, who clutched her snowman prize and fled the room.

Had Miss Thornbridge or Mr. Delaney done something here to irk the killer… like hawk-nosed had rattled the broad-shouldered woman with the snowman peppermill?

What was the motive?

"Maybe you should shop somewhere else, asshat," a teenager cursed hawk-nosed. The teen stretched up and grabbed one of the mugs, this in the image of a cartoon moose head. "Maybe the sheriff should arrest you for misconduct." She gestured to Piper, and then continued perusing the gaudy wares.

How had the killer selected his victims?

Why Conrad Delaney and Abigail Thornbridge?

Piper saw an opening and stepped in, grabbed the sole Merry Christmas mug, and headed toward the counter, the questions tumbling over each other and begging to get out.

SIXTEEN

The final chords of *I Saw Three Ships* played as Piper reached the front of the line.

She placed the Merry Christmas mug and the box of cards on the counter, the bag with her treats beside them. "I'd like these... and I'd like to talk to the manager."

"That would be me, Sheriff," returned the thirty-something woman at the cash register. She was stunning, in a claret pantsuit with a dainty sprinkle of beads around the collar, long neck which helped show off dangly crystal snowflake earrings. Her blonde hair was cut short and her nose slightly upturned, bringing to mind the image of a pixie. Her makeup was *Cover Girl* quality. "Is there a problem?"

"Two of them," Piper said. Abigail Thornbridge and Conrad Delaney.

Several minutes later, after the manager found a clerk to take her place at the counter, they sat at the small table near the Santa throne. All of the goodies had sold out of the bakery case; the sweet shop was closed, though Piper could still pick out the heady scent of chocolate.

"I need to find out who bought a few of these." Piper took the Merry Christmas mug out of her bag and set it in front of her.

"We sold a lot of those mugs, in red and green." The manager passed over the list of employees and their phone numbers that Piper had requested. "But I don't think any of my people bought them." A pause. "But I remember a man who bought a lot of them. And I'm the one who rang him up."

"When was it? When did he buy the mugs?"

The manager's forehead wrinkled while she thought. "I think it was a Wednesday, maybe a Thursday. The first week of December. We were so busy busy busy that week. I hadn't seen him in here before, but that doesn't mean he wasn't. I couldn't give you a name. You'll have to ask the girls... if they'd seen him before, knew him. One of them might. We get oodles of customers all year, especially in December. I'm only good with the regulars. And I'm good at coats and hats and spotting great high heels." She smiled wide. "Awesome to see your father back here, by the way. How is he doing?"

"Good. He's doing good." Though Piper didn't know that to be true. She pulled a small recorder from a pocket, unzipped her jacket and shrugged out of it. "Do you mind?"

"Record me?" The manager touched her nose. "I guess so. Sure. Go ahead."

"You are—"

"Vivian Moss." *Mrs.* Piper thought, noticing the ring on the woman's left hand.

"Thanks for taking the time. I know you're busy. Before we're done here today I'd like to see some video, Mrs. Moss, of customers at your counter, from that first week of December. It's important, and—"

"We don't have any video, Sheriff, though the owner has thought about it. We have some theft, but not a lot, all things considered. Especially given how many people come through. Minor, really. It's just smalls that get stolen. We all keep a pretty close eye on folks, though. Catch a few every year. And we prosecute, no matter what their story."

"Fine, no video. Then can I see the credit card receipts from that week, Mrs. Moss, from the day that you sold the mugs, and—"

"Viv, please. He paid cash. I remember that. And he counted change out, like he wasn't sure he'd have enough money. In fact, he didn't, was twenty or thirty cents shy. I put in the rest and told him Merry Christmas. So no credit card records either, no check. Cash. Bought the three big Merry Christmas mugs that were on the shelf, and had asked if we had any more. That's why I remember the sale. He said he wanted *all* the red Merry Christmas mugs we had. And said if we didn't have more, where could he order them? There was a half-dozen green ones like it, Merry Christmas, but he said they had to be red. I found more in the back room. He ended up buying eleven, I remember because it was one short of a dozen. He could have had a dozen, but he didn't want that one. Plus, he was a tad short on the eleven as it was." She tapped her index finger on the rim of the Merry Christmas mug Piper had purchased for a dollar and set on the table between them. "The design on that one is crooked, see? That's why I marked it so cheap. One dollar. Originally they sold for ten-fifty."

"Eleven mugs."

"Yes, Sheriff. All we had," the manager returned. "Well, all we had with the design printed correctly and that were red. Pick it up. The mug has a good feel to it. And they sold well. We'd moved a dozen before Mr. I Want Them All came in. Moved all the green ones, too, eventually. We won't reorder them for next season, though, as we always try to bring in new designs each year. I like the company, good product."

A husband and wife walked through the room, headed toward another part of the store. The man sang boisterously to *Good King Wenceslas*: "Mark my footsteps good, my page, tread thou in them boldly. Though shalt find the winter's rage freeze thy blood less coldly."

Piper hefted the mug and stared at the inside. Ceramic, heavily glazed, a little over-sized and shiny as Rudolph's nose, it would hold maybe sixteen ounces of coffee. She set it back down. "What did he look like, Mr. I Want Them All?"

Vivian leaned forward. "What's going on? Katie said you've been showing a picture of Sweet Abby T around."

Piper let out a breath, strong enough to ruffle her bangs. "It's an ongoing investigation."

"Into what?"

"I can't say."

"Oh, come on."

Take a chance, Piper thought. Abigail Thornbridge's death was public record, and it would be in the paper, maybe in tomorrow's edition. Conrad's death would be in there, too. "Abigail—"

"Sweet Abby T—"

"Was found dead yesterday, and—"

"Really? Well, she was up there." Vivian scowled, tiny cracks showing in her apple red lipstick. "And what does that have to do with our big red Merry Christmas mugs and the man in the Colts jacket?"

Piper felt like she'd been struck in the stomach. "Colts jacket?" Her voice was soft. There was a man in an Indianapolis Colts jacket on Conrad Delaney's driveway. And at the quick stop shortly before the truck ran her off the road—and he'd looked familiar, looked right at her while she was eating her late lunch. Oren would have the man's name, said he had everyone's name from the Hagee New Year's Eve party, and had talked to them. Maybe they could take the man into custody before lunch. She'd radio Randy from the car.

Vivian had been saying something, but Piper missed it. Didn't matter, she was recording the conversation.

"The jacket—"

"Yes. The man who bought the mugs… the man in the leather Colts jacket. Was probably quite expensive, that jacket. Leather. You get something 'officially licensed' by the NFL, like some of our ornaments, and it costs more than it really should." Vivian clutched at the mug. "Is he related to Abby? The man in the jacket? Are you trying to find him to notify—"

"No, it's not like that." Piper didn't like to lie. It was in the sheriff's department records—that were public—that Conrad Delaney had been murdered. The report on Abigail Thornbridge listed it, too… though only a handful of specifics would be in either set of records. Ongoing investigations, lots of things would be left out for awhile. "Abigail Thornbridge was murdered. We found her body yesterday morning."

"Murdered?" Vivian looked a shade paler. "I'd figured a heart attack or stroke or just her years caught up. Murder?"

Piper dropped her voice again. "What did the man look like? In the Colts jacket?" She wanted a description; there was bound to be more than one man with an Indianapolis Colts jacket in the county. Too much of a coincidence though, for this not to be "the guy."

"A murder? In Spencer County?" Vivian's knuckles went white against the mug.

Apparently news hadn't reached her yet about Conrad Delaney. *Two* murders in Spencer County. A savvy reporter from a big-city newspaper would link the deaths, would talk to the Hagees and discover Conrad had been posed, maybe find Abigail's pastor and learn about the white Christmas ribbon. But sleepy Spencer County didn't have an investigative reporter like that, her father had said over breakfast.

"The man, Viv, what did he look like?"

"Did he... do you... do you think that man killed Sweet Abby T? A murderer? Why would you think—"

"What did he—" Piper figured she'd gone about this wrong. MP training? Yeah, she'd aced it. But never a murder investigation, an *actual* investigation. Textbooks and *Law & Order* reruns and commanding officer lectures hadn't prepared her enough for the real thing. Inexperienced, she likely should have taken a different approach, maybe not have talked to the manager here... found her at home, visited the clerks at home... Maybe she should've taken the autopsy and sent Oren here, or Randy.

"He was several inches little taller than me and had a Colts stocking cap pulled over his ears to match the jacket, stubble on his face. I remember it being cold the week before Christmas. Hadn't snowed much. We only had a dusting on the sidewalk when I opened up. I could use a broom, didn't need a shovel. He had nice eyes, a good smile."

"Go on."

"He was polite, respectful, called me ma'am, which made me feel a tad old. Good voice, a little deep. I'd heard him singing to one of the

Christmas carols. Some of our shoppers sing along, you know. A favorite comes on and you can't help yourself. You start singing."

"Yeah, I know."

"His eyebrows were brown except there was a streak of white, maybe paint, maybe just white hair, in one of them. I don't remember which one."

Piper remembered that the Colt-jacketed man in the quick stop had the makings of a beard. He might have had a streak in his eyebrow; she couldn't summon a clear enough mental image, hadn't looked at him but for a moment.

Vivian closed her eyes and shook her head. "I'd recognize him if I saw him again. It was buying all those mugs, wanting just the red ones, being a couple of dimes short, that's why I remember him... having to go in the back room to get more mugs, him paying cash. That was memorable."

Piper had taken pictures of the people shivering on Conrad Delaney's driveway. She'd go back to the office, print them out, and have Vivian look at them.

"He didn't buy anything else," she continued. "Oh, and he looked strong. The jacket was tight around his shoulders. I remember wondering if he was an athlete. Jay Cutler was born here, you know." Another pause. "And I wondered what he was going to do with the mugs, maybe give them to people where he worked, fill them with candy. Some people buy our mugs and fill them with candy, tie curly ribbons on the handles."

He filled Mr. Delaney's with coffee, Piper thought, *Miss Thornbridge's with tea—and used curly ribbons to tie the mug to her hands.*

She shivered.

He'd bought eleven mugs.

SEVENTEEN

"You don't like her do you?"

Oren looked across the table and shook his head. "Nope." He stirred the cottage cheese with his spoon. "Do you, Annie? Do you like her?"

Dr. Neufeld pushed her tray aside, finished with her meal, the plate as clean as if his cats had licked it. They were in the hospital cafeteria, the lunch crowd dispersing around them and the chatter of competing conversations dying. "I don't know, Oren." She crossed her arms. "Verdict's out as they say. I don't really know her. Can't judge what I don't know."

"She said you were finishing the autopsy on Delaney when she got here yesterday."

"I started early, and I hadn't bothered to let her know."

"Good." He stirred the cottage cheese some more. Oren knew he should have been hungry, but the Thornbridge autopsy, reasonably quick though it was, had unsettled his stomach. He hadn't touched his meal, other than to move things around.

The coroner's preliminary ruling: asphyxiation due to strangulation. Tox panels were set to run, but they expected to find nothing beyond whatever plethora of prescriptions Mrs. Thornbridge had been taking. Dr. Neufeld showed him the marks that indicated the killer had used his hands, apparently with gloves on. Large hands, giving further strength to the notion they were looking for a man.

"I should have let her know," she continued, "that I was starting Conrad's early. I would have let you know."

He nodded.

"She's young, Oren."

"Same age as my granddaughter. Twenty-three." Oren set the spoon down and pushed the tray to the side. "I should have retired. Maybe I should retire now, but—"

"She might not pass the sheriff's exam come spring."

"There is that."

"Why don't you hold off on that retirement until then? Besides, what would you possibly do with all that free time? You can be boating every day, especially in this weather." Dr. Neufeld smiled sadly and reached for Oren's sandwich. "You're not going to eat this, are you?"

"Nope." He was amazed she could have an appetite after cutting someone apart. "Help yourself."

"Thanks."

"This murder… *murders*… they're keeping me occupied. And the sheriff's in over her head. Way the hell over. She gave me a choice this morning—the autopsy or the Ho Ho Ho place in Santa Claus. A *choice*. Paul Blackwood would never have given me a choice. Paul Blackwood would have given orders. She doesn't know what she's doing. Maybe I'm in over my head, too. Never had something like this here. In all my years in the county. Nothing like this. It's sick."

"I don't disagree on the sick part." She worked on his sandwich.

He noticed a divot in the tabletop. Oren had worked two murders when he was with the Rockport police department, the first when he hadn't been on the job long. They were simple, he remembered. One was the result of a drunken dispute between farmers after a bar had closed down, accidental. The larger farmer had leveled a haymaker at the smaller, dropping him onto the sidewalk, where his neck snapped. The other case involved a man running over his mother-in-law—

intentional, he was sentenced to fifty years. Oren wondered if he was still kicking in the pen.

There were a few others murders in the county in the past twenty years, also solved without a great deal of work, domestics for the most part.

But this?

Oddly, he found it both disheartening and exciting. Sleepy Spencer County had a nutcase that had it in for two old people and dressed them up to look like Christmas cards.

"Whatcha thinking about?" She'd finished the sandwich and eyed his cottage cheese.

He nudged the bowl toward her.

"That Abigail Thornbridge was Conrad Delaney's fourth grade teacher, and that she later was the principal when Conrad's kids went to that same grade school. So that's the connection between her and Conrad. And apparently Conrad's wife, Sara, went to Abigail's church. Conrad didn't go to church, his neighbors said, at least not often enough so's they'd notice."

"Small county like this, a lot of people are connected." Dr. Neufeld started on the cottage cheese. "I just want you to get the son of a bitch. Conrad Delaney was my very good friend. I've hardly slept."

"Yeah, I want me to get that son of a bitch. When we were young, Conrad was my good friend, too." Oren wanted to solve it on his own, maybe with Randy's help, didn't want the State called, didn't want the new sheriff's fingers in it. But she was in it, wasn't she? She'd been run off the road, and Oren believed what Piper believed, that the killer had done it. Randy wasn't sold on that notion yet, but he always looked at all the angles before picking a conclusion. Oren figured Piper had seen something—or the killer *thought* she had seen something—and he wanted her eliminated because of it.

Oren wanted her eliminated, too, but from the department and not in any permanent way.

"I don't know what she saw, Annie, what Piper Blackwell did—"

"—to get the killer's attention?"

He'd shared that bit about the crash with Dr. Neufeld during the autopsy.

Oren shrugged. "Something. Just something she saw."

"Maybe the sheriff didn't see some*thing*. Maybe she saw him."

Oren sat straight. "And maybe she didn't know it. Hell, probably didn't know. Twenty-three. Helluva thing, Annie. Twenty-three and she's running the sheriff's department."

"She has to pass the test come April to keep the office." Finished with the cottage cheese, she reached for Oren's chocolate chip cookie.

"Or not pass it." He caught her studying him like he was a sample under a microscope. "Conrad, Abigail, they knew their killer."

"Sure. They probably sent him Christmas cards."

"And probably let him into their house." He stared at the divot. "If they knew him, maybe we know him… saw him, talked to him. Small county, like you said."

"Probably."

"So maybe he's been around in the county a while."

"Probably."

"And maybe something sent him over the edge this year."

"Definitely."

He growled softly. "It's in front of me, Annie. It has to be, and I just haven't made the pieces fit right." But maybe he'd make them fit a little better. Randy had called, said he was bringing in a few people to question again, something not sitting the way it should. Oren was going back to the office to catch the interviews. "I'll make them fit, Annie, all the pieces. Before Piper Blackwell does."

"You really don't like her, do you?"

"She's twenty-three," Oren said, as he grabbed his coat.

EIGHTEEN

"I've been going over it and over it, Chris, and the times don't fit right." Randy sat across from Chris Hagee in the small room. A six-foot table was between them, two chairs on each side, not much wiggle room for anything else.

Oren squeezed in and took the other seat opposite Chris. He was surprised Hagee was one of the folks Randy had called in to talk with again.

"Looking through our notes," Randy continued, "Oren's and mine, a couple of things don't match."

Chris didn't say anything. He wore the same green coat he had on when the department got the call about Conrad Delaney. Oren still smelled the cigarette smoke on it and saw the pack outline in Chris's front pocket. Chris unzipped the jacket and shrugged out of it. He had a heavy flannel shirt on underneath, no t-shirt, wiry gray wisps of chest hair showing where he'd not buttoned it at the collar.

Oren didn't say anything, either. His mind flitted between the image of Conrad Delaney in the sleigh and Abigail Thornbridge in her living room. Sick bastard to do that. Oren never had a high opinion of Chris, but he hadn't thought him the sort who could do something so evil.

Randy tapped his notebook, and then pulled a recorder out of his pocket and set it on the table. "I'm gonna record this, Chris."

"Suit yourself." Chris rested his elbows on the table and cupped his chin in his hands. Oren heard him tap his toes.

"Like I said, things don't match." Randy waited.

A phone rang in the other room, three times before the dispatcher answered it; not the emergency line, that had a different sound to it.

"What doesn't match?" Chris said after a few more moments had passed. "I done told you everything I know. Told Oren that night... morning... of my party." He belched. "Excuse me. Told you the next day. Ain't got nothing else to say about it except I feel bad about Conrad... and I told you that earlier, too."

Randy waited. Oren knew the detective played with silence, that it could make people feel uncomfortable and that they needed to fill it up with noise, even if that noise was the sound of their own voice. The phone again; she picked it up after two rings. A moment later a gentle shushing sound—the main door opening and its rubber strip sliding along the mat. The door closed. Muted voices; probably the next interview showing up early.

"So what doesn't match?" Chris tapped his foot faster, and his elbows slid off the table. He sat a little straighter and folded his hands. He didn't meet their eyes, instead looked at a whorl in the table.

Oren saw a vein in Chris's jaw stand out, an indication of fear or worry. All of it was a "tell," proof that Chris was hiding something. What had Randy picked up on that he'd missed? Was he really getting too old for this?

"What doesn't match, huh?" Chris persisted, his eyes still down. Oren saw a vein standing out at Chris's temple.

Randy glanced at his notebook. "You said you went over to Conrad Delaney's about eleven-forty."

"Yeah, twenty to midnight. I wanted to get over there, make an invitation he'd decline, and get back before the ball dropped, you know. Told Oren that. Told you that."

The dispatcher stuck her head in the doorway. "Buck radioed and said no go on talking to the roofer. On vacation, he said. Apparently no one wants roofing work done in the winter."

"Thanks." Oren waved her away.

Randy tapped a pen to the notebook, in time with the tapping of Chris's foot. "Well, you're consistent on *that* story. But it doesn't match what some of your guests told me."

Chris shifted in the chair.

Oren's interest was definitely piqued.

"Your cousin said you went over a few minutes *after* eleven, that you were there a little while, and then came back, talked to your wife in the kitchen."

"Maybe I got the time wrong."

"He said you went back over... at eleven forty. Said you made two trips."

"My cousin, he was drinking. Hell, everybody at my party was drinking. He probably didn't know what he saw."

Randy put the pen down. "Three other people at your party said the same thing, Chris, that you went over to Conrad Delaney's *twice*." He let a little more silence settle and Oren watched Chris's jaw clench. "Dispatch said your call came in at eleven fifty-five."

Oren knew Teegan talked to Chris a few minutes, and then called Piper Blackwell, apparently timing that call at midnight, when the new sheriff officially took over. Then Teegan called Oren.

"I waited outside, just like the dispatcher told me to. I told Oren that."

"You also told Oren that you called your wife from the phone in Conrad's living room. But phone records don't show that, only the call to the dispatcher at eleven fifty-five."

"Well, I called Joanie. The records are wrong. I called and they all came over for a peek."

"Actually, Chris, your cousin said everyone was curious and came over a few minutes after you went to the Delaney house the *second* time. You didn't need to call your wife and tell her about Conrad because she already knew. You'd told her after your first trip, didn't you?"

Chris didn't answer.

"And the people from your party, they all came over on their own, curious, wanting to take a look." Another stretch of silence. "Four people from your party tell the same story. Did they all get it wrong? Do I need to have Joan come in and ask her the same questions?"

Chris worked his jaw, his eyes beads fixed on his fingers.

"Why two trips, Chris? Why did you go to the Delaney house twice? And why did you wait to call the dispatcher until your *second* visit?"

Oren cursed himself for not asking the guests the questions that would have led to the two trip discovery. But he figured Randy must have only made the connection late this morning, which is when he called Oren during the autopsy, told him he was bringing some people in, that things didn't match.

Maybe he really was getting too old for this. Maybe he should retire.

"What's it matter if I went over there once or twice? What's it matter, you know? Conrad was dead dead dead. Dead dead dead, I say. Frozen like an icicle. Dead. What difference does it make how many times I went over there? What if I went over a hundred times? An icicle just sitting there, I told you. Dead dead dead."

And apparently Conrad had been sitting there—dead dead dead— for two or three days and no one had noticed, Oren reflected.

"I only went in the house once."

"But you went over there *twice*." Randy's voice had an edge to it.

"I didn't kill him." Chris sounded angry. "I wouldn't kill nobody. You know that. So what's it matter if I went over there twice?"

"Because the truth matters," Oren said. He watched Chris's expression soften a little.

"So tell us the truth," Randy prompted. "Tell us the truth and maybe you can go home."

Chris plopped his elbows on the table again and fidgeted with his fingers, like his thumbs were dancing with each other. "My Joanie, it mostly happened the way I told Oren. She saw Conrad sitting in the sleigh, you know. Around eleven she saw him and told me to go over, invite him, that he shouldn't be alone. So I put on my coat, you know, and went over, stopped at the end of the driveway and lit up. Joan don't want me to smoke in the house. I saw that Conrad wasn't moving, figured he was dead. I really did think he'd had the big one, you know. He'd had a heart attack some years—"

"Go on," Randy said.

"I finished half my cigarette and walked over. I saw them boot tracks I told Oren about, walked right inside 'em to keep the snow out of my dress shoes. Went right up to the sleigh... them tracks went up to the sleigh, around the sleigh, up to the sidewalk. I saw that Conrad was dead. Dead dead—"

"—dead. Yeah, I get that." Randy crossed his arms and leaned back. "So why didn't you call the dispatcher then, the first time? Why didn't you go inside the house on your first trip? Or better yet, why didn't you call the dispatcher when you went back to your house after your first trip? Why did you wait and—"

"Because I took the damn sleigh bells, that's why." The anger had returned to Chris's voice. "Because I walked around the sleigh, in them boot tracks, and pulled the sleigh bells off. Antiques. My Joan likes antiques. Conrad was dead. Dead dead dead. He sure didn't need the damn sleigh bells. His loser of a son... he didn't need the damn sleigh bells neither. So I took the bells. What's it to you? They were out in the yard, that's pretty much public property, you know. They weren't inside the house. Conrad would have liked my Joan to have 'em, you know. I took the bells and I put them in my garage, went into the kitchen and told Joanie about Conrad having the big one, about him being dead. Someone took his damn Teddy bear a few years back. That wasn't me by the way. Someone took that damn bear 'cause it was sitting outside. Well, the bells were outside, too."

Chris was red-faced, and the veins stood out even more pronounced. He took a deep breath and coughed, a smoker's cough, and continued. "My Joan, she said we should call somebody. She said we should *really* make sure Conrad was dead and just wasn't, I dunno, unconscious or something. I said he was dead, and she asked me a few more times if I was sure. Of course I was sure. He didn't blink when I unhooked the bells. He was frozen solid like an icicle. But I went back over there anyway, to keep Joanie happy, made sure he wasn't breathing, and went inside... that's when I went inside, only once... and I hollered, just to see if his loser son was around, went into the living room and called 9-1-1. See... it happened mostly as I told Oren, but two trips instead of one. And when I came back out, all my guests and Joanie were on the lawn around the sleigh. I told 'em not to touch anything. Happy now?"

Randy didn't say anything. Oren watched the red fade from Chris's face.

Oren decided to try one. "Your brother Mike, he tried to buy Conrad's gas station, didn't he?"

Chris glared. "Mike made him a couple of offers, but Conrad... he wanted too much for that damn little gas station. Wasn't worth what he was asking. Everybody around here knows that, knows that he asked too much."

"Maybe we should talk to Mike again," Randy said. "Bring him in and—"

"Mikey didn't kill Conrad, and certainly not over some stupid gas station."

"He didn't come to your New Year's Eve party."

"Mikey doesn't drink."

"And he lives just lives down the road from you, doesn't he?" Oren and Randy both knew where Mike Hagee lived. "Not far from—"

"Hell, call him in if you want. Call the whole town in if—"

"Calm down," Oren cut in.

"I didn't kill Conrad," Chris repeated. "I wouldn't kill nobody. You can't possibly think that I—"

"Do you know Abigail Thornbridge?" Randy fired out the question, keeping it present-tense. Oren figured word of the Thornbridge murder might not have reached across the county yet. "Down the road from Fulda, Miss Thornbridge?"

Chris blinked. "Sweet Abby T? The retired school teacher?"

Randy nodded. "So you know her."

Chris shrugged. "Sort of, but not really. I know who she is. I didn't go to that school, my son didn't either, but I know *of* her. Always popped up and popped off at the county school board meetings, you know, and I was on the board a couple of years back when my kid was in track." A pause. "What's she got to do with this? Had Conrad willed her the bells?" A longer pause. "Do you think *she* killed Conrad? That's not possible. Abby T's gotta be pushing a hundred, you know."

"Eighty-two," Oren said softly.

"And she sure as hell didn't put him in the sleigh."

"Somebody did," Randy said. "And he'd sat there a while."

"And right across the street, apparently you didn't notice," Oren put in.

Chris looked defiant and defeated at the same time. "You don't get it. That damn spotlight on that damn sleigh. I avoided looking at it, that's probably why I didn't see Conrad sitting out there. Come night, Conrad would leave that damn spotlight on, sometimes to ten, eleven, sometimes all night if he forgot to turn it off. Our bedroom's at the front of the house and that light… even with the shade down… had a helluva time getting to sleep sometimes, you know. Inconsiderate, I tell you."

"I guess you won't have to worry about the spotlight anymore," Oren said.

Chris's foot stopped tapping. "Can I go now?"

"Bring the bells into the office before we close today, Mr. Hagee." Randy turned off the recorder. "Otherwise I'll come out and get them —and you. Understand?"

"They're just bells."

Randy made a humming noise. "Trespassing, vandalism, theft… by your own admission. Disturbing a crime scene. Tampering with evidence. And about fifteen other charges. Back before we close up, you hear?"

"Yeah, I get you." Chris stood and reached for his coat, eyes on the floor as he left.

"He didn't do it," Oren said.

Randy put the recorder in his pocket. "He lied, didn't tell us he'd went over there twice. Stole the antique bells. I don't trust a liar. They never stop at just one lie. Lives right across the street, retired, no alibi for the window we're setting for Conrad's death. And therefore no alibi for Abigail's either. Claimed he didn't really know Abigail. That's bullshit. Called her Sweet Abby T and mentioned the school board meetings. He knew her. And Chris is a drinker. I checked on that. No arrests, but Rockport police answered a couple of calls at a bar on Main last year, and Chris's name was mentioned. The bartender says he's a regular—and regularly drinks too much. I'm putting him on the boss's whiteboard as our current suspect. Motive: he was pissed about the sleigh display. Means and opportunity: had that out the whazoo. Maybe got drunk and offed Conrad and figured he might as well get Abby T while he was at it."

"You put his name up on that board, and I'll be erasing it." Oren stood and stretched, looked down at Randy. "Chris Hagee didn't kill Conrad Delaney." He decided he wasn't too old for the job, after all. "Yeah, you caught Chris in a lie. Ha! Maybe he was the one who stole that stuffed bear a few years back. But a liar doesn't make a murderer. Sometimes a liar is just a liar."

"And what makes you so sure he's innocent?"

"Well, innocent of murder. Chris wouldn't have set Conrad up in that sleigh. Oh, he probably could have lifted him, dragged him... Conrad was a little hefty, but not *that* hefty. But Chris wouldn't have put him up on display like that. Killing was premeditated, and so some planning was involved. Chris is more of a spur-of-the-moment fellow, outside of his annual party... and he's been doing that for so many years it's probably by rote."

"I don't know, Oren, I think—"

"If Chris was the doer, he would've killed Conrad in the house, left him there, and unplugged the spotlight in front of the sleigh before he went back home."

"There is that I suppose," Randy said.

"And he didn't kill Sweet Abby T either. Might not have liked her from his school board days, a good while back—and yeah I'm sure he probably knew her better than he let on. But Chris is retired, and he retired *early*. He's on the lazy side, and setting Abby T up like that with the curling ribbons and everything. Setting Conrad up for that matter... too much work, too much thought into it, and like I said, too much planning. Probably took all his effort to make his lit'l smokies for that New Year's Eve party. So I'd say the only thing Chris Hagee is guilty of is stealing some old sleigh bells and trying to lie about it."

"You should have won the election, Oren."

"Yeah, I should have."

The next man in wore a leather Indianapolis Colts jacket.

"We've got a few questions for you," Oren began.

NINETEEN

THURSDAY, JANUARY 4TH

The man in the leather Indianapolis Colts jacket was Elias Gerald Hagee, a nephew of Chris, and he had a solid alibi for the window of both Abigail Thornbridge's and Conrad Delaney's murders. Piper listened to Randy's recording of the interview and read the follow up verification before she called her shift done for the night.

Elias Gerald, as he preferred to be called, had been in the Bahamas with his ex-wife, and showed off his sunburn to prove it. They'd taken a weeklong reconciliation vacation and flew back on a red eye that got into the Louisville, Ky., airport at 5 a.m. on December 31. He wouldn't have had enough time to kill Conrad, set him up on display and let the body freeze. Elias Gerald told Randy and Oren that Freeport was fun, and lots of sex and alcohol were involved, but at the end there was no reconciliation. Elias Gerald said he slept most of the day, then got up and went to his uncle's annual New Year's Eve bash and drank more than he should have. His ex- did not attend, apparently having found a different party to go to.

Elias Gerald had an alibi, too, for when Piper was run off the road. He worked at the Rockport power plant; the shift manager saw him clock out right at 5. Piper had left the Delaney house five minutes after that, and he could not have met her on the road in time to put her in a ditch. Besides, Elias Gerald drove a Chevy Equinox, and didn't own a truck.

Piper yawned and clicked on the radio and turned up the window defrosters. She was headed to the Indianapolis airport. According to MapQuest, it was three hours and twenty-one minutes from her apartment. She'd set the alarm for 4 a.m. and put it out of reach so she couldn't hit snooze, showered fast when it chirped, wolfed down two frosted strawberry Pop-Tarts without bothering to toast them, and allowed herself an extra half hour of travel time... in case. In case of what? In case someone tried to run her off the road again? She was still sore from the first joust and had a deep purple bruise on her chest from the seatbelt.

She had been so certain the man in the Colts jacket was at the heart of this. She'd returned to the store in Santa Claus just before it closed yesterday, showed the manager pictures of the people at Conrad's party—and according to her not one of them looked like the man who bought the Merry Christmas mugs.

Now they had to pursue another possibility—the roofer Abigail and Conrad had in common. Maybe he had a Colts jacket, too. Unfortunately, one of her deputies reported that the roofer was on an extended vacation.

Anthony Delaney's flight was due in at 8:20, and if it was on time she'd be back in the office before noon. When she'd told Anthony about his father during their phone call, he said he wanted to come back for the funeral, hadn't seen his father in four years—since his previous trip to the States. He arranged travel immediately, which entailed a bus ride to Bangkok, a flight to Los Angeles, and then a fast connection to Indianapolis.

Anthony had planned another bus trip that would take him to Evansville, where a friend would give him a ride to Fulda. Since Piper wanted to talk to him anyway, she said she would pick him up. Piper wondered how he was paying for this; maybe the temple had a fund for family situations. *Maybe it's none of my concern*, she thought.

Whoever had rented this car before her had set the radio to an oldies station. She was about to remedy that when a favorite tune came on: Chicago performing *25 or 6 to 4*. It had a heady, relentless beat that she set her thumbs tapping in time to against the steering wheel. One of her soldiers during her second tour in Iraq played a trumpet, and *25 or 6 to 4* was his go-to piece, others around him banging on footlockers or knocking their boots together in accompaniment. He'd told her that Robert Lamm composed it when he lived with hippies above the Sunset Strip. In the Hollywood Hills, overlooking the city one very early morning was where Lamm supposedly sculpted the classic. It was either 3:35 a.m. or 3:34 a.m.—hence either twenty-five minutes to four or twenty-six minutes to four—when Lamm looked up from working on it.

Piper's trumpet player was killed shortly before her unit returned to Fort Campbell. IED, downrange assignment, prophetically closing in on 4 a.m. It could have been her had she went into that trapped house, but she'd been checking out the one next door. They played *25 or 6 to 4* at the memorial service.

Piper brushed the memory away and instead turned up the volume and focused on the road. Loud music was therapeutic, she believed. If you cranked it high enough it wouldn't let you think.

His flight had arrived early, and he was waiting for her at the gate. Piper had a small picture in her pocket that she'd taken from the Delaney house. She hadn't needed it to recognize him. Anthony was bald and wore heavy dark orange robes, a backpack slung over one shoulder. He walked straight toward her. Piper was the only soul in a sheriff's uniform.

"You're going to be cold," she told him as he slid into the passenger side and placed his backpack on the seat behind him.

"My robe, Sheriff Blackwell, will keep me warm. It is so designed that way. Beyond a reminder that I am a member of a great universal community and have pledged myself to lofty spiritual ideals, this robe wards off cold, heat, insects, and the wind." He buckled the seatbelt. "But I intend to ask my brother to take me to the J.C. Penny outlet store in Owensboro so I may acquire jeans and a sweatshirt and something to wear to my father's funeral tomorrow. I did not have time for such shopping before my flight left Bangkok. It is important I look nice for my father's funeral. I did not attend my mother's, and though I am not supposed to carry regrets, I cannot seem to lose that one."

Piper had turned off the radio. "So you have a little money to spend. For clothes?"

"An allotment of baht for my expenses. I will need it converted to dollars."

Piper had a better idea. She had a Kohl's card and stopped at one of their stores on the way out of the city and bought Anthony a pair of jeans, a sweatshirt, dress shirt, blazer, tie, and nice pants for the funeral—everything off the discount racks, including a pair of Nunn Bush Bourbon Street oxfords that were half-price. He wore the jeans and sweatshirt right then, declining a winter jacket as he was certain something of his father's would fit. At the checkout she added a cheap prepaid cell phone, and in the car she programmed her number into it and collected his number as well.

"In case you need to contact me," she told him.

"You are gracious, Sheriff Blackwell."

"Don't mention it."

"And I will pay you back after I get my baht converted."

She didn't give him the grisly details of the staging of his father's body, but Piper did confirm he was murdered, and that Abigail Thornbridge was strangled, too.

"Sweet Abby T," Anthony said. "She was nicknamed that because she always had a glass of ice tea on her desk. Every year she sent me a fruitcake for Christmas, even this past year. They were always awful, at least I thought so. But old Chaow—one of my mentors—loved them. Every year my father sent me a card and a few mystery novels for Christmas. The books were always good and welcome, and those I did not pass along to old Chaow until I'd read them twice. I am especially fond of the works of Robert Crais and Jeffery Deaver." He stretched around behind him and fumbled in the pack, brought out the Christmas card she'd asked him about.

His smoothed, tan face was handsome, Piper judged, with a strong jaw, perfect nose, and bright brown eyes highlighted by long lashes. Anthony came close to resembling the picture in her pocket, though in it he had hair and his cheeks looked fuller.

"This is the last thing he wrote to me," Anthony said. "He knew I wasn't Christian, but he still always sent a Christmas card, always a photo one."

Piper noticed the writing on the back was tiny so Conrad had been able to fit a long note on it.

"Read it to me, will you? I gotta keep my eyes on the road."

"Dear Anthony." He laughed softly. "He always called me Anthony, never Tony, the name I used in school. Or Tiger, my nickname for most of my life here… Tony the Tiger because I ate Frosted Flakes and played for the Fulda Wildcats. Always called my brother Zachary, too, never Zach. Dear Anthony, I hope this finds you well and happy. The doctor says my heart is fine, and I have my blood pressure under control, so I'm up for travel. I thought I'd come visit in April. I know it is hot then, and that we'd talked about July, but the airfare and hotel prices are too good to pass up, probably because of the heat, you think? You know me and sales. I found a package for a jungle tour, meeting hill tribes, a place to ride elephants, a boat trip to Shampoo Island. I'm not interested in the beach part, so I thought we'd spend time together then. I might take a little side trip to Vietnam. My friend Nang went last year and stayed in Hoi An, said he loved it. Better go before I'm too old, you think? Past time I spent some of the money from selling the gas station. I put my sleigh out again, painted it a glossy black this time. You'll see it on my next Christmas card. Your old school friend Jacob took my picture in it when he was here setting down a new kitchen floor for me. He put a roof on the house back in September. Best prices I could find in the county for the work. Seems young to have his own business, but then everyone seems young to me. Love, Dad."

Piper had plenty of questions. She'd jotted them down last night and read them over several times, essentially memorizing them. She had a recorder in her pocket, too, but decided not to use it. That wouldn't feel right, taking the conversation all formal.

"So the last time you saw your father was four years ago?"

"Yes. I was with a small delegation to California, and my father flew out to visit for a few days when there was an airfare war going on. Buddhism is one of the largest religions in the States, more than a million practitioners, and a great percentage of them are in California."

"I didn't know that," Piper said. "How did you—" She paused, trying to find a way to phrase it, but he intercepted the question.

"Become enlightened? I was doing a paper on Eastern influences the first semester of my senior year in high school, and as part of my research I read about Buddhism. Something clicked for me, like all my issues started falling into place. I found a temple in Louisville and visited, and right before Easter went on a weekend retreat at the Buddhist center in Furnace Mountain. That's in—"

"Clay City," Piper said. It was a town near the Daniel Boone National Forest in Kentucky that she'd road-tripped through once.

"I announced to my parents I was Buddhist, and that I wanted to be a monk. It probably had the same impact as if I'd said I was gay. Maybe they could have handled that easier. They were in denial, disbelief. Fortunately Zach stood by me. In the end, love won out. My high school graduation present was a round-trip ticket to Bangkok. They wanted me to go to college, but they also wanted me to get 'Buddhism out of my system.' I never used the return half of the ticket; I still have it, non-refundable back then, worthless now. I use it as a bookmark."

"So it was a one-way trip."

"Yes. I stayed. I was at peace, and it took me two years before I was welcomed as a monk. Twenty was a magic age for the temple I chose. I guess they wanted me to be sure, too. And so I have been serving in the Pathum Thani Temple for the past eight years."

"And you're happy."

"I am at peace," Anthony repeated. His face was serene. "Buddha said, 'Peace comes from within, do not seek it without.' Though I suppose I sought it by going to Thailand. Yes, I am happy."

"So you haven't been back to the house since you left after high school?"

"No. It will be good to see it again, even though the circumstances are sad. I plan to stay there while—"

"We haven't released the house yet," Piper cut in. "Though I'll check with my detective and see if we can hurry that up, and at least get you a winter coat out of the closet."

Anthony looked puzzled.

"I understand your father didn't have a will, and you and Zachary are the only relatives. If there are no claims on the estate, the house belongs to both of you. But at this time we're still treating it as a crime scene. And because it is a crime scene—"

"Ah, I understand. I will make other arrangements for a place to stay. I still have friends in this area, Evansville and Rockport mostly. Jacob… Jake… lives in Rockport and—"

"—is on vacation. We've been trying to talk to him."

He frowned. "Perhaps I will stay with my brother, then. Owensboro is just across the river. It is unfortunate that Jake is not here. He and I were very close, and he went with me to the temple in Louisville our senior year. He did not find enlightenment, but he was a good sport about it. I was looking forward to catching up."

"What can you tell me about Jake… Jacob Wallem?" That was chief among her questions.

A semi- barreled by, throwing slush on the windshield. Piper pumped the brake and turned on the wipers, sprayed washer fluid and watched as the icy gray stuff melted and left a slime trail across the glass.

"In high school he excelled in shop classes and in the summer worked for a builder. He started his own company three or four years ago. Jake told me about it in a Christmas letter and sent me emails with pictures of his projects. He knew I was Buddhist, but old friends like Jake still send me Christmas cards. I welcome the correspondence. Christmas is always a good time for keeping in touch. And Jake occasionally skyped with me."

"Did you get a card from Jake this year?" Piper had been driving under the speed limit, but she sped up now, two miles above it. She wanted to get back to the office and find out where Jacob Wallem was vacationing.

"Yes. It was machine printed, and I suspect it was the same letter he sent everyone. You know, one of those newsletter-things, an accounting of the year."

Piper remembered that Conrad had received a Christmas card and newsletter from Jacob.

"But at the bottom of the letter Jake scrawled a personal note about doing some work for my dad and about volunteering at the animal shelter because his business slowed in the winter. He loved dogs." He closed his eyes and his lips worked. Piper thought maybe he was praying. "I was hoping Jake would be at the funeral tomorrow."

Piper intended to go the funeral; Randy and Oren were planning on it, too.

"Anything else you can tell me about Jake?"

"We stayed in touch. But I haven't seen him in ten years, I can tell you that. When we were in high school he was a magnet for trouble, like my brother. But Jake wasn't into drugs. It was staying out late, skipping classes, a little graffiti, some minor vandalism. Your dad picked him up once and gave him a 'talking to' I guess you'd call it. Scared the crap out of him. When I started following the tenets of Buddhism, I tried to get Jake to take a look, thought it might smooth him out. I think his roofing business did that, though, his energy turned into construction rather than destruction." He touched his fingers to the vent and adjusted it so the heat blew against his face. "I truly was hoping to see Jake again."

"Maybe his vacation won't last much longer."

"Maybe. I plan to stay two weeks."

"Listen, Anthony... you know, I don't know what I should call you. Is there some title for a monk, or—"

"Call me Tony." He smiled.

"Tony. Tony, my dad has a guest room. You can stay with him until we clear your father's house, maybe only a day or two, then you can move in there. And my dad will have an extra coat you can wear.

Should've bought one at Kohl's." *How had that popped out?* She *had* offered to buy him a coat at Kohl's, and he'd turned her down. *Let him shiver if he wants to.* Piper mentally kicked herself for volunteering a room at her father's, and the coat. She should have asked first… could have called him, as Randy had found her cell phone and it was riding in her pocket. It had a cracked screen, but still worked.

"That is most generous. I will thank your father. I remember when he used to be the sheriff." He waited a beat. "I remember when he arrested Zach and warned my friends about spraying graffiti."

"He arrested a lot of people." *Four terms,* Piper thought. Thirty years with the department roughly. Was she going to make it through one term? "Yeah, Paul Blackwell was a fixture with the sheriff's department for a lot of years."

"It is good you follow in his stead. Tradition can be important."

"Yeah, it's ducky."

She reached the northern part of the county when the dispatcher radioed her about a suspicious death.

"Maybe the CCK," the dispatcher said. "But it's not an old fart this time."

Dear God.

"Send Oren and Randy out. Give me the address and tell them I'll head right over."

She called her father about his houseguest, dropped Anthony off, watched him go inside, and then sped away.

The killer had bought eleven Merry Christmas mugs, the store manager had said.

Please, dear God, don't let there be an equal number of bodies.

TWENTY

He dropped the pickup off with his girl and told her to keep it hidden because people would be looking for it, and if they connected it to him there would be serious prison time. "Speaking of time, it is time for me to get a new ride, sweetheart," he'd said. But he kept the license plates—he'd need those for whatever he picked out.

Later the next morning he walked to a gas station, bought a root beer out of the machine and discovered by the brick-like feel of the can that it was frozen. He stuck the can in an empty pocket, and used his cell phone to call a cab—which deposited him at a car dealer on 41 in Henderson. The soda had warmed up just enough so it was more of a slushee. He drank it while he walked up and down the rows of cars and trucks, thought maybe he'd buy himself a six pack of A&W, stick it outside, and have root beer slushees tonight. No more alcohol for a while. It muddied his thoughts, and he needed to stay clear-headed.

The hybrids were out of his price range, as he'd decided to only spend the money he'd pilfered from old woman Thornbridge's underwear drawer.

He settled on a Ford Focus four-door, a 2002 automatic—a lot more age to it than he wanted, and it had a hundred and twenty-three thousand miles on the odometer. The high mileage helped him talk the salesman down about eight hundred. They settled on three grand and he paid cash, pulling the wad out of his pocket.

It was a pretty ice-blue thing with leather interior. He'd not had a car with leather seats before. Running his fingers across them, he decided all future rides would have leather. They gave him a complimentary full tank of gas and sent it through the car wash, and then he was on his way back to Spencer County. This car would do until he could afford something better, a new Prius maybe, a red one; he sure liked the look of those things.

He needed to look in on the sheriff, since she hadn't been killed—he'd called the department to check and the dispatcher said she would be in the office this afternoon. He crossed the bridge to Evansville and then headed east to Spencer County.

"I messed up," he'd told his girl when he dropped off the pickup last night. "I should've crawled down that slope and strangled her like I did the others. Should've. But I'll take care of it. Maybe I'll find some money in her underwear drawer, buy you something nice with it."

With all his planning and killing during the holidays, he'd forgotten to buy the girl anything for Christmas. "I'll make it up to you, babe," he'd said. "I promise. Stick a needle in my eye and all that shit."

She'd just stared at him, so no use apologizing. But he definitely would have to buy her something nice. *Maybe a music box. Should've stopped by that Santa Store for their after-Christmas sale; might've found a fine music box there, one with an itty bitty snow ballerina on top that twirled to some Nutcracker tune.* Years and years ago he used to be better about remembering to get people presents.

He got a map at the Chamber of Commerce across from the power plant. It didn't have enough of the streets displayed for Rockport, so he swiped a phonebook from a convenience store and found a map in the back that was more helpful. The book also listed Paul Blackwell's number and address. "Aces," he pronounced.

It was a little before noon when he found the big house. It figured that a guy being sheriff that many years could afford a two-level with a honking big garage and a level above it, too. He'd asked around and learned that Piper Blackwell also lived here. "Double Aces." With luck, he'd get both of them, leaving just the old Jew to handle the murder investigation. And that would mean he'd be safe.

Parking across the street and a few houses down, he scampered through the neighbors' backyards, not worrying about tracks. There were plenty of tracks in the snow from kids who'd been playing. And fortunately there were lots of hedge-like evergreens so he could likely approach the rear of the Blackwell house with no one noticing. He figured the sheriff wouldn't be home, was out looking for him. But her dad... he'd heard that poor Paul Blackwell had cancer. He'd be home, resting, and not able to put up a fight. He'd get her dad, and then he'd wait. Piper would come home sometime. Maybe the Blackwells had a well-stocked fridge; he was getting a little hungry.

And hopefully the Blackwells were like everyone else he'd targeted... leaving a door open 'cause they thought they were safe in a tiny town.

He hurried to the sliding glass door he spotted at the back, tried the latch, and cursed. Locked. These sorts of doors were easy to break into, but it would make noise and that—

"Huh?" Curled in a dog bed near a kitchen counter was old woman Thornbridge's pug. Paul Blackwell was a few feet away, shoulders hunched, and it looked like he was talking to the dog.

Well, the dog would have to find yet another home, wouldn't it?

Hey, maybe he'd keep the dog himself. He still had about a thousand left from old woman Thornbridge. He could buy it food, a few toys. It'd been some time since he'd had a dog. His girl wouldn't mind... at least he hoped she wouldn't. And he'd be getting her a late Christmas present to ease things over. Should've taken the pug to begin with after he'd offed the old lady.

There was another way in, a smaller door on the side. He stepped to the corner of the house and froze when he saw a car pull in the driveway. It wasn't an official sheriff's department car, but it had one of them bubble-lights sitting on the dash. Hey, maybe it was a loaner 'cause he'd trashed the real sheriff car. A man got out, bald, wearing jeans and a sweatshirt. He reached in the backseat and pulled out a pack. Piper Blackwell was in the driver's seat, wearing her uniform and hat.

The man looked fit. He didn't think he could take the man *and* Piper. Paul Blackwell? That'd be easy. Old guy with cancer, wouldn't even work up a sweat over that. But Piper *and* the bald dude? Not today.

Interesting, the bald guy went to the front door, and Piper drove away. He could take the bald guy, right? If he had to? Probably a chemo buddy to Paul Blackwell. Chemo made your hair fall out, he'd read. But he looked fit, so maybe the chemo hadn't wrecked his body yet. Taking Paul *and* his chemo buddy during daylight might be foolish... and he was far from that. Maybe he'd just dawdle around, wait for night, wait for the bald guy to leave and Piper to come back and get the Blackwells as they snoozed.

And maybe while he considered his options, he could do some more exploring. *Good idea.* He scuttled to the back of the garage, found a door there, and slipped inside. Two cars, a Chevy Tahoe SUV, and a little red thing that'd crush like an aluminum can if it got hit—that must be Piper's. Dad would be too smart and have too much money to buy something so small. A disposable car.

Drive My Car, the Beatles; *Fast Cars*, U2; *Get in My Car*, 50 Cent—that was a great one; *Stop Draggin' My Car Around*, Weird Al—that was a stupid one.

The garage was orderly, like it should be pictured in Home Depot ads. He could see pretty good in here with light coming in through windows in the garage door. One wall had hooks that held all sorts of tools—rakes, hoes, shovels. There were shelves above that with jars and boxes, all labeled. A neat freak.

A set of stairs lead up, and he decided to have a look, see what treasures the Blackwells stored up top. Some of the steps creaked, like they were grousing that he was trespassing on them. A door at the top was locked, but it was old and he got it open with his pocketknife. He stepped inside and was surprised to see an apartment. The door opened into a small living room.

"Well hello, Sheriff Blackwell," he whispered. She lived here, not in the big two-level. Probably wanted her own space, probably was the only way her old man could lure her back to boring-as-hell Rockport. "Stay above the garage, honey, and I'll stay out of your hair. I don't have hair, I have cancer."

There were a couple of framed photos on a small desk, of young people in battle dress uniforms, Piper in one of them... that's how he knew this was her crib. And there was a framed picture above a gray futon couch—the only wall decoration that he noticed. It was over-sized for a photo, maybe eleven by seventeen, matted to make it look even bigger, a Christmas tree in the background, Paul Blackwell and maybe his wife—ex, he corrected as he knew a lot about the old sheriff—and two little girls. Couldn't tell which one was Piper. The frame was wood, pitted, maybe old or maybe it was designed that way on purpose—some people liked the battered-look stuff.

The place had shag carpet that looked like dingy fire, oranges with yellows woven into the mix, faded near the window where the sun had come in and bleached a perfect square. Did they still make shag carpet? He knelt and took off his gloves, ran his fingers through it, expecting it to feel good. Instead it was scratchy and there were places where the nap had worn away, showing the canvas weave beneath. *She could do with new carpet, something from the past two decades*, he thought. But she wouldn't have to worry about it, would she? Piper Blackwell would be dead before the week was out. Somebody else could put in new carpet.

Maybe she'd be dead before this day ended.

The kitchen connected and was also small, furnished with a table for two with a Formica top and padded straight-backed chairs covered in vinyl. *Could be a set out of* That '70s Show, he thought. He used to catch the reruns on Netflix. And, oh my, avocado green appliances—fridge, stove, dishwasher. Bet you couldn't buy something in that color now unless it was a special order. The Sunbeam microwave looked new, small, still had a price sticker on the door, $53.85. A glance in the fridge: carton of milk, which he opened, took a big swallow of and then spit in... just because; jug of orange juice with the seal still on the cap; three apples on a shelf; a half-used pack of turkey slices; a big bottle of Gatorade; a carton of eggs with six inside; and a package of Kraft American slices that hadn't been opened yet. He liked cheese, even that garbage, but he tamped down the urge to dig in. The freezer held three frozen dinners, the good kind, Marie Callender's Sesame Chicken, Three Cheese Tortellini, and Golden Batter Fish Fillet. Maybe she didn't eat beef. Cabinet above the sink had a little box of chicken flavored Rice-A-Roni, a jar of Bustelo Supreme freeze-dried coffee, a container of sugar cubes, and three cans of tomato soup.

Not many groceries, even for one person. He wondered if she ate out a lot and didn't like to grocery shop.

Two doors off the living room, the one standing open led to a good-sized bathroom with a claw-footed tub and shower. He peeked in the linen closet: two bath towels, a couple of smaller towels, four bars of Zest, an unopened box of toothpaste—the tube in process on the sink—shampoo and conditioner, a four-pack of crap paper. *Not much stuff*, he thought. Not into loading up on extras.

The closed door yielded up a bedroom, a double bed with a plaid comforter, old leather easy chair by the window next to a stick lamp, footlocker at the end of the bed. Nothing on the walls, though when he looked close he saw tiny holes where pictures used to hang, spotted a little nail that she'd neglected to pry out. The nail bothered him, should be covered up. The closet didn't have many clothes in it, mostly casual, a nice suit—probably had worn it campaigning—only one dress, so dark purple it looked black at first glance. The footlocker had tennis shoes and a pair of army boots in it; a handgun—he didn't know what kind, as he wasn't into them—and a box of bullets; and another box that he carefully opened—medals—a decorated war hero, eh? A Purple Heart. Impressive. There was also a cheap plastic frame with a certificate in it bearing a Screaming Eagles logo. He took it out and closed the footlocker... after he made sure everything else was the way he'd found it. Then he carefully hung the certificate on the nail. Maybe she wouldn't notice. And if she did, so what? She wouldn't have to puzzle over it long.

A small jewelry box on top of a chest of drawers was next. He lifted the lid and a shelf raised with it, four small compartments filled with pierced earrings. Underneath was a tangle of necklaces, some real gold... he knew real gold. He pulled one of those out, guessed it was eighteen inches, a thin ropy thing that caught the light coming in through the window, had a pretty little butterfly charm hanging on it. Hadn't intended on taking anything, but he'd not gotten his girl a Christmas present. Late, sure, but when she saw it was real gold, she'd adore him for it. He dropped the butterfly necklace in his front pocket and closed the box. The chest of drawers was narrow, and the four drawers weren't filled all the way. Underwear, which he carefully moved around—no money, she knew better. T-shirts, a couple of sweatshirts, one tan with an eagle head in a black shield 101st in block print, had some wear to it, a couple of nightshirts, an assortment of socks.

Smiling at his secret exploration, he backed out of the bedroom, closing the door, surveying the living room one more time and spotting a small stack of books on the floor next to the futon.

"Whatcha reading, bitch?" He padded over and knelt, tipping his head sideways so he could read the spines. Library books from the plastic covers and labels on the bindings. One a biography of Truman, Michael Moorcock's *Tales From the End of Time*, Philip Kerr's *A Five-Year Plan*... looked like some sort of mystery or thriller. No books that looked to be her own property or that were current bestsellers, though maybe she had a Nook or Kindle or some such and bought the electronic editions. Less clutter that way, certainly less to pack. Observation: Piper Blackwell lived here, but it didn't look like she intended to stay. Maybe she figured her dad would die soon and she could move into the big house, where there was plenty of furniture and most assuredly better carpet; he probably had a lot of books, too. But that notion didn't explain the lack of boxes, the relatively small selection of clothes. Seemed like everything she owned could fit in three big suitcases. Maybe she embraced a minimalist style, was one of those souls who could be happy in the tiny houses they advertized on the Internet. Or maybe she hadn't been out of the Army long enough to accumulate stuff. No collection of refrigerator magnets or paperweights, no action figures, no Beanie Babies, nothing to let him get a good read on her.

Didn't matter, did it?

Soon she wouldn't have the opportunity to accumulate anything.

He crept toward the desk, finding a slight dip in the floor. Whoever lived here next might want to fix that—get up in the middle of the night and walk over it, you might trip. A telephone was on the back corner, one of those old banana shaped things like he'd seen on *That '70s Show*. He lifted the receiver: no dial tone. She probably relied on her cell, that's what most younger folks did, right? Only one drawer, and he tugged it open to find a thin laptop inside. He took it out, set it on the desk, then eased into the chair, which was wood and old and he didn't want to break it.

The laptop wasn't full-sized, not more than ten or eleven inches across. Acer was the brand; he'd never heard of it. There was also a cable for it in the drawer, but he turned it on without plugging it in, discovered it had enough battery life.

"Let's look into your soon-to-be-short life, Sheriff," he cooed. But when the startup screen faded, it asked for a password. "Oh, piss." He turned it off and put it back in the drawer, just as he'd found it. No use trying to fathom what code she used, probably something from her Army days or the name of a childhood pet.

"Pop this popsicle stand," he decided, leaving and closing the door. It still latched, he'd only jimmied the lock, hadn't broken it.

Out the back of the garage and through the neighboring yards, keeping close to the hedges before coming out to his pretty ice blue ride. Maybe he'd just go cruising for awhile, go buy that six-pack of A&W at the Rockport grocery store, head to Owensboro and stop in at the mall on Frederica, the Macy's or Penny's there, or better yet the Rue21—trendier. He could come back late tonight; it was easier at night, especially if he could catch them sleeping... like he had with old woman Thornbridge. Easier to get both of them now since they had separate digs. It was stupid to come here during the day, feeling all cocky because he'd got a car. He hadn't brought any of his signature mugs along, had forgotten them in his closet. He couldn't kill Piper and Paul Blackwell without a mug... even if neither had sent him a Christmas card.

Well, he could kill them without his signature mug, but it wouldn't be proper. Besides, he might as well use some of the mugs he had left. Only needed to save one; something to drink a root beer slushee out of. He laughed at that thought as he drove away.

"You're gonna love this pretty gold necklace, Babe. Got it special, just for you." He'd poked through old woman Thornbridge's jewelry, but it was big clunky stuff, not at all elegant. This chain Sheriff Blackwell had offered up... that was classy. It was a good thing he hadn't killed her when he'd run her off the road the other night. He wouldn't have thought to come to her place, and so he wouldn't have acquired this shiny little thing.

He laughed louder.

TWENTY-ONE

Samuel Reynolds lived at the edge of New Boston. His ex-wife Nicky had found his body when she'd come back to pick up some toys and clothes the twins forgot.

Sam's corpse was posed against the largest of three snowmen in his front yard, arms around the middle section and tied in place with twine, and affixed to one hand was a bright red Merry Christmas mug. His lips were pressed against the side of the snowman's face as if kissing it, and they shared a long red scarf wrapped around both their necks.

Piper parked on the shoulder near the end of the long driveway. Nicky leaned against her car, which was butted up to a barn-like garage.

Oren pulled up before Piper had taken a dozen steps, and he was quick to trail her.

There were no houses directly across the road, so no lookie loos to contend with, and also perhaps no witnesses. But the cars that drove by slowed, some to a near stop, the drivers and passengers twisting their necks to gawk.

Nicky stuck her hands under her armpits. "I'm staying right here," she hollered. "Don't want to look at him again. You can come back here if you wanna talk."

"Fine," Piper said, too soft for Nicky to hear. She looked over her shoulder. "Let's chat with her first. Obviously our victim isn't going anywhere. I called Dr. Neufeld. She said she'll probably be an hour." Piper was surprised Randy wasn't already here. She knew he'd been re-interviewing some of the Hagee partiers.

The driveway hadn't been plowed for a few days, so there were tire ruts in the snow. If there'd been any tread to point to the killer's vehicle, it had likely been obliterated by Nicky driving her Escape over them. Piper walked through the snow, avoiding the tire tracks… just in case Randy could lift something useful. It was several inches deep and came up over the tops of her ankle-high boots. The cold winnowed its way in as she crunched through it.

"Hi, Sheriff," Nicky said.

No tears, Piper noticed. Nicky's cherry red face was colored from staying out in the cold. She was skinny, about five-five, Piper put her, with blonde hair that didn't match her darker eyebrows—so from a salon. The cut was clearly professional, a reverse bob, and her mascara thick, eyelashes curled. One of her friends at Fort Campbell had said, "A woman can never have too much money or mascara." Said friend had re-upped and was posted to Spain.

Nicky wore a parka with a fur-lined hood that flopped down between her shoulder blades, probably hadn't wanted to wear it and mess her hair. She had a distressed flap handbag sitting on her trunk; it looked pricey. The car was a BMW, but an older model, and there were half-dollar size rust spots on the fenders.

Nicky rocked back and forth and bobbed her head. The image of a pigeon sprung into Piper's head.

"I called you all right away," she said. "Used my cell. I haven't been in the house, and there's some stuff in there I need, kids' clothes, a few toys they forgot. That's why I'm here, they kept hounding me, wouldn't shut up about the stuff. Gave me a migraine. Anyway, I knew he was dead when I turned in the driveway. Seen him frozen to the snowman. I didn't want to get close, you know, so I pulled up here where I couldn't see him and called. Took you long enough to get here. I'm freezing. Can you get me in the house so I can get the stuff and get out of here? I don't have a key and the back door's locked. Sam... he'd never locked the back door before."

No trace of grief whatsoever, Piper decided, a woman as cold as this winter day.

"Ma'am," Oren said. He tipped his hat to her. "Your husband—"

"Ex-" she cut in. "Ex-husband. God, but I don't know whatever I saw in him. Married him right out of high school. I think I just wanted out of my folks' house. Got pregnant too young. Love the twins, though. We have... I have... twins, a boy and a girl—Samantha and Keven with two Es. Sammy had them for a week at Christmas and they left some stuff. That's why I came back."

"I see," Oren said.

Piper took a step back and watched Oren, didn't mind if he asked the questions. She heard music, faint, must be coming from inside the house.

"Sam drank too much," she continued. "My dad had drank too much, and I'd married into the same damn problem. One of the reasons I called it quits, Sammy's beer. That and this little farm. He inherited it from his dad, was hell bent on making a go of it. Cue the *Green Acres* theme song, baby. I'm no Lisa Douglas, but I wasn't cut out for something this rural." She paused. "Court gave me the kids, but he had visitation rights, like this past Christmas." A longer pause. "The kids said they had a good time. I'm glad they got to spend it with him."

"Did Sam have any enemies?" Oren asked.

Her eyes grew wide.

"Someone he'd had an argument with, owed money to, anything, anyone—"

"Holy! You're thinking someone killed Sammy. I figured he did himself in, drank too much, wandered out to get a little something on with the snowman—I don't think he was seeing anyone, hadn't ever since our divorce—and passed out like that, froze to death. You think someone—"

"Just asking you a few questions," Oren said.

155

"I'm sorry. I really don't know if someone had it in for him. Maybe he owed somebody money. He had to work at the power plant over by the bridge, couldn't make enough money with this dump."

Not grieving now, not going to be later, and still obviously bitter about her stint as a farmwife, Piper thought. *She's not a suspect.* "What is it you said you need from inside?"

"Clothes, my kids' clothes, a couple of sweaters, Samantha said. Crap. I have to tell them Sammy's dead. Maybe they're too young to understand."

"How old—" Oren started.

"Six. Six years old. Me and Sammy were married less than two years when I got pregnant. After I had the kids, after he decided he wanted to stay on the farm, after he kept drinking, I filed for divorce. And you don't need to think—"

"We don't judge," Oren said.

Piper didn't like Oren, but she had to admit he handled the woman well.

"Let Sheriff Blackwell take a look inside, and then—"

"Door's locked," she said again.

"Let the sheriff take a look and we'll see if you can take the things you want and be on your way. All right?" Oren looked at Piper, as if asking her if Nicky would be free to go.

"Do you know Conrad Delaney?" Piper asked.

She shook her head.

"Abigail Thornbridge?"

"Who?" Nicky screwed up her face. "How long is this going to take?"

"Wait here," Piper said. She went to the back door, and while it was locked, it was old and easy to force. She'd put booties in her pocket, and she slipped them on along with a pair of white gloves, before going inside.

The house was probably built in the 1940s, but there were obvious updates to the kitchen, the cabinets looking practically new and the bronze knobs shining. The table was old, though, and she spotted a stack of seed catalogs on it, and a beer can in front of the only chair that was pulled out. A glance at the floor. It gleamed in the light that streamed in through the windows. Everything looked clean.

The music came from a radio on the counter, Ed Sheeran's *Photograph*.

The lights were blinking on the Christmas tree, and an old train chugged around and around the base, endlessly going nowhere. The tree was artificial; she resisted the temptation to unplug the lights. Christmas cards were stacked on the coffee table. She nudged the pile to spread them out, probably two dozen, flipped one over and read it.

Samuel, I haven't seen you for a few years and we haven't exchanged cards in longer than that. But I was going through my attic around Thanksgiving and saw some of Anthony's and Zachary's toys. I'd not tossed them. There's a little John Deere tractor and couple of attachments, some Hot Wheels that I remembered you and Zachary used to race, a little track for them that's still got the box. Have a big box of Tonka trucks as well. I remember at the summer picnic you telling me you had twins. How about you give me a call after the first of the year and come over and get this stuff. I'd rather you have it than someone I don't know. And, honestly, I don't know how to sell on eBay. Happy Holidays, Conrad.

Piper didn't see a card from Abigail.

No signs of a struggle here, she moved on to the bathroom, which also looked clean, then the first bedroom she came to—twin beds inside, a few toys on the floor and sweaters folded on the end of the bed near a square depression in the quilt where a suitcase might have sat.

The master bedroom was not as neat, men's clothes tossed on the floor, the bed a rumpled mass of blankets and pillows, just how she might picture a single man leaving it.

She grabbed up the toys and clothes and went outside. "This what you're looking for?"

"Yeah, I think so. Samantha has been pitching a big one because of that stuffed bear. I bought her a new one, but it wasn't her 'Bubby Baby,' so I drove all the way over here just for that damn thing. Should've done it yesterday and saved twenty-four hours of my sanity. Left the kids at my mom's. Crap. Now I gotta tell them about Sammy when I pick them up. Crappity crap."

Nicky juggled her prizes and opened the passenger door, dropped them on the seat. "So I can leave now, right?"

"When was the last time you talked to Sam?" Oren asked. He leaned against the trunk, blocking her from driving off.

Nicky gave out an exaggerated theatrical breath, which barely moved her perfect bangs. "Yesterday. I called him on my lunch break at the shop, probably noonish, said I wanted to come get the damn stuffed bear and whatever else the kids left. He argued with me, said he'd take good care of everything and they could get it when they came up again. It's like he thought I wouldn't bring 'em back. I have to 'cause of the court order, but not until summer. Anyway, he finally caved and said I had to get up here before two. He works—worked— the three to eleven shift at the power plant."

"So he was alive yesterday," Piper mused.

"Sure. It wasn't his ghost I talked to."

Piper had a few more questions. "Did you get a Christmas card from Sam?"

She shook her head, again her hair barely moving, evidence it had a good amount of spray or gel on it. "Haven't gotten a Christmas card from him since a year after the divorce was finalized." Nicky gave a wistful smile. "But he always sent the kids one, well two. He sent them separate cards, though they were always the same design. Sammy bought boxed cards, and never those variety mixes."

"Do you remember the design from this year?"

Nicky set her hands against her hips. "Really?"

"It could be important."

"Really?" She asked it louder. "I couldn't tell you, no reason to pay attention. Snowmen. It had snowmen on it. Sammy always sent cards that had snowmen. He liked snowmen."

"Do you know if he had any work done on this house in the past year?" Piper looked for the thread that would connect Samuel to Conrad and Abigail. "Roof work maybe, some—"

"He had new kitchen cabinets put in, and Lord knows he didn't do the work himself. Oh, Sammy was handy around a farm, but wood-working… he flunked shop in high school. I remember that. Couldn't build a birdhouse, and then senior year when he was working with a blowtorch he lit another kid's farts. That story was all over the school, and it got him sent home for three days. Kitchen cabinets. Don't know where he bought them or who put them in. What's it got to do with—"

"It's just a question," Oren said.

"Well, I've got a question, can I go now?" Nicky headed around the front of her car to get to the driver's seat. "Seriously, can I go now? I got Shelly running the shop today, but I told her I'd be back to close up. I'm gonna have to hurry to make it."

"Sure," Piper said. "But we want your phone number, where we can reach you, in case we have more questions."

"I probably ain't gonna have more answers." Nicky grabbed her handbag off the roof and looked inside, her manicured fingers—complete with snowflake decals on blue polish—darted in and brought out a business card. She waved it and Piper came over to get it. "I'm sorry about Sammy," Nicky said softly. "He wasn't all bad."

Nicky's Beauty Boutique was printed in raised hot pink letters against a pale pink background. "That's my shop number, and the one under it is my cell. Sammy had a will. He told me he'd drawn one up a year ago, worried he might have an accident plowing or planting or something. The kids are in it, get everything. He said I'm not. If you go through the house, you can bag up all his clothes and take them to Goodwill. People need clothes this time of year. The kids aren't going to want his clothes." A pause. "They're not gonna want this damn farm either." She got in, and after Oren moved, drove away.

"Cold," Oren said.

"As this winter day." Piper walked back down the driveway, stop-ping even with the snowman display. "What the hell's keeping Randy?" The yard was unbroken white, except for a path from the front door to the snowmen where it looked like the snow had been brushed.

"The killer covered his tracks," she said. "He hadn't bothered to cover them at Conrad's—the nosy neighbors did that for him—and there weren't any tracks at Abigail's because her staging was inside. Here, he covered his tracks."

"Nervous maybe." Oren followed her. "This is a later kill, probably less than twenty-four hours ago. So maybe he's grown wary. But still at it. We need to find one of the cards Sam sent out. I'll check with the neighbors, look inside for an address book." He shook his head. "He's one of ours, you know, the killer."

"What do you mean?" She looked for the best way to approach the snowmen without disturbing too much of the scene.

"One of us, a county man. The people he's killed were born here, Randy checked. All of them born here. Never lived anywhere but this county, except for Conrad when he served in the Marines. Oh, they moved around to different little towns, but always *in* the county. They have... *had*... deep roots, so I'll wager whoever killed them has the same ties. Just got to figure the connection, figure out what set the guy off. *Gornisht helfn.*"

"And figure out who he is. We need to find that roofer." The possibility of calling the State flickered in her mind. Maybe she should call the State, maybe it would keep someone else from dying. But if the killer was a local, someone from the State would be at a disadvantage; they wouldn't know the people like Oren and Randy did... and her father. She'd pick her dad's brains again tonight and see if he had any ideas.

Three bodies in nearly as many days.

He'd bought eleven Merry Christmas mugs.

"My case," she whispered. "My damn case." She'd never backed down from anything. She wasn't ready to call the State. "Where the hell is Randy?"

Piper picked an approach and gingerly stepped out into the yard. "There's a connection between Samuel Reynolds and Conrad Delaney," she said loud enough for Oren to hear. "No thread to Abigail... not yet."

She heard the crunch of snow behind her, Oren following, and then she heard a car shush by. It stopped in front of the house, as the driver craned his neck to get a better look. After a moment, it kept going.

"Conrad sent this man a Christmas card. I saw it on his end table. I don't recall if Conrad received one from Samuel Reynolds." She'd read the cards over and over, had some of the verses and the names of the senders committed to memory. But Sam, Sammy, or Samuel didn't surface in her thoughts. "Nearly forty years apart in age, but they were connected by a Christmas card."

"Small county. Lots of people are friends with each other, regardless of age, but anyone who's—"

"—spent a good amount of time here knows that," Piper finished. "Yeah, I know." She carefully edged near to the corpse. Samuel Reynolds was held in place with twine. The Merry Christmas mug had tipped, half of its contents spilled. She could smell that it was beer. Apparently the killer knew enough about his victims to stage them with their favored beverage.

Oren crunched closer, and she wished Randy would have showed up rather than her chief deputy. Where was he? She'd radioed him on her way over.

"Look at his eyes," Oren said. "See the tiny red spots?"

"I can spell," Piper returned sharply. "P-e-t-e-c-h-i-a-l."

TWENTY-TWO

J acob Wallem's driveway hadn't been shoveled in days, and there was a drift across it that went three feet up against the side of the house. It was a ranch with a low-pitched gable roof, ash gray vinyl siding with black shutters on the irregular sized windows, and a one-car attached garage, which had a deep drift against it. The roof was charcoal and had flecks of something that sparkled. A roofer would have a nice-looking roof, Randy figured. In fact, the outside of the entire house, though the design hinted that it was built in the 50s or 60s, appeared in first-class order. It was probably well landscaped, too, just couldn't tell under the mounds of snow.

Randy parked on the street and looked in the mailbox—it was stuffed, he doubted that another envelope could be jammed inside. A mix of letters and catalogs on first glance; he'd go through it later if he needed to. If Jacob had gone on vacation, he forgot to have his mail held.

Maybe Randy needed to think about a vacation for himself, or simply go somewhere else… other than out to Samuel Reynolds's house, which would be next after he checked on the roofer. Maybe he needed to go to another county. Vanderburgh, one county over, had a much bigger sheriff's department, probably higher wages, and he knew the man who assumed the head post a couple of days ago. While they weren't friends, they were friendly. There was going to be an opening in a month or two, the chief deputy retiring—he'd read that in a state newsletter. And while he wouldn't be in line for that post— he was certain someone in-house would be moving up—he'd get strong consideration for whatever spot was left vacant. More than one hundred and eighty thousand people lived in Vanderburgh County, and more than half of them were in Evansville. There was a university, arts, theater, museums, a zoo, and a big old showboat on the river where you could gamble and sip fancy drinks. He liked the city in the summertime.

Forty was looming. Born on Valentine's Day, he'd be seventeen years older than his boss then. It wasn't sitting well on his tongue, tasted pretty awful in fact. He imagined it sat ten times worse for Oren.

Randy had been satisfied here, if not outright happy. He enjoyed his role as sole detective, had lots of friends, roots, was suited to small-town life, and he wouldn't have considered looking elsewhere until Piper Blackwell took office three days ago. He'd started casting his eyes toward Vanderburgh when she won in the fall, but hadn't been "all in" on the notion until he actually saw her in the sheriff's uniform. Too small, too young, and way the hell too inexperienced. She had no business heading up a department she'd not previously served a day in.

What the hell had Paul Blackwell been thinking, encouraging his daughter to run for sheriff? As many years as Paul had been sheriff— and with the department in general—Randy had thought the man would have put the department and the county first. *Just what in the holy hell had Paul Blackwell been thinking?* Had the chemo warped his brain? Randy had heard the term "chemo brain," and wondered if Paul hadn't been thinking straight.

Randy had considered taking a run at the office himself… fifteen years with the department was more than enough experience to qualify him for sheriff. But Oren let it be known that he wanted it bad, and Randy was good enough friends with the chief deputy—respected him—that he wasn't going to compete. Besides, Oren said Randy would move up to chief deputy. So he supported Oren, campaigned for him, and watched in disbelief with him from the country club dining room as the election results came in and gave Piper the win. He believed that the county residents weren't voting *against* Oren because of his age, they were voting *for* Piper because of her last name. Hell, most of them probably thought they were voting for Paul Blackwell all over again.

So even if Randy had thrown his hat in, the Blackwell name would have steamrolled over him. Twenty-three years old. Twenty-frigging-three years old and she was his boss. He'd been civil about the whole thing, polite to her even, followed her orders to that proverbial "T," though he hadn't zoomed right out to the Reynolds's house when called a little while ago. He had an itch to stop here first.

He couldn't say he disliked her. Oren had asked him more than once about that. He didn't know her well enough to like or dislike her. He liked Paul Blackwell, respected him and had been proud to serve in Paul's department. But he couldn't say he respected Piper. And how do you work for someone you don't respect?

Randy figured Oren would have retired before Piper moved in. Then Randy was certain he'd be in line for the chief deputy post. He could have handled the situation better then, with the promotion, waited it out to see if she passed the sheriff's exam in the spring... moved into the sheriff's spot on appointment if she hadn't, or stuck it out four years as chief deputy if she had and then campaigned for sheriff himself the next go-round. By then everyone would know that Piper was not Paul, and they would not vote for her again.

That way he could stay in the county.

But Oren was holding on, hoping Piper'd fail come April. And if she did fail, Oren would get the sheriff's appointment again, just like he had when Paul Blackwell stepped down because of the cancer. Either way, Randy would be sitting around another term before his shot at a run. Forty-four would be looming.

What was it Oren liked to say? *Gornisht helfn*—beyond help.

Randy decided he'd call the Vanderburgh County Sheriff sometime tomorrow and ask about that vacancy. In the meantime, he was going to settle the itch about the vacationing roofer.

He slogged up the drive, the snow wrapping around his knees and the cold easing in deep, feeling the way with his feet and finding the sidewalk, and then following it to the front porch steps. The snow had drifted over the lowest one, and he nearly tripped. He stood on the top step and brushed the snow off his pants.

A shiny red ribbon hung from a big wreath on the front door. The door was a showpiece, stained mahogany with sidelights from top to bottom, and it had a brass handleset and lock. Randy gave out a low whistle. "That's pretty."

He stepped up to the door and knocked, knowing that it wouldn't be answered—if Jacob Wallem was home, smoke would be trailing up from the chimney, the mailbox wouldn't be full, and someone would have shoveled… at least a little. Buck said he had been over here a few times, but evidently hadn't bothered coming up to the house, merely reporting that, "Jacob Wallem, that roofer you're looking for, is on vacation." Buck said he'd checked with the neighbors, who confirmed Jacob was away. Randy wondered if Buck had bothered to look in the mailbox.

Randy hadn't known Buck to skimp on an assignment, was usually known for being thorough. But he'd take him to task about this. Buck should have checked the doors and windows, taken a look inside—but there'd been no tracks leading up to the house except the ones he just made. Maybe Buck had a problem working for a twenty-three-year-old boss, too.

The radio squawked on his belt, probably the sheriff wondering where the hell he was. He ignored it.

Randy well knew he was supposed to be at Samuel Reynolds's house right now, had taken the call from Piper about the body found in the front yard—the third victim of the CCK. He said he'd be over directly, but he stopped here first anyway… it was sort of on the way. Piper could wait just a little while; the body wouldn't get up and walk off on her. It felt good, this little act of defiance.

He knocked louder.

Nothing.

"Mr. Wallem!"

He thought he heard something, someone moving around.

Randy tried to look through the sidelights, but the glass was beveled, designed to let in light only.

One more knock.

"Mr. Wallem! Sheriff's department, Mr. Wallem!"

A dog bayed, a beagle or basset. Then it started barking and scratching on the other side of the door.

Randy pressed his ear to the wood. There must have been a little crack between the door and its frame; nothing sealed perfect, did it? He smelled the pine of the wreath and some type of sealant on the mahogany, but he also picked up an awful reek.

Jacob Wallem—or whoever else was in that house—hadn't gone on vacation.

He retraced his steps to his car, while he clicked the radio on his belt.

"I found the roofer, Boss," Randy told her. He'd been calling her boss, didn't respect her enough to say 'Sheriff.' "At least I'm pretty sure I found him. Somebody's in the house—dead. It's Rockport, so we're obligated to call the police department." It was one of two towns in the county that had a police department; the other was Santa Claus, though it had only four officers and often relied on the sheriff's department.

She answered him, "Oren's got this scene, and JJ and Buck are on their way over to help him. I should be to you in about twenty. Can we make the police call after we take a look?"

"Good idea, Boss." This was the sheriff department's case after all. "I'll wait out front for you, we can go in together." Randy settled back against the seat of his Crown Vic and closed his eyes. Oren had let him go first into Abigail's house; Randy would let Piper have the honors here. "I'm thinking it's related," he added.

"To the CCK?"

"Yeah," Randy replied. "If Wallem's our killer, maybe he committed suicide and saved us the trouble and expense of a trial. And if he isn't our killer, I'll bet he has a Merry Christmas mug in his hand."

TWENTY-THREE

R andy forced open the beautiful door and gestured.

"After you, Boss."

She glanced at a bagged weekly newspaper sitting on the snow near the porch, stepped inside the house, and put booties on as she went. The stench was a thick barrier she had to struggle through. No other smell compared to death, though it varied in intensity depending on how long a body had been destroying itself. This ranked as high as some of the kill sites she'd marched across, likening the odor to a monstrous creature that burrowed into her lungs and held on with sharp, insidious claws. Her shoulders hunched and though the Pop-Tarts were a memory she felt bile coming up.

Piper concentrated to keep from retching, figuring she was being tested, her detective wanting to watch her toss her cookies and flee to the front yard. She was used to being tested. In Iran there were soldiers who didn't accept a woman as an equal, let alone as their commanding officer—despite her having endured the same rigorous training they had and facing the same ordeals. She'd had to win respect during both of her tours; though it came much easier after the downrange night she saved her unit. She suspected some of her deputies would never respect her.

She barely registered the dog at her feet. It pawed her leg, tail wagging madly, tongue lolled out. It yipped happily. Piper stared at it. The dog was missing half an ear, and where one of its eyes had been, the skin was stitched together to cover the hole. It had three legs, the left front one a one-inch stub. She picked it up to make sure it didn't run out in the yard.

"Keep this door open," she told Randy. "And protocol or no, we're going to open some windows."

"Sure thing, Boss." She noted the quaver in his voice—the stench had burrowed deep in his lungs, too.

She opened the door as wide as it would go and left it that way. She cradled the beagle closer and discovered that the dog's intact eye was milky white. Blind and three-legged, and skinny—the ribs protruded. But the dog was so very pleased to be in the company of someone living. The dog raised its snout and lapped at her chin. The tag on the collar said her name was Merry.

"I'll get my kit, Boss."

"Randy," she said as she turned. He was standing on the step just outside. "Good idea you had, stopping here. Who told you he was on vacation?"

Randy whirled and slogged down the steps without answering. "I'll get the video camera, too."

"Call the Rockport police while you're out there," she hollered.

The dog quivered in the crook of her arm. Piper put it at about a dozen pounds, a smallish beagle.

"Take a good look," she told herself, again fighting the urge to join Randy outside and puke in the yard. One of her MP instructors taught her: "enter a scene, stay still, and take visual stock. First impressions are all-important." Look patiently, diligently, and clues would appear.

There was no corpse with a Merry Christmas mug in its hand. But she saw the mug almost immediately. It sat in the center of the mantel of the living room fireplace, which was draped with pine garland decorated with red glass ornaments. Little ceramic buildings with snowy roofs filled the rest of the mantel. Where the outside of the house had been devoid of Christmas decorations, save the simple wreath on the door, the inside was overdone to Piper's eyes. But she thought her father would approve.

The tree in the corner was big and beautiful, an artificial flocked spruce covered with gold and red glass balls, gold and red strings of beads applied with precision, and a gold and red star on top, everything perfectly spaced. The tree skirt spread out into the room, thick tiered red lace, like it had been the skirt of a wedding dress dyed for the holiday. Seven unopened packages in fancy foil paper and topped with big lavish bows circled the trunk. The coffee table held one of those miniature villages, a mirror serving as the skating pond on which little figures were posed. A shelf above the widescreen TV was occupied by two dozen of those floppy-legged "elf on a shelf" stuffed toys. Pictures on the wall had been covered with wrapping paper and bows, making them look like Christmas packages.

The throw on the couch depicted Santa in his sleigh flying above colorful rooftops. Pillows on the furniture were needlepoint, each different—a snowman tipping his hat, Rudolf with a glittery nose, elves making toys, cardinals stringing ribbon on a snow-covered tree, and a Golden Retriever puppy tugging on a Christmas stocking. Her gaze drifted back to the Merry Christmas mug on the fireplace. The beagle licked her chin. Piper couldn't smell the dog; the stench of a rotting body overpowered everything.

She heard Randy stomping on the porch, knocking snow off. He came in behind her, setting down the evidence kit.

"Putting on booties, Boss. The body's got to be close," Randy said. "I'll start recording here." He stepped around her, the video camera to his face. He was pale; she suspected she was, too. "In all my years, I've never smelled anything so awful."

I've smelled worse.

"Maybe in the kitchen—"

"No. The body's in the fireplace," she said.

"How do you—"

"The boots hanging… dangling above the hearth? They're not part of the decorations."

"Oh God."

Piper recalled that among the Christmas cards Conrad Delaney and Abigail Thornbridge received that were identical, there was an illustration of Santa's boots dangling down in the well of a fireplace, a plate of cookies and a glass of milk sitting on the floor nearby. The plate was there, empty, and the glass that was tipped over had milk residue in it. Probably Merry had devoured Santa's treats.

"Oh God," Randy repeated.

"God had nothing to do with this," Piper said. "Did you call Rockport police?"

"Yeah, someone should be here in a few. I told them to bring booties and gloves and that it was our crime scene. The dispatcher said the chief might argue with that. But I'm thinking he won't. I'm thinking he might stay on the front stoop." A pause. "Think that's Jacob Wallem stuffed in there?"

"Yeah. We can take him off the suspect list."

She padded close to the fireplace, still holding the beagle, squatted, held her breath, and looked up the chimney. "I can't be sure, but I think he was stuffed up past the damper so he could sit on the smoke shelf." She rose and looked in the Merry Christmas mug on the mantel —filled with eggnog that she was certain had spoiled, but she couldn't smell it. Piper could only smell the decomposing body.

She backed to the center of the room, her legs bumping against the coffee table and rattling some of the figurines. "Can't tell who it is," she said. "What I can see of it, hands at the sides, is black and bloated, Santa pants stained, fluids have darkened everything. But it has to be the roofer. The only thing that makes sense. And it's not going to be pleasant or easy getting him out of there."

"We'll need to wait for the coroner. She's going to wish she hadn't run for reelection."

Maybe I shouldn't have run either. Piper's fingers registered the feel of the beagle's coat, smooth and soft. Again she felt the protruding ribs. "Dead at least a week, maybe as much as two, the way he's so swollen in there. Fluids have drained onto these fake logs." She tipped her head back. "Who the hell would do something so... so... awful?"

"Mailbox supports that time frame. It's stuffed. I'll take the mail before we go, check the dates. Phone records will show the last outgoing calls. Poked around in the snow, found another newspaper under it. I'd say dead at least two weeks. S'pose all his friends thought he was somewhere south to beat the cold."

"We'll take the phone records from all the victims, lay them out side by side, see if any incoming calls were from the same person. Maybe the killer, eh? Christmas cards from here and Reynolds. Something connects all of them." She shuddered. "This is nasty, Randy. We need to get the son of a bitch."

"We should call in our people with days off, on vacation. Put everybody on this, Boss."

"We should call the State," she admitted. "I don't want to. But, it's time. Past time. Probably contact the F.B.I., too. Maybe our guy didn't limit himself to our county."

"Boss, we can—"

"It's a serial killer, Randy. A fucking serial killer. And as much as I want to solve this on my own." She wished she could have swallowed those last three words, hadn't wanted to confess that to anyone. But she kept going. "As much as I don't want to holler for help on my first case, I know we have to. You're a great detective, everyone says that. This... this is beyond us. We've no lab, limited equipment, we're no experts, and we don't have the resources for something like this. You know that. We're Mayberry RFD. This is a fucking serial killer and this has to stop now." She turned to face him. He took the video camera away from his eye. "Did you know the sicko bought eleven of those Merry Christmas mugs? Eleven. We've got four bodies now, all related. And we might have seven more. Eleven mugs."

"Okay, Boss. We need some outside help. I agree."

"I hear a car outside, probably Rockport police. Go get some clean air, see if the cops'll stay out for a little while. I'll open some windows. Can you call the coroner while you're out there? Have her come here first; Samuel Reynolds is second on her list now. Snowy Samuel Reynolds is a piece of cake next to this. Then come back and video the rest, bring the camera for the close-ins."

"Sure thing, Boss."

Piper, clutching the beagle a little tighter, moved through the doorway and into the kitchen, which was just as decked out. Flocked tablecloth, similar to Conrad Delaney's, Santa chair back covers, poinsettia centerpiece dead from lack of water, candles with holly bases on the island. She opened the first window she came to and sucked in the cold air. On the floor was a large casserole dish, empty, but from the mark near the rim looked like it had been filled with water; and a sliced open bag of dog food, also empty—and no telling how much had been in it when the killer left. The beagle's food and water bowls, on a holiday mat, were empty, so no telling how many days the dog had been starving.

"No wonder you're so thin." Piper picked up the dry water bowl, keeping hold of the dog with one arm. She sat the bowl in the sink and filled it with water, put it back on the floor and placed the dog in front of it. The beagle practically inhaled it, and then barfed it up, only to drink again. "We'll worry about getting you some food in a little while, eh?" When the dog was done, Piper picked it up again and started looking for a leash, passed by another window, which she opened, the back door, which she opened, and went through a doorway to the utility room. She opened the window there, too.

The floor was dotted with feces, mostly clustered on a spread of newspaper, as if the dog, despite being blind, was trying to be good about it. Nothing looked fresh; the dog hadn't eaten for some days. Next to the washer and dryer was a small plastic kennel. Piper put the dog inside and closed the door. It started to whimper.

"Just for a little while," she told it again. "Somebody will get you out of here, I promise." *And to the animal shelter, where you'll probably get the needle because who wants a blind, three-legged dog.* Not her father; the pug was more than enough, Piper decided. "Maybe Jacob has a friend who'll take you." But apparently he hadn't had a close enough friend to notice him missing for a couple of weeks, or a nearby relative. *Otherwise he would have been found before now,* she thought.

She heard voices in the other room, returned to find the Rockport police chief standing in front of the fireplace. No gloves on, but at least he'd put on booties.

"Sheriff." He gave her a nod.

Randy was recording the living room. The cord from the digital camera dangled out of his pocket. "I called the coroner," he said. "She's on her way. She's not happy, said something about bodies dropping since you took office. Said she'd be about a half hour."

Randy moved past her and into the kitchen.

"Heard about the Merry Christmas deaths in the county," the chief said. "Lots of chatter on the scanner." He pointed to the mug on the mantel. "This related?"

"Yeah. No question."

"Fine, this one is yours. I got people on vacation, though I can spare one if you need him. Just keep me in the loop on everything. I want copies." He turned and walked to the door, bent and removed the booties. "You're calling the State, right? This is what... the third body?"

"Fourth," she said. "We have one out in New Boston. Call came in for that about two hours ago."

"Lovely. Why the hell did a serial killer decide to decorate for the holidays in our county?" He made a move to shut the door behind him.

"Leave that open, please."

"Good idea."

She heard him talking to someone outside, heard the crunch of feet over snow, then a few moments later the sound of a car pulling away. Piper heard more voices and looked out the door—a dozen lookie loos had gathered on the sidewalk across the street. The sidewalk in front of Jacob's house was snow covered. She wondered if the city had some sort of ordinance that required residents to shovel... and whether it was enforced. It was probably something she should look up. Her dad had always shoveled his sidewalk, though she'd been taking care of that since she'd been back—it was good exercise.

Piper walked through a doorway near the tree, following a short hall that opened to a bathroom and a bedroom. What probably was designed as a second bedroom served as an office. There were a plethora of Christmas decorations in each room. The bedroom dresser was littered with snow globes, and in the center one of those ceramic trees people made in craft classes.

"I'm thinking Jacob Wallem was gay." Randy had appeared in the hall behind her. "Can't imagine a straight man going to all this work."

Piper knew her father used to go "all out," though not quite to this extreme. He used to put something Christmassy in every room, red and green towels in the bathrooms. One year he bought candy cane toilet paper... but that was a good while back.

"And everything is like you'd see it in a magazine, Boss. No straight guy would do that."

"I think you're wrong. But it doesn't matter." She looked him in the eyes. "Whether Jacob Wallem was straight or gay or came from another planet had nothing to do with why he was put into a Santa suit and stuffed into his chimney. It's not who or what he was. It was who he knew."

"It's just like in one of the cards Conrad received," Randy returned. "Boots hanging down a chimney, miniature Christmas village on the mantel. Milk and cookies, though I'm thinking the blind dog got to the milk and cookies."

Pretty astute, Piper thought, that he remembered that particular card on Conrad's and Abby's tables in the sheriff's department office.

"I wonder if Samuel Reynolds got one of those boots cards."

She shrugged. "Oren's going to bag those cards." *And anything else that might yield clues.* "We'll bag the ones from here; they're stacked on his desk." Despite not liking the chief deputy, she trusted him with evidence and a crime scene, figured he would do his best to show her up... and that wasn't a bad thing if it got this solved faster.

She opened the window in the bathroom, stuck her head out, and breathed deep. "He has lights strung on the pines in his backyard. And there are birdseed wreaths—well picked over—hanging on a clothesline."

"Definitely gay."

It doesn't matter.

The stink had abated just a little. Piper's eyes had stopped watering, and she resisted the urge to rub them. Randy's eyes were red and watery, too.

"I'll record the rest of the house," Randy said. "Then start lifting fingerprints, and—"

Piper's cell phone chirped, and she glanced at the caller ID. Didn't recognize it at first, only a number, not a name. Then it clicked, Anthony Delaney on the disposable phone she'd bought him. "Just a sec," she told Randy. She took the call, welcome for the brief distraction from the crime scene. "Hello Anthony, I'm kinda busy, but what do—"

Piper felt the remaining color drain from her face. "Okay. Okay." She listened as her chest tightened and she leaned against the bathroom wall, fearing her knees might buckle. "Okay. Yeah, I know where it is." After a few more moments she hung up and stuck the phone in her pocket. "My dad's in an ambulance, on the way to a hospital. They think it's a heart attack."

"I've got this," Randy said. "Go."

TWENTY-FOUR

Her apartment wasn't far, and she briefly considered going there to change out cars, take her private vehicle rather than the loaner rented by the sheriff's department. Going to see her father was not department business. But she didn't want to spare the minutes. Besides, her suggestion-of-a-car didn't have flashing lights and a siren. She opted to use the former as she sped out of Rockport, the scanner chattering away in the background.

It was all about Paul Blackwell, the talk, no mention of the two bodies and the crime scenes.

Cars pulled to the side of the road as she raced by.

Shouldn't be using the lights, she admonished. *If someone else's father was heading to the hospital, they wouldn't have lights.* Still, she didn't turn them off.

Traffic was scant anyway, it being mid-afternoon, people still at work.

Teegan came on her scanner's direct channel. "Sheriff Blackwood, any word on how he is?"

"Nothing yet, I'll let you know after I get there."

Dear God, don't let him die. She still wore the white gloves she'd put on at the roofer's. They weren't good enough to keep her fingers warm, but she didn't want to waste the time it would take to swap them for the good gloves riding in her pocket.

He couldn't die. Not to a heart attack, not to cancer. She'd quit the Army to come back here and be with him, the only family that mattered to her... now that her Army family was out of reach. Wrong of him to even think about dying after she walked away from Fort Campbell and what a commanding officer had assured her would be a promising military career. He was only fifty-five.

He'd been fine yesterday, more than fine really. In that silly Santa Claus store he'd been grinning like a kid, looking at the ornaments and decorations, shopping, having *Mr. Wrinkles* personalized on the pug ornament he'd picked out. You don't go from more than fine to a heart attack in one day. You just don't.

St. Mary's Warrick Hospital was in Booneville, a county over. Spencer County's lack of a hospital was rarely a concern given the close proximity of hospitals in the neighboring counties. St. Mary's was only fourteen miles from Rockport. But it seemed like a very long fourteen miles. And why take him there? Why not a little farther to a larger hospital with no doubt better equipment and more staff. Her dad should have the best. Had she been at home, she might have insisted they take him to one of the big hospitals in Evansville.

Was his condition so bad that they couldn't risk the extra miles?

Sure, the little hospital in Booneville had an ER, but probably only three or four dozen beds for overnight care. Small. Was it good enough? Was anything good enough?

She parked in the ER lot and dashed through the doors, seeing Anthony, bald head gleaming in the fluorescent lights. He stood at the nurse's station. His call to her at the roofer's house had been brief: "Sheriff Blackwell, your father was making coffee, and then he grabbed his left arm. I knew what it was. I called 9-1-1, though he argued with me, and I found aspirin in the cupboard. I gave him two. The ambulance came, said I could ride with him. I think they assumed I was family. The driver said we were going to St. Mary's. You know where it is, right?"

Thank God the Buddhist monk had been with her dad. Thank

God Anthony could not stay at the Delaney house; that she'd imposed on her father to take him in. If she hadn't drove to the airport to pick up the monk... Her dad believed everything "happened for a reason." In the past handful of days everything had been happening for very bad reasons.

Anthony turned to face her, reached out, and touched her cheek. "The doctors are with him, Sheriff Blackwell—"

"Piper." She leaned around him and saw a nurse. "Paul Blackwell, he was just brought in and—"

"He's in the ER—"

"I know. I know. I need to see him."

"We'll let you know when you can." The nurse gestured toward a collection of chairs around a low table littered with magazines.

"Is he going to be all right? When—"

"Please." The nurse pointed to the chairs again. "Honest, as soon as I know something, I'll tell you."

Piper let Anthony lead her. He sat next to her and took her hands, tugged the white gloves off and dropped them on the table. Then he cupped her hands in his. She was shaking.

"Visualize," he said. "Your fingers, hands, visualize them as a bowl."

She nearly pulled away, but didn't want to argue with the man who'd helped her father.

"We make bowls, from clay, metal, even our hands. The material doesn't matter. It is what we put in them that matters." His voice was even and soothing, and she imagined he'd be good at hypnotizing people. "In this bowl you have made a place good thoughts, Piper. Place a prayer for your father. Buddha said, 'All life is temporary. Why worry about anything that is temporary.' So do not fill your bowl with worries. A worry will take you nowhere, will accomplish nothing. Fill it with prayer and good thoughts. Let peace enter. The bowl does not leak that way."

She closed her eyes and tried to do that, to picture her father standing in front of his "Deck the Halls" kind of tree, tried to pray to a God she was angry with for letting Paul Blackwell get cancer—again, for allowing her fellow soldiers to die in horrible ways in Iraq, for permitting a sicko serial killer to carve a path through no-longer sleepy Spencer County. Her shoulders hunched like she was a turtle and she cried, her tears spilling into the bowl she'd made with her hands.

They sat like that a long while, Piper thinking about her dad, prayers tumbling through her head followed by questions of "does God exist... 'cause if so, how could this happen?" She was angry—at God for all manner of things, at her father's heart, at herself for not being there when it happened. The Army had taught her to be strong and to compartmentalize things, like shoving a problem or bad attitude in a drawer and locking it away so you could focus on something more important. One of the men in her downrange squad was Jewish, but was fond of quoting Buddha. "Holding onto anger is like drinking poison and expecting the other person to die." He quoted that one a lot... because in war anger seemed ever-present. She shoved her anger in a drawer and took a deep breath.

And here, a virtual stranger—a Buddhist monk, Anthony Delaney —was helping her, had helped her father, hopefully had saved his life just by being in the house and calling for an ambulance. And this stranger was comforting her when he'd just lost his own father... to a serial killer. Piper suddenly realized that when she'd picked Anthony up at the airport she never gave him the customary and polite, "I'm sorry for your loss." They were hollow words anyway because everyone said them and didn't really mean them. But she should have said *something*. Should still say something, but not now. Above that, she should call the State in the morning and together get the man who killed Conrad Delaney... and Abigail Thornbridge, Samuel Reynolds, and Jacob Wallem.

She'd stopped crying. The sounds of the emergency department swirled around her. A woman nearby talking on her cell phone, annoyed that she hadn't gotten to see a doctor yet when her "ankle was swollen like a softball."

My father's heart attack trumps your ankle.

The cell phone in her pocket buzzed, muted because it was next to her driving gloves. Not important, she decided, someone from the department wondering about Paul Blackwell because they couldn't wonder to her about it on the scanner.

Anthony whispered something soft and musical in a foreign language, maybe a prayer in Thai; it was no doubt an effortless language to him after all these years. The alien words sounded nice and became a susurrus that had a calming effect. She focused on them and the irritated woman with the swollen ankle drifted to the background.

Get a grip on this.

Piper thought back to New Year's Eve, sitting at the table in her father's kitchen before she took the call about the first murder. Though he'd looked faded, he'd seemed happy, talking about her starting the next day as "head honcho of the Spencer County Sheriff's Department." He was proud of her. Piper hadn't the heart to tell him then that she wasn't sure it was right for her. She'd embraced the campaign because it distracted him from the cancer and treatments. But she honestly hadn't expected to win. Over her head, and committed to four years.

But isn't that what she'd initially committed to the Army? Four years. It had turned out better than she'd expected. Maybe she needed to embrace this job like she had the MP school. Piper wasn't anxious about the sheriff's testing she'd have to take come April. If she'd managed the rigors of Army training, successfully completed every downrange assignment her unit tackled, and if she could keep her head and keep control of the department during the terrors of this CCK thing, she could damn well pass that test.

Piper wanted her father around to see her do it.

Get a grip.

She pulled her hands back and stood, shifted her weight from one foot to the other and took off her coat; the waiting room was so warm she'd started to sweat. How long had she been sitting there?

"Thanks, Anthony, for being here and—"

"I do not need your thanks." He stood up next to her, took her coat and gently laid it on the chair next to him. "It was an honor to help."

"You have my thanks anyway," she returned, offering him a hint of a smile. She started to say something else, but a short woman in blue scrubs came over, pulling down her mask.

She had broad shoulders, a broad face and wide-set charcoal eyes, gray hair at the temples; the rest of her hair was bunched up under something that looked like a shower cap.

"Dr. Kilduff," she said, thrusting out a hand. "Your father is going to be all right."

Piper let out a breath she'd been holding. "Can I—"

"They're admitting him, to an ICU bed, so it'll be several minutes. Check with the desk to get a room number."

"How bad—"

The doctor seemed to anticipate all the questions. "A heart attack is always serious, but there are degrees. And as that goes, this certainly wasn't major. Otherwise the ambulance crew would have stabilized him and taken him to Evansville. Your father said he has no history of heart problems, but he's been receiving chemotherapy, a second round. Some forms of chemo are hard on the heart, and it might have triggered it, or at least helped along a problem that had been simmering. We'll forward our records to his oncologist in case that drug regimen needs to change. We're going to give him a beta blocker because there was a myocardial infarction at the root, maybe an ACE inhibitor, but I don't think there's any congestive heart failure involved. I won't have all the blood work back for a while, and I want to see that before I start prescribing. We did a 2D echo, and though the flow looks good, there is some blockage. Tomorrow mid-afternoon I've scheduled a percutaneous coronary intervention—"

Piper took in more of the doctor's words, but she didn't understand them, shoving them in a mental drawer until Dr. Kilduff started using layman speak.

"—it's nonsurgical, going up through the leg. We'll inflate the balloon to compress the plaque. We might put in a stent. It's a common procedure. We can do it here. He'll do fine." After a moment she said, "Relax."

Piper hadn't realized she'd been holding her breath again. "When will you know how long he'll be—"

"It's hard to say how many days he'll be here. Extremely variable. Depends on how he responds, and we have to fine-tune the dosage of medicines. We'll flush his arteries, make sure there's no bleeding, so I'll want him here four or five days at least. He's going to overnight in the ICU before we move him to a regular room. Maybe he can go home Tuesday. We'll see." The doctor put her hands in her pockets. "We'll take good care of him, Sheriff, I promise. I'll have an ICU nurse come get you."

Anthony tugged her back to the waiting room, where she made another bowl with her hands.

TWENTY-FIVE

"**A**ny word on Paul?" It was Oren, calling Randy on his cell. Both were still at their respective crime scenes.

It was 5 p.m., and Randy had just watched Jacob Wallem —at least he was pretty sure it was Jacob Wallem—extricated from the chimney, put in a large black bag, and taken out of the house. The coroner, who had brought two assistants and came in wearing an impressive facemask, hadn't said much more than a dozen words, including, "I'd say he's been in there two weeks, maybe a little longer."

Jacob Wallem definitely had been killed *before* Christmas. Days and days before Abigail and Conrad. Was he the first victim? Were there more out there?

All the windows open, the stink was still strong.

"Hey, Randy... you there?"

"Sorry, Oren. The body's out of here. Coroner's headed your way next. The boss called a half hour ago, said Paul's in an ICU bed, that they're going to do some sort of procedure tomorrow. He'll be there a few days at least, maybe a week. She also said he probably would have died if Anthony Delaney hadn't been with him. Apparently she hadn't known what to do with Conrad's Buddhist monk son, and had dropped him in Paul's lap."

Oren made a *hmmphing* sound. "You gonna go see him?"

"Paul?" Randy thought about that a moment. "Yeah, I checked with the hospital... they took him to Booneville of all places, so it must not have been too serious. If I get there by nine I'm good and can get in. But it's ICU, so the visit will be short. So, yeah, I'm going over when I've finished some stuff here and back at the office." He was about ready to disconnect when he added, "Buck there with you? Good. The Christmas cards you bagged from your scene, ask Buck to take them to the office now—before he heads home. And that he's to wait for me if I'm not there. You and me can connect tomorrow, share what we've found." Randy figured Buck was about ready to clock out for the day, usually railed against working overtime no matter what was going down. He wanted to talk to him. "I'm heading to the office in a little bit. Marsh and me have fingerprints, about two dozen evidence bags to send off to the lab, some stuff I'm taking back with me. Got some guys going door to door asking about Wallem and any visitors they might have noticed. I'll lock this up in a few and be back at it later tomorrow."

"The first funeral's tomorrow."

"First of four," Randy said. Conrad, Abigail, Samuel, and Jacob. He'd already loaded his kit and video equipment in the trunk. "Don't know if I'll make it to Conrad's funeral. Have to talk to the boss about that. Got some things not sitting right I got to dig into."

"Hell, nothing's sitting right." Randy heard Oren whisper something else, about "twenty-fucking-three."

Marsh started closing the windows.

Randy had a bag with Jacob's Christmas cards in one hand and an animal carrier with a three-legged blind beagle in the other.

He stopped at the grocery store and bought a sack of dog food, two plastic bowls, and a couple of kitchen towels. He'd found the dog's leash hanging on a hook by the back door.

Randy couldn't have dogs in his apartment, and didn't especially like them, would have dropped this one off at the shelter, but one of the "things not sitting right" was the victims' pets. Studies showed that a lot of serial killers started out being cruel to animals. The CCK appeared to be the opposite, though he hadn't left enough food down for the beagle. Or maybe he just figured it wouldn't have taken so long to find Jacob's body.

Jacob's neighbors had assumed he was on vacation, said his parents —who'd years ago moved to South Carolina—usually booked a cruise between Christmas and New Year's because of the discount rates. They thought maybe Jacob had gone with them, because he had in previous years. Randy had learned from the Rockport police that a worker at the animal shelter had called a few days ago, saying Jacob had missed a couple of volunteer shifts and she was worried; he hadn't been answering his phone. She did not file a missing person's report. It wasn't clear if the Rockport police had pursued it, but it didn't look like they had.

Randy walked the beagle around the edge of the parking lot at the sheriff's department and watched as it squatted against the tire of a silver Sonata. Then he tugged the dog inside and set up the crate in his office, filled the plastic bowls with food and water, and spread the kitchen towels out on the floor for it to nest on. There had been a dog bed at Wallem's, a comfortable-looking one. But Randy knew it would reek because of the body. Hell, the dog stank and needed a bath, had picked up the *eau de corpse rot* fragrance. It seemed to get around pretty well for being blind, though it did bump into a few things before it found the food.

"You got a dog?" Teegan was on shift and she leaned in the doorway.

"It's temporary. Her name's Merry."

"Belonged to one of the dead guys, huh? Didn't want to take it to the shelter? Don't blame you, it's overcrowded, that old thing'd get the needle for sure."

"I don't know if it's old. It's just—"

"Not adoptable. And it stinks." She smacked her gum and did a hair flip. Randy thought she was a Goth-embracing teenager trapped in a forty-year-old body. "Heard anything new on Paul?"

He shook his head. "But I'm going over there in an hour or so. Buck come in yet?"

"Nah, but he and JJ are on their way in to and drop off some evidence bags. Christ, this is awful stuff, eh? I got a call from an *Indianapolis Star* reporter when I came on. She's coming down with a photographer tomorrow for the Delaney funeral. Bet there'll be more. The *Evansville Courier* will be next, you think? I can see the headlines: Slay Bells in Spencer County. Nobody from the local rag has called us that I know of, but Joe stopped in to look at the blotter. Oh, and Chris Hagee came by with a box of big antique bells, apologized for not getting them back yesterday. I could've sworn I smelled pot on him." A pause. "Not that I know what pot smells like. Have fun with the *Star* tomorrow."

Randy shuddered. Media to deal with on top of this. Really? But that might be a good thing. He wanted to solve this personally, be the brilliant detective to uncover the sick son of a bitch, use it as a jumping off point to something better… to a sheriff's posting somewhere, if not here. Media attention, his name in the first paragraph; that ought to boost his career. If he could somehow solve it by the morning, he'd make sure he was at the funeral so he could talk to the press.

"Hey, Randy, do you think—" The phone buzzed in the other room and Teegan waggled her fingers and disappeared.

A radio played softly; rarely could Teegan deal with silence. It was some country station. Randy barely tolerated country music. The dog started crunching. He looked over the top of his desk and saw her tail was wagging wildly while she ate.

"And what the hell am I going to do with you?" he mused. "A bath tomorrow, definitely. But after that?" He'd keep the three-legged beagle here for a while; if anybody raised a fuss he'd call the dog a piece of evidence… because in a way she was. Why did the CCK take steps to make sure his victims' pets had food and water? Why care about dogs and cats when you were throttling their owners? It couldn't be a statement that the killer thought the owners abusive, because it appeared that Abigail Thornbridge, Conrad Delaney, and Jacob Wallem had taken fine care of their pets. Wallem had bought top-of-the-line dog food, according to the price sticker Randy saw on the empty bag, and had volunteered at the shelter and with some beagle rescue group. Oren said there was no evidence Samuel Reynolds had any pet. So the pets weren't a connection... and yet pets were somehow connected to the killer. Because he liked them? Probably more than he liked people.

He dumped Wallem's Christmas cards on his desk; he'd put them with Conrad's and Abigail's cards later, see what names matched. There... Conrad in his sleigh. He flipped it over.

Jacob, Somehow that new roof you put on has cut my heating bill... and it's beautiful to boot! Very pleased with your work. I can remember when you and Anthony used to play Cowboys and Indians in the backyard. Time goes too fast. I've got some other things around here I'd like fixed up, my bathroom redone. I want one of those fancy bathtubs put in, the walk-in kind. There's some sales on them coming up. I intend to stay here until they drag me out in a box, so I want the house accessible. Those bathtubs are expensive, but cheaper than an assisted living place. My knees are starting to really bother me. But you don't need to hear about my old-man woes. You need to hear MERRY CHRISTMAS from me. Thanks again for your good work. Regards, Conrad

He found the card Abigail had sent Wallem, too, the design of a woman in a rocker in front of a Christmas tree. A shiver went down Randy's spine. A very sick bastard had posed the old woman just like her card.

Jake, So happy you've been coming to church again. God is good! Young man like you, it's a great place to meet single women, and there are more than a few in the congregation. I can introduce you if you'd like. Sally's granddaughter is pretty and still without a fellow. Otherwise, I'll mind my business. I talked to Conrad the other day, and he's apple pie pleased I gave him your name and number. He didn't know you had your own business, said he gave you a couple of jobs. I should have you do a little more work for me after the worst of winter passes. I'm going to move to one of those retirement villages in Tennessee, where the weather is kinder and there's more music. This old house will sell better with a little fixing. I'll give you a call. All my best to you and Merry. Love, Abby T

No card from Samuel Reynolds to Wallem. Maybe they didn't

know each other. But the killer clearly knew all of them. The relationship of the killer to these people… that's what he needed to discover if he was going to beat the State to the solution. Damn, but he wanted to clear this on his own. Media attention was coming… Chief Deputy Randy Gerald.

Randy pounded his fist on the desk and the beagle stopped crunching.

"It's okay, Merry," he said. Randy felt sorry for her, and hoped Oren could place the dog somewhere. "Really, it's okay." After a moment, the dog went back to eating.

He leafed through the cards, seeing no other senders' names jump out that matched the ones in the other room addressed to Conrad and Abigail. He'd look at those all again, just to be sure. A lot of the cards to Wallem were basically photographs, pictures of pets or children with pets, flipping them over and reading the notes and guessing they were from other people involved with the shelter.

"Teegan… how old is the coffee?" he hollered. Maybe he'd take a Thermos full when he headed out.

"Probably goes back three or four months." That was Buck Hannoh's voice. He came into Randy's office, sat opposite the desk and plopped the bag filled with Samuel Reynolds' Christmas cards in front of him. "Oren said you wanted these now, couldn't wait for the morning. Said you wanted to talk to me. What's up? I'm in a hurry to get home."

Buck had been a police officer in Santa Claus before Paul Blackwell took him into the sheriff's department a half-dozen years back. The sheriff's department paid a little better, and always there were local cops trying to get on. He was good looking, like a roguish young Harrison Ford complete with the Indiana Jones stubble, and his wife, a real estate agent, was a stunner. Randy and his on-again off-again girlfriend played miniature golf with them in the summer. Buck smiled, his teeth so shiny Randy figured he'd had them professionally whitened.

"Earth to Randy. Oren said you wanted to see me. What's up?"

Randy stacked the cards he'd been looking at, tugged open a

drawer and pulled out a notepad he'd scribbled on earlier. He didn't say anything, letting the diffused strains of someone singing about an old pickup truck filter in. The dog had finished eating and was slurping at the water now. He'd have to walk her again.

Nervous people needed conversation, he knew from experience, and Buck was fidgeting. Randy thought maybe he should have discussed this Buck business with Oren, who was the chief deputy after all. Maybe should have said something to Piper, too. Maybe. He could justify not reporting this to her easily enough... didn't want to disturb her while she was at her father's bedside. Yeah, he was being considerate that way.

"So whatdya want? Huh? I need to get going. And how's Paul Blackwell? Heard anything?"

Randy pursed his lips and shook his head, waited a beat. "He's in ICU. Boss is with him."

Buck snorted. "You call her boss, I call her—"

Teegan poked her head in, looked down at the dog. "Oren called, says he's going to stay out there for maybe another hour and then stop at the hospital before heading home. Says he'll bring in the stuff to send to the lab in the morning. No more mail's going out today anyway and—" The phone rang and she disappeared again.

"—an embarrassment," Buck finished. He stuffed his hands under his armpits and harrumphed. "I call her an embarrassment. Hell, Randy, I'm thirty-six. I've got a college degree in criminal psychology, worked in Santa Claus five years before I got on here, and I'd made sergeant. I don't care if she'd made sergeant in the Army. It's not the same thing, you know that. I don't want to answer to no—"

Teegan came in again. "That was Sheriff Blackwell with an update. Paul's sitting up, talking. I'd phoned the florist over there before they'd closed, sent a bouquet. I'm assuming you'll chip in. I put everyone's name on it." Another call. "Busy busy. Better catch it."

Buck and Randy nodded.

"I'll give you some money in a few," Buck hollered.

"You told me you'd checked on Jacob Wallem, Buck, and you told me his neighbors claimed he was away on vacation."

Buck shrugged. "So?"

"You couldn't have checked on Jacob Wallem. There wasn't a boot-print in the yard. And the neighbors told me no one from the sheriff's department asked them about Jacob or asked about anything for that matter." That was a lie, Randy hadn't asked the neighbors a single question, Marsh and two other deputies were still interviewing them now. "So who told you Jacob was on vacation?"

"Oh, people."

"The people at the animal shelter?"

"Yeah, them."

"Funny, the shelter folks said no one from the sheriff's department talked to them either, but one of them had called Rockport police, concerned Jacob had missed a few shifts." Randy let the silence settle again, and he glanced at his notepad. The tune in the other room changed; a woman singer this time, sounded like maybe Dolly Parton. He didn't like what he called goat-roping music, but he liked Dolly.

"You had me checking on quite a few people, Randy. I might have missed a few things."

More silence.

"Buck, honestly, did you check on Jacob Wallem?"

"I drove by the Wallem house the other night, okay. No lights on. It was obvious the guy wasn't home, nothing shoveled, mailbox stuffed to the gills. Construction business... no one hires roofers in the winter. I figured he went to Florida or something." He laughed. "Hell, if we're going to have another winter like this, I'll take all my vacation and go to Florida."

Randy was thinking Buck might have a lot of vacation time on his lazy-ass hands.

"I didn't know he was dead, Randy, that roofer. Had no reason to think that. Why the hell would I have a reason to think that when you had him on your suspect list?"

"All that mail built up, you didn't think that odd?" Randy idly flipped the notepad over because he noticed Buck was trying to read it. "What about Elias Gerald Hagee?"

"Who?" Buck honestly looked puzzled.

"Relative of Chris Hagee, the guy who hosted the party across from Conrad Delaney's. Elias Gerald Hagee."

"Oh, him. Yeah, what about him?"

"You said you did a follow up on him, and his ex-. You were assigned follow-ups on five people, including Elias Gerald and Chris."

Buck shrugged. "So if my report said I followed up, I followed up. You know I'm not great on names."

"Damn, Buck." Randy felt his face warm with ire and he grabbed the edge of his desk. "Maybe I don't want to work for a twenty-three-year-old either."

"Twenty-three-year-old *girl*," Buck cut in. "Who ain't never worked in a sheriff's department ever before this, who ain't got no right to be the boss. Damn fools in the county thought they were voting for her dad, I'll bet."

"Did you follow up with any of these people?" He flipped the notepad over again and pushed it at Buck so he could finally see the names.

Buck glared at the page. "You talked to all of them first, right? Said you and Oren did. You're the detective. I'm not going to learn anything that you two hadn't already. Would've been a waste of my time. Had plenty enough to do anyway, all the calls that weren't about the dead bodies, DUIs and—"

"So you didn't double-check a single one of these folks' alibis. You didn't follow up with even one of them."

"I don't like how this conversation is going, Randy. I've been in this department six years. Busted my butt here for six years. But it won't be seven. I don't have to worry about vacationing in Florida next winter. I've been talking to the new sheriff over in Vanderburgh. He's got an opening coming in two months when his chief deputy retires. I'm on his list, likes my experience, my degree, my record, and I can get three weeks of vacation there automatically. Been looking at apartment listings in Evansville ever since the *Courier's* last Sunday classifieds came out, started making calls when I got a look at her in that sheriff uniform. Ain't no Christmas Card Killer over there in Vanderburgh. Now, if you don't have anything else... because I don't work for you. At the moment I work for a twenty-three-year-old *girl*. I'm going home. My feet hurt. Got a problem with me, tell the *girl* about it. Better yet, I'll tell her about it in the morning when I turn in my notice. I quit."

Buck hadn't even unzipped his coat. He glanced down at the dog as he pushed out of the chair, snorted, and left.

"Son of a bitch," Randy said, looking at his list. "Son of a bitch." Buck wouldn't get the Vanderburgh job, not if he called the sheriff, mentioned the shoddy work, and said that he wanted the job instead... which he would do in the morning. Calling the Vanderburgh sheriff about this at home might only piss him off.

Randy looked through the bag of cards Buck had brought. Samuel Reynolds hadn't received as many as the other victims, and apparently hadn't received ones from Abigail or Jacob Wallem. Received one from Conrad, mentioned giving old toys to Samuel's kids. No apparent thread to connect them all... but there had to be one.

He walked the dog in the parking lot, and then put it in the little kennel with some water. Merry looked up with sightless eyes, sniffed, found his hand through the grate and licked it. Then he grabbed his coat and the notepad.

"Teegan, I'm gonna take a run over to St. Mary's and check on Paul." Then he was going to tackle what Buck Hannoh hadn't, all the double-checking that was never done, and see if Marsh had been just as careless, too. Piper Blackwell had been so busy she couldn't have known that at least one of her deputies wasn't working to full potential... she was trusting her department. Naïve of her. But, hell, she was twenty-three. He would have liked to take a shower first, knew some of the stink was clinging to him. But he didn't want to take the time.

"Look in on the dog for me, will you, Teegan? Give her a little walk before you clock out and put her back in that crate. She likes to pee right next to your car."

TWENTY-SIX

Oren walked into the ICU of St. Mary's hospital just in time to see Randy stepping out of Paul Blackwell's room.

"He's pale," Randy said. "About as white as the sheet he's laying on."

Neither said anything for a moment. Oren heard the rattle of a medicine cart being pushed somewhere nearby, smelled the strong antiseptic cleaner used in places like this. He'd attended the autopsy yesterday for Sweet Abby T, and the smell was similar in that hospital —until of course he entered the room where Dr. Annie Neufeld was working. That room didn't smell similar to anything.

Three bouquets of flowers sat at the nurse's station, as well as a big basket of fruit topped with a loopy blue bow, a helium Get Well balloon floated above it. Oren glanced at the attached cards, all to Paul Blackwell, the largest bouquet from the sheriff's department with everyone's names on it—he'd have to chip in for that. Other flowers were from the Rockport Police Department and someone who must be a neighbor, name not familiar. The fruit, supplied by a local grocer, was from Dr. Neufeld. Word had traveled like lightning about Paul Blackwell's heart attack.

Yesterday he and Annie had talked about fruit. She mentioned to him that she'd just put in an order with an online company for a tray of olives, dates, figs, and pomegranates to commemorate *Tu B'Shevat*, which was weeks away. It was a large order, she'd said, and would he like to share it with her and Bebe? The Jewish festival meant "New Year of the Trees" and was something Oren acknowledged but typically never celebrated. It had come to be an ecology awareness day, and some people planted trees in celebration. Too cold to plant a tree at his Santa Claus home. He had enough trees in the yard anyway.

"Sure," he'd told her, wondering if she'd made the offer because if the killings kept going they'd be seeing more of each other anyway. "My wife would like to catch up with you two." Oren was good friends with Annie, had been since they were young. But he felt "itchy" when Bebe was in the picture. Oren's wife seemed more accepting of the coroner's same-sex marriage.

"They won't let him have that stuff in his room," Randy said, catching Oren looking at the flowers and fruit. Randy had a box of chocolates in his hand, nothing fancy, probably grabbed at the store on the way over here. Oren knew better than to bring something because of ICU rules, and he knew he'd be tossing money at Teegan for his share of the flowers. Randy placed the candy next to the fruit basket. "You give that to Paul Blackwell when he gets moved into a regular room, okay?" he asked the nurse. She nodded.

"How's he doing?" Oren figured he should say something to Randy.

"I only stopped in to say 'hi,' didn't ask how he was doing. He just doesn't look good to me." Randy shrugged. "Boss is in there with him. She said the doc claims it was a fairly minor heart attack... if there's such a thing."

"There is."

"But he looks like a ghost, I think. Hope he bounces out of it. He's a good guy, Oren."

"I know. A real good guy."

"But cancer... twice, and now a heart attack. And he's only what, fifty-eight?"

"Fifty-five." Ten years younger than himself.

"Yeah, that's not *that* old."

"We all get different cards," Oren said. "Some of us get dealt a better hand."

Randy shook his head. "Hope he bounces out of it," he repeated. "Hey, listen, I need to go. I'm in a hurry, actually. Some things still aren't sitting right with—"

"A helluva lot's not sitting right."

"Buck's been skimping."

"Yeah, I got that feel from him. Doesn't like the new sheriff." Oren might not have liked the new sheriff either, but it wasn't in his makeup to skimp on work.

"I don't know if any of the others haven't been following through. I don't know how widespread the malaise is."

"Malaise." Oren rubbed his chin. "Not a word I use."

"It means—"

"I know what it means. Marsh was kind of shoddy on some Thornbridge stuff, but I had a talk with him this morning. He hasn't missed anything that I can tell, just hasn't been as thorough as he should be. I think the new sheriff is clueless about department morale. People just aren't liking to work for someone so young and with no experience." Oren rubbed at a mark on the back of his hand —his years showing in a few liver spots. "But JJ... hell... JJ loves the new sheriff and is working harder than ever." He laughed. "Helluva thing all of this." He sniffed and wrinkled his nose. "What did you step in?"

Randy ignored the question.

The medicine cart clattered by. The orderly pushing it nodded to them.

"So, I'm going to backtrack on everything Buck was supposed to do, just to be safe. And Buck claims he's putting in his notice tomorrow. Really, I gotta get going."

Oren unzipped his coat; it was warm in the hallway. "Buck... he's never been all that hard of a worker anyway, you know, Randy." A pause. "Are you staying? With the department? Annie said there's an opening coming in the Vanderburgh sheriff's office. She figured you, maybe Marsh, were casting your eyes over there because of little Piper Blackwell."

Randy gave a clipped laugh.

"I'll take that as you're thinking about it. I'm not looking. I'm not moving. But I'll write you a recommendation if you want." *I'm too old for the sheriff there to pick me up.* "If you stay, I'd make you my chief deputy come April if—"

"Oren!" Piper was in the hall, had just come out of Paul's room. "Good of you to stop by."

"Yeah, that's the thing," Randy continued. "If she *doesn't* pass it. Like I said, I gotta run." He zipped up his coat, looked over his shoulder. To Piper, "I've got some things to check on, Boss, before I call it a night." Then he stepped around Oren and disappeared around the corner.

"He's still awake," Piper told Oren. "But they won't let you stay long."

Oren took his hat off. It gave him something to do with his hands. "The bald guy in the waiting room back there, that Anthony Delaney?"

"Yeah."

"Good thing he was with your father. He give you anything? About Conrad? Enemies?"

"Not much." She put her hands in her pockets and seemed to study a design on the tile floor. "But Anthony's been gone from home a lot of years. He was friends with Jacob Wallem, though. I need to tell Anthony about that. Randy said he's pretty sure it was Jacob in the chimney."

"Dentals will take a while."

"Yeah." A pause. "I'm gonna go get a cup of coffee. You want some?"

"Nah. Just here to see Paul. I won't stay long." Oren watched her retreat down the hall, probably in the direction of some vending machine.

"Keep it to fifteen minutes, please," the nurse said as Oren walked by.

"No problem."

The antiseptic odor wasn't as strong in here, and Oren detected a hint of pine. Maybe they tried to make the place smell better for people in critical shape.

Randy was right—Paul looked awful. Pale, haggard, like an *old* man, eyes hollow. He was propped up because of the adjustable bed, and something clear from a bag dripped into a tube connected under some gauze tape to his arm. Colored wires poked out from the top of his hospital gown and fed to a machine monitoring probably everything. Oren hoped he never ended up like this; if he had a heart attack he'd like it to be lights out, let's see if something is on the other side.

"Paul," Oren said. He took a seat next to the bed, but pushed it back a bit. "They taking good care of you?" He didn't know what else to say. *Hope you're feeling better* didn't seem right.

"I suppose. They've stuck so many needles in me, and all these monitors... I feel like I'm in a science fiction movie."

"They said I can't stay long, but I wanted to stop by. Check on you."

"Thanks." Paul shifted a little and one of the lines on the machine jumped then settled down. "Geeze, Oren, you look like a raccoon, the dark circles. You getting any sleep?"

"Working late. We all are. This is bad business."

"I think Piper's barely sleeping." Paul's forehead creased with worry lines. "Is she doing okay, Oren? Is Piper handling stuff okay?"

Funny thing to ask, Oren thought. No, she wasn't. Piper Blackwell is twenty-three years old, no experience in a sheriff's department, not even a certificate from a community college. No, she wasn't handling stuff okay. He should be the one "handling stuff" and wearing the sheriff's badge. Piper should have stayed in the Army.

"Considering," Oren said. "Considering we're dealing with a serial killer, she's doing okay. Never had one in the county before."

"Ever," Paul said. "Sadly exciting, isn't it?"

Oren noticed Paul's eyes gleam with a little life.

"It is that. Never had a serial killer on my plate before. Hope I don't ever again. But while it's there... all served up on the table... yeah, it is sadly exciting."

Paul motioned for a cup of water that had a bendy straw sticking out of it. Oren obliged him, held it while he drank, and then set it back on the tray. "She's not saying much about it to me. Hasn't asked for a lick of advice. Wants to stand on her own feet, maybe doesn't want to worry me. Probably figures I have enough to worry about."

Cancer and a heart attack, Oren thought. Yeah, that's more than enough to worry about.

"We're pretty clueless," Oren admitted. "She bought a whiteboard, has it all filled up with victims names and how they're connected, has collected all the Christmas cards. You know they're posed like the cards, right?"

Paul nodded. "Randy says they're calling it the CCK—Christmas Card Killer."

"Helluva thing."

"Suspects?"

"Thought we had somebody good for it, a roofer in Rockport... a thread that connected to Delaney, Abby T, and Sam Reynolds. He did some work for all of them. But we're pretty sure he's the body that was stuffed in his chimney. Glad I was dealing with Sammy the Snowman, a better looking corpse."

"I hadn't heard about that one, the roofer. So four victims?"

"Yeah. Scene's still active. Him and Sam Reynolds found dead the same day." A pause. "But the roofer's been dead a while. Annie's thinking he was killed a few days before Christmas."

"And nobody missed him?"

"That's Randy's scene. I'm working on Sammy the Snowman." Oren laughed. He hadn't laughed for a while. "Helluva thing, a serial killer, more bodies than... well..."

"Calling in the State?"

"Yeah, Randy says she's calling them tomorrow. Don't like it, but I don't see that we have a choice."

"Spencer County," Paul said glumly. "Things like this, serial killers, ain't supposed to happen in a place like Spencer County."

"Damn straight."

"Wonder if there are more bodies out there? From this killer?"

Oren shrugged. "In between things JJ's checking with sheriff departments in Kentucky, seeing if they've got any Christmas corpses. Nothing else in Indiana that's popped up. But something in Henderson might be related, she said. Something marked as an accidental death that she got the report on. If there's a thread, somebody will drive over there tomorrow after Conrad's funeral and talk to Henderson police."

"Piper said the guy bought eleven Merry Christmas mugs. Did you know that, Oren? Eleven. Didn't buy the last one in the case because the design on it was crooked, Piper said. Eleven."

"Didn't know that," Oren said. But he'd been avoiding working with the new sheriff, avoided being in the same room with her when possible. "Good time to be Jewish, eh? Make sure they take good care of you, Paul. I'll try to get back here Saturday."

He stopped in the waiting room to introduce himself to Anthony Delaney, who was sitting cross-legged on the floor, hands on his knees, eyes closed, and lips working. He waited for the monk to finish whatever he was doing. When Anthony opened his eyes, Oren could tell he'd been crying.

"I'm Oren Rosenberg, the chief deputy."

Anthony stood and held out a hand. "Pleased to meet you. Actually, I think I remember you. I was younger."

"I used to be younger, too." Oren put on his hat. "I'm sorry about your father, sorry for your loss."

"Thank you." Anthony bowed his head. "And for Sweet Abby T, Sam Reynolds, and Jake. Detective Gerald told me that Jake is dead, too."

"Yes, I'm sorry for all of them."

"Life is temporary," Anthony said. "And Buddha posed that we should not worry about temporary things. But it should not be a murderer's purview to decide how temporary someone's life is."

Oren didn't have a response. He waited a beat. "I'd like to ask you about your father." Oren figured Piper had plenty of time to talk to him, driving him back from the airport. But she might not have asked the right questions. Randy had obviously talked to him, too.

"Everyone seems to want to ask about my father." Anthony let out a deep sigh. "Actually, I'd have time to talk on the way back to Rockport. Give me a lift? Detective Gerald suggested I ask you for a ride. I came here in the ambulance with Mr. Blackwell, and a little while ago he asked me to go back to his house and take care of his pug. He gave me a key. I'm staying there for a few days, and—"

"Sure, I'll give you a ride." He noticed the monk didn't have a coat. "Did you get any dinner?"

A head shake.

"We'll stop at this little diner on the way. My treat. I'm hungry, too."

Oren figured what's one more long night, right?

TWENTY-SEVEN

Randy wanted to solve this by himself. He knew Oren was just as driven; neither had been faced with a serial killer in the county before, and neither wanted a twenty-three-year-old first-time sheriff to take credit for catching the guy.

Randy wanted that credit.

"Do you like her?" Oren had asked him more than a few times.

He still couldn't say that he *didn't* like her. Piper had given him no reason not to like her... other than her age, which by itself wasn't enough reason. But he didn't like working for her. She'd probably ream him a new one if she knew he was pursuing a suspect without writing the name of the guy on her precious whiteboard and telling her about it. She'd have every right to be pissed... suspected she'd be seriously pissed when she found out how lax Buck had been. He could wiggle around the chain-of-command thing; tell her he didn't want to burden her about a lead when she had her father to worry over.

Randy figured he would benefit more from the victory of solving the case than Oren would. At sixty-five, Oren was likely going to retire soon, maybe real soon if Piper passed the sheriff's exam in April. So solving the case wouldn't do the grizzled chief deputy all that much good—outside of going out on a high note and grabbing some headlines. And Randy could slip into the chief deputy job if Oren left, but the more he thought about, the more he knew he really didn't want to work for a twenty-three-year-old newbie.

For Randy... solving a case like this would open a lot of doors and get him out from under Piper Blackwell. There would be plenty of headlines; and not just in the itty bitty county weekly. Headlines in the big Indianapolis paper, in the *Evansville Courier*, and it would make the national wires—because serial killers were gruesome news that people all over the country were fascinated with. Hell, maybe Randy would gain enough notoriety that he could push for the chief deputy posting over in Vanderburgh, and then he'd run for the top spot there come the next election. Catching a serial killer would give him a great campaign platform. Sheriff Randy Gerald.

But to make the catch, he'd have to work fast. Piper was calling in the State sometime tomorrow. They'd probably send investigators down over the weekend. And she'd mentioned the F.B.I., too. Crap. Serial killer? Four victims? The big Fed guns might turn out in force and try to take his glory.

The killer was a county man, or someone who had county ties. Randy had always been rock-solid certain of that. And so he should be caught by a county deputy... by the county detective. Maybe Randy would get enough material to write one of those true crime books. A case like this, posing people to replicate Christmas cards, that ought to sell, right? Maybe someone would make a movie out of it, if not a big theatrical release staring Matt Damon or Daniel Craig, then at least one of those made-for-TV Lifetime shows. He'd be happy with either.

If Buck had been thorough, had given half a shit about doing his job, the clues would have fallen together faster and Randy might have been driving to Owensboro two days ago to follow this lead, not getting ready to do so right now. He stopped back at the office to look at one of his reports, just to make sure he had the right address—no use storming into Kentucky if he didn't know where he was going. He checked on Merry while he was there, and walked her out to pee next to the car tire.

He glanced up, the sky was clear and the stars out in serious numbers, diamonds scattered on black velvet, one of his former girlfriends used to say. The only lights that competed were at the edges of the parking lot. In a big city the stars were harder to see because of all the street and business lights. The sheriff's department sat near the downtown, but there wasn't much operating along the main street anymore. A few taverns, an antique shop that opened when the aging owner had the whim, Harlan Crook's law office. God, he loved this small town and this rural county; he liked the *feel* of it. The air was good here. Still, he was going to be destined for greater things in a much bigger place if this played out the way it was looking. And if his hunch was wrong, he'd pull in Oren and they'd come up with another suspect to chase.

But he hoped he was right.

His breath puffed away like he was sending smoke signals to God. *Dear God, let me be right.* The dog hunched near the sidewalk. Randy hadn't brought anything with him to pick up the poop. He went back inside and tucked Merry in the kennel. Time to get going.

"I thought you were done for the day," Teegan chimed from her office. "Didn't you say you were done?"

"Still working," he said. "I've got another thing to check on."

"Something good?"

"Very strong lead. I'll radio you if it turns into anything." He looked in through her doorway. "Hey, I still need you to walk the dog before you go. I need to keep her here for a while, understand? Consider her evidence." *Because she really is.*

"Sure thing." She smacked her gum. "How's Paul?"

"Still breathing."

"Breathing's good."

Randy headed south and across the bridge that led to Kentucky.

The scanner chatter was light. He listened to a report of a DUI north of Rockport; apparently someone had stopped at a tavern after work, drank too much, and then while attempting to go home instead plowed into a tree. DUIs... the number one ticketed offense in Spencer County.

He pulled the recorder out of his pocket, sat it on the passenger's seat. Randy had spotted Anthony Delaney in the ER waiting room, recognizing him—even without hair—because of the pictures at Conrad's house. Randy stopped to chat with the monk before visiting Paul, and he recorded the conversation just as he had when he'd interviewed others these past few days.

And when Randy was through, he almost didn't stop to visit Paul. He was excited, thought he might be onto something, wanted to pursue this angle right now. But he'd bought the chocolates, and he was only a dozen or so yards away from the former sheriff. Still, he hadn't stayed long at Paul's bedside, not even five minutes, bumped into Oren on his way out, and that stalled him. He nearly grabbed Oren by the shoulders and told him about the discovery. But fortunately he'd stopped himself. He really couldn't afford to share this. Oren most certainly would want to go with him, and then the credit would be divided.

Fifteen years with the Spencer County Sheriff's Department, the lone detective, this would be his. He wouldn't have to call the twenty-three-year-old sheriff "boss" much longer.

He turned down the scanner, pressed play on his recorder, and cranked the volume.

"Do you mind if I record this?"

"No. That's fine," Anthony had said.

"How do I refer to you? Brother? Or—"

"Please call me Tony."

"Tony, good. I'm sorry about your dad, Tony. No one deserves to die like that, murdered. The neighbors all spoke well of Conrad." The faint clatter of a wheeled medicine cart was heard in the background. "It's our job to find the man who killed your father... and Abigail Thornbridge and—"

"Sweet Abby T. She'd sent me another fruitcake some weeks ago. I'd told the sheriff that."

"Did you know Sweet Abby T well?" Obviously, Randy had thought, otherwise she would not have sent him a fruitcake.

"She was the principal at my grade school, had been one of my father's teachers... when she was right out of college. I liked her. A small place like this, it is easy to become friends with people of all ages, to see them at picnics and church socials. I'd stayed in touch with her when I left the States."

"We think the murders are connected."

"I understand that."

"There's a connection with Jacob Wallem, too."

"Jake? My dad wrote that Jake did some work for him and—"

"Yeah, well we're pretty sure Jacob Wallem was murdered by the same guy." Randy had paused, gauging Tony's reaction. The monk's stoic face had shifted to disbelief, then sadness. He'd wished Piper had broached the death of Jacob Wallem, but he realized she'd not had the time, just coming from Wallem's house, no positive ID made. "Samuel Reynolds is dead, too."

"Another childhood friend of mine."

"Yeah, I'd gathered that from a Christmas card your dad had sent Sam, mentioned some of your old toys he wanted to give to Sam's children."

There were no words for a few minutes, the click-clack of some-one's heels against the tile, the *shoosh* of double-doors opening as a man came into the ER coughing up a lung. On a chair in the waiting room across from them a young woman had hummed. Randy had noticed she had earbuds and a cord leading to a shiny blue mp3 player in her pocket; looked healthy, probably waiting for somebody who wasn't.

"Related, all of it," Anthony had pronounced. "But why would someone kill these people? Harmless people. Good people. I'd heard from all of them at Christmas, got cards and letters."

Randy had wondered why people would send Christmas cards to a Buddhist monk. But then he recalled that Conrad Delaney had sent a Christmas card to the Jewish coroner. Maybe they were all just keeping in touch, and Christmas gave them an excuse to do that.

"We're working on that, a motive. It doesn't appear to be robbery."

Anthony had shaken his head. "Sammy didn't have much money. He struggled to keep his farm. He would email me sometimes, ask about the weather in Thailand, tell me about his bills. I should have emailed him back more often, but I limited my time on the computer."

So Buddhist monks used computers. Not so primitive as he'd imagined.

"Better than here, the weather in Thailand, I suspect," Randy had said so softly the recorder barely picked it up.

"Do you have suspects, Detective?"

"I'm not at liberty to discuss that." Randy had heard that particular line several times in cop-themed television shows. "I can tell you, however, that we've been talking to a lot of people. Interviewing people who knew the victims."

"Like you are interviewing me?"

"Yeah."

"Have you talked to my brother? Zach might be able to help. He knew all of those people, too. A few years ago he used to help Jake with the beagle rescue group. He might have a better idea who would mean those people harm."

"I'll probably talk to him again tomorrow after your dad's funeral."

"It is a sad occasion, the funeral, but I look forward to seeing Zach again. He is going to pick me up at Mr. Blackwell's house, where I am staying, drive me to the funeral and to the cemetery."

"How long will you be staying, Tony?"

Another cart clattered by and the sick man kept coughing. Thankfully, a nurse appeared and ushered the man down the hall. Probably pneumonia, Randy had thought.

"I planned for two weeks, but my return ticket is open-ended. I might stay a little longer, attend the other funerals, look in on old friends. Sheriff Blackwell says my father's house will be cleared soon and so I can stay there. Though this is sad, it will be good to spend time with my brother."

"You haven't seen him in a while."

"We email from time-to-time, have for several years, but I have not seen him since I left the States after graduation. Too long, I realize, but the time was like butter, so easily it melted."

"Yeah." There was more silence, and Randy had noted this wasn't like the previous interviews he'd conducted. The other people thought they needed to fill up the silence with small talk, but the monk just sat there. Eventually, Randy started again. "I imagine Zachary will be glad to catch up with you, too."

"Face to face will be better than our scant emails. I hope I can help him find a new job, help him with his resume, look through all the classified ads in the paper and on the Internet."

Randy had been puzzled. He'd remembered Zachary saying he worked at Plank Manor out on Heartland in Owensboro, that he'd been there a while and was going for a promotion, and that he could only get three days off for Conrad's death.

"He been out of work long, your brother?"

"Since around Thanksgiving, I believe. He said it was a seasonal lay-off, too many employees. But I knew better. Zach always had trouble holding a job. He'd done something to get himself fired, I know. He has not yet found inner peace. Perhaps I can help with that, too."

Randy hadn't known what to say after that, but his mind churned. Zachary Delaney had been on Buck's list of people to double-check, verify alibis. Buck had signed off on Zachary, but he couldn't have made any calls, or he would have flagged the fact that Zach had lied in the initial interview about being employed and punching a time clock. Lie about one thing… lie about something else.

The silence got to Randy for a change. "You mentioned your brother knew Jake, something about beagle rescue?"

"My brother loves dogs."

Randy had sat down at that point, rubbed his chin and felt the stubble he'd forgot to take a razor to this morning. Randy couldn't explain it, but the hairs on the back of his neck fairly danced. He was getting close to something important.

"Loves dogs?"

"We had one when were kids. What is the saying?" The monk

pursed his lips in thought. "I remember. Everyone believes they have the best dog in the world, and every one of them is right. Duke was the best dog ever."

"Tell me about it, please."

"Sure, but what does that have to do with your investigation? How will that help find my father's killer?"

Randy had been quick to answer. "I'm trying to find out more about your father. Even years back to when you were a kid. I paint a picture of the victim, and that helps with the solution. So, go on please."

Randy remembered that Anthony had smiled sadly, his eyes focusing on something far beyond the ER waiting room.

"Zach, when he was young, had the most amazing mutt, Duke. Maybe a Golden Retriever mix, maybe mixed with a Great Dane. He was huge. Dad had bought him for Zach's seventh birthday. So naturally he was more Zach's dog than mine, even though I enjoyed Duke, too. They just fit together, Zach and the dog, did everything together. Duke slept on Zach's bed." Anthony stopped.

"Go on," Randy had urged. "I'd like to hear about Zach and Duke."

"This isn't about my father, it's about a dog."

"I know, but your father bought the dog."

"My brother did not kill our father."

Perceptive, Randy had realized. The monk had figured out that Zach was his suspect.

"Oh, I know he didn't. I've already interviewed your brother. He's definitely not a suspect." Randy could lie effortlessly to someone if he needed to. "We had a nice long talk, your brother and me. So, go on about the dog."

"He was only seven, Duke, when he started falling down and having seizures right after Halloween. We took him to the vet's. I'd just gotten my driver's license, so I drove. Zach held him in the back seat. There were x-rays and blood tests, and the vet called it a form of pancreatic cancer. Zach cried so hard." Another pause.

"I used to have a dog, too," Randy had lied again. "I remember losing that dog was just terrible. It broke my heart."

"The vet offered some promise, called it 'great risk and great reward,' a surgery they could do at the veterinary school at Purdue in West Lafayette. It was going to be expensive. I don't remember how much, but a couple thousand dollars, said it would buy Duke maybe four or five years more of life if he survived the surgery; that's a good amount of time for a big dog, a natural lifespan. Me and Zach... I was sixteen, he was fourteen then, we didn't have that money. Mom was sympathetic, said okay, but Dad shut it down. Said he wouldn't' spend thousands of dollars on an animal, especially something considered risky."

"What happened?" Randy put on a good sympathetic face.

"Zach begged and begged for the money, but Dad wouldn't relent. Zach and me called everywhere trying to find odd jobs to raise the cash, but nothing happened fast enough. Duke? He had all these seizures in our bedroom one morning in early December. Dad didn't come in until after he'd finished setting out his sleigh. Duke was dead by then. He said surgery might not have saved the dog anyway, risky and all. But I think that the surgery might have saved Zach. See, Zach was holding Duke when he died, never got over it. That year, Dad had had these Christmas photo cards printed with Zach, Duke, and me on them. Even though Duke was dead, Dad sent the cards, said he wasn't going to buy new ones. That made things worse with Zach, those cards. Zach stopped going to church with Mom, said there was no God. Said no God would let an animal suffer like that. Took over-the-counter sleeping pills after that, said otherwise he had nightmares and couldn't sleep. Stole the pills when he didn't have the money for them. I never snitched on him, my brother and all. I sometimes wonder if he started playing around with other drugs to forget that awful day with Duke."

"Do you think they smoothed things out, Zach and your dad?"

Anthony had shaken his head. "That dog had been everything to Zach, and he never forgave our father. I know I've been away for years, that things can change, but not that one thing." A pause. "But Zach would not have raised a finger against our father. Especially not after all these years. He could not have done such an awful thing. He couldn't have because he wouldn't have come near our father."

"I know that," Randy had purred. "Zach isn't a suspect. He gave us a rock-solid alibi. I just was asking because it told me a little bit more about your father, about him not wanting to spend money."

"Money was always important to him, sure." Anthony let out a deep sigh. "Maybe too important. He did not understand the vow of poverty I took. But overall he was a good man, Detective, and he was going to spend some of his money and come to Thailand this year. I believe he'd found a tour package with a fair price."

"I got the impression your dad was lonely."

"Especially after my mom died. I couldn't come back for the funeral, and Zach refused to go. Zach had avoided our father after that awful morning, dropped out of school at the first opportunity and took off. He wouldn't have killed Dad, if for nothing more than he wouldn't have been in same room with him. Zach is only going to the funeral tomorrow because of me."

Randy remembered Zachary claiming he and his father had patched things up, were getting along.

Lie and lie and lie.

Randy decided right then that he was going to go have a talk with Zachary tonight, double-check his alibi, see what kind of ride he—

"Dad had offered to get us another dog from the shelter, I remember that. But Zach said no. So did I. Sixteen, I figured I'd be off to college in two years, so I wouldn't be around to take care of it. That was before I discovered Buddhism. I really think Dad should have paid for the surgery. Things might have turned out differently with him and Zach... even if the dog died anyway. It would have been in the trying. Zach might have found peace."

Randy had nodded. "Your dad had a couple of cats. Do you know how long he had them?"

Anthony had shaken his head. "We have cats at the temple. Beautiful, graceful creatures. I hope someone is taking care of my father's cats. Zach can't take them; he is allergic to cats."

"Yeah, we got that covered, your dad's cats."

Randy played the recording one more time before pulling into the parking lot of Zachary Delaney's rent-by-the-week apartment.

He got out, reached to his holster and clicked the safety off the gun, then looked up at the night sky. The stars weren't so bright in Owensboro, too much light pollution, and the air didn't smell quite as clean.

Dear God, let me be right.

TWENTY-EIGHT

No answer at Zachary's door, but the manager let him in the apartment; flashing a badge sometimes had the effect of waving a magic wand.

Randy flicked on a lamp on the bureau. The place was old and beat down; the furniture scored with pits and scratches and melted spots where someone had rested cigarettes. It was one good-sized room, basically an efficiency with a tiny kitchenette and a double-bed that sagged in the middle. The place looked sad, and it smelled of mold.

"I tried to kick him out New Year's Day. He was more than a month behind on rent," the manager said. "And I'd been more than easy on him. Supposed to pay every week here." He pointed to a few boxes in a corner. "Brought him those and told him to pack up. I'd filled out eviction papers. But yesterday he handed me a wad of tens and twenties and gave me a six-pack of root beer. He paid up back rent and through the end of this month. Said he might be moving out after that. Had his eye on some place in Rockport. No matter to me what he does, we're square."

"I'll let you know when I'm done here so you can lock up."

"Sure thing. Hey, Zach's not in trouble is he?"

"I'll stop by your office when I'm done."

"He didn't rob somebody, did he? I mean, he had a stack of money, and I know he'd been fired from Plank Manor."

"What kind of vehicle does Zach drive?"

The manager, who looked as beat-down as the room, paused a moment. "He had a late-model pickup, silver, a Ford, I think, with a red door. But I haven't seen it for a couple of days. I think he must have traded it in and got a car, something with better mileage. He was also complaining about the price of gas."

A silver pickup could look gray in a snowstorm.

"Thanks. I'll stop in when I'm done." Randy dismissively waved his hand and shut the door behind the manager so he could poke around undisturbed. There was a little ceramic Christmas tree on the desk next to the phone. It was similar to the tree he'd seen at Jacob Wallem's, a dust catcher somebody's aunt probably made in a craft class. Stacked next to it was a small pile of Christmas cards.

Randy pulled out the chair, sat, turned on the desk lamp, and counted them: twenty. The card on top had been folded then smoothed back into shape. It had three snowmen on it, and a man tying a red scarf around the neck of the largest one. He opened it. The verse read: *Have Yourself A Snowy Little Christmas*. It was signed *Sammy*. No note. Randy figured that must be Samuel Reynolds. And according to the department scanner he'd listened to, Reynolds had been found next to a snowman. Randy shuddered and looked through the rest of the cards, finding the one of Conrad in the sleigh, which he turned over: no note, signed *Dad*; the woman in the rocker in front of a tree, opening up to see it signed *Abby T*; and the dangling boots in the fireplace, opening it to see the signature *Jake*. Some of the other cards had notes in them, just a line: *Merry Christmas, Zach; Stay warm and stay in touch; Best wishes in the New Year*; but half of them just had signatures.

Twenty cards, not many compared to what the murder victims had received. Randy looked through the cards again, noting names. Zachary had gotten his kill list from the Christmas cards he'd received. But why? Money? The manager mentioned Zach had a stack of tens and twenties. Nothing had appeared stolen at any of the residences, but that didn't mean Zach hadn't found some secret stash in someone's underwear drawer.

Were there more victims that no one had discovered yet? People who lived alone, maybe out in the sticks and so their absence wasn't noticed. Neighbors thought them on vacation, as had been the initial assumption with the roofer. Were there victims in other counties? In Kentucky? He recalled the Henderson report JJ had flagged, a printout of it was in the basket on the front desk. Was that death connected? It had been logged in well before Christmas. He should have read it closely before coming here.

How long ago had Zach started killing?

Randy was convinced it was Zachary Delaney behind the murders. It made the most sense. He was available, supposedly laid-off, and he had ties to everyone dead. The Christmas cards in this stack proved that... Conrad, Abby T, Samuel, Jacob.

Means: Zachary had been working at Plank Manor, a physical job. He looked strong, certainly capable of strangling Conrad, Abigail, and Samuel, arranging them just so. How Jacob died was yet to be determined.

Opportunity: Laid-off, time to kill... literally.

Motive: Couldn't be over a dog that died when he was fourteen. That was a dozen years ago. Had to be something that happened recently. But it likely explained why he didn't hurt the pets; no malice toward them. So money, right? Had to be money. But Abigail didn't appear to be particularly well off. Samuel certainly wasn't—especially if what the monk said was true; he was having trouble staying afloat. Jacob the roofer... he looked to be comfortable with the appearance of his house, but not extravagant. Randy had taken a look in Jacob's garage, finding a van with a considerable amount of rust on it. Conrad Delaney had done well for himself... nice house, had sold his gas station for the asking price. Zach would inherit.

An inheritance would definitely land Zachary Delaney in a far better place than this rent-by-the-week dump.

Randy put the cards back the way he'd found them, opened the drawer and saw a laptop—he'd go through the computer, maybe back at the office—and a small leather notebook. Opening it, he realized it was Conrad's Christmas card address book. He got up and closed the drawer, nudged the chair against the desk. Another look around... the bathroom was small, a shower, no tub, the shower curtain moldy at the bottom. The medicine cabinet had a straight razor, shaving cream, toothbrush, toothpaste, and a bottle of Advil PM all on the lower shelf. On the middle shelf sat empty bottles of Prozac and Clozardil—the first an anxiety medication, the second... who knew what, both dated October. Maybe he couldn't afford to have them refilled since losing the job and health insurance. On the top shelf were seven unopened boxes of Advil PM 120-count. Apparently Zachary could still afford them and still had trouble sleeping.

The closet near the bed was small and had only a few garments hanging in it... including an old, leather Indianapolis Colts jacket with holes worn on the elbows, and a nice winter coat that looked new and too large for Zachary.

"Bingo." Randy took the new coat out by the hangar, cursed himself for not thinking to put on gloves for any of this. He'd just been so excited. He fished around in the pockets, finding paper in one and bringing it out, hanging up the coat, which he noted was size XXL —too big for Zachary, not too big for Conrad. He was closing the door when he saw a big shopping bag on the floor, next to a pair of boots... the kind that left noticeable tread marks. The bag was from the Santa Claus store. Tugging the bag out with his free hand, he saw three Merry Christmas mugs in a divided box inside, all the other compartments empty.

Three mugs.

Piper had reported that the killer had purchased eleven.

There were four with the victims in Spencer County. Plus these three. Seven.

That left four more mugs unaccounted for. Four more victims yet to be discovered?

"B-I-N-G-O and Bingo was the name-O." He replaced the bag, making sure everything was the way he'd found it. Went to the desk and spread the pieces of paper out under the light. Receipts, one from the grocery store in Rockport.

Folgers Coffee, classic roast: $12.78

Friskies Savory Shred Cat Food: $18.94

Randy remembered reading Oren's interview with Chris Hagee, who said he saw Conrad in the grocery store the Tuesday before the party, that Conrad had coffee and cat food in his cart. Tuesday, December 26th, the date on the receipt. He'd have to ask Chris if Conrad was wearing a nice winter coat, because Randy had a strong suspicion this coat was Conrad's.

And that meant Zachary had taken it from Conrad's house after December 26th. Lie and lie and lie. Zach said he saw Conrad Christmas Day and then left, hadn't spent the night. He went back to the closet and looked at the jacket again, just to make sure. The size label definitely read XXL. Zach could wear it, but it would be big on him. The other coat was a size L, the flannel shirt hanging next to it, L. Yeah, Conrad's coat.

"Bingo again."

Randy would go back to his car, park at the edge of the lot, and wait for Zachary to show up. He'd take him in, call Oren, and then call the sheriff in Vanderburgh County. He'd ask for the chief deputy job right off the bat. He'd run for sheriff the next election.

Smiling, Randy turned off the lights and opened the door.

"Randy Gerald," Zach said. He'd been standing on the other side. "The man with two first names. Nice to see you again."

TWENTY-NINE

FRIDAY, JANUARY 5TH

Piper dreamed of Iran, and swore she was plodding across a stretch of sand, heavy pack on her back, the sun turning the world into an oven that made it difficult to breathe. She woke gasping at 4 a.m. to the sound of a wheeled medicine cart. She'd slept at the hospital, on a chair in the hall outside her dad's room. The nurse with the cart stopped to *again* check on her dad's vitals. They'd been waking him every two hours to check on him, and each time—because she woke, too—they told her he was improving. How was a man supposed to heal with all the interruptions?

She slipped inside the room.

"Hey, Dad."

He looked groggy, pale, old, and exhausted. But he smiled. The nurse, however, scowled at her and made a shooing motion.

"They're moving you into a regular room in a couple of hours," Piper said. "There'll be flowers waiting. You're loved."

He made a move to sit up, but she shook her head.

"I have to go. I've got—"

"A lot of things to do," he said. His voice was hoarse, sounded like a smoker's though she'd never known him to smoke anything. "You've got more things to handle than I ever tackled all at once." The nurse handed him a cup of water to sip.

"I'm sorry, Dad, and—"

"Sorry nothing. Call me later and tell me how it's going. Scoot. Catch the bastard."

She kissed his forehead, put on her coat, and headed for home. Piper wanted to change before going into the office and then to Conrad's funeral. Anthony had said his brother would pick him up, so that was one less thing she had to worry about. Again, she realized that dumping the monk at her father's had been a blessing.

Piper radioed in to tell dispatch she was coming back to town and would be in the office soon. God, but she wanted to take the whole day off, spend it with her father. Not possible. She didn't mind driving in the dark, liked the shine of the snow piled up on the sides of the road and the absence of other cars. She stopped herself from turning on the radio, instead talking to herself, running the clues over and over. She had a headache centered over her left eye, probably from not enough sleep, and her neck throbbed because she'd spent hours oddly curled in a less-than-comfortable chair. The fourteen miles to Rockport went by much faster this trip; and she didn't use the flashers this time.

She showered and dressed in her only other clean uniform—she'd have to do laundry tonight—and took a few minutes for makeup. She hadn't bothered with any primping the past few days, but the dark circles were too pronounced and needed covering. Piper wanted to look her professional best at Conrad Delaney's funeral later this morning. Too, she didn't want to appear faded in front of her deputies; most of them seemed to tolerate her, but Piper sensed she lacked their respect.

She stared at herself in the mirror, thinking she looked haunted, and for the thousandth time she wondered if running for sheriff had been a foolish idea.

Piper hurried back downstairs, noticing a light on in her dad's kitchen. She peeked in the window and saw Anthony feeding Wrinkles. She almost went in the back door, to chat and share some coffee with the monk. But the pleasantries would slow her; too much to do.

She fought the yawn as she slid into the rental and backed out of the driveway, so fast she nearly clipped a metallic blue Ford parked across the street that hadn't been there when she pulled up. Somebody else keeping early morning hours.

The scanner crackled with a deputy—Piper didn't recognize the voice—reporting that he was arresting two teenagers parked in the lot of the Pioneer Village. It was a touristy spot on Fairground Drive, open daily from May to October, but in the winter it kept weekend hours. The deputy reported into dispatch that they'd been drinking, apparently fell asleep, and he was surprised that hadn't frozen to death. "They're mostly sober now," he continued. "Cold as hell and cranky. I'll get them on trespassing at least."

Piper figured that was a good call. A DUI charge probably wouldn't hold up since they weren't driving. But they could add underage drinking. When things calmed down in the county, she'd take a look at the DUI issue. Right now, the serial killer trumped everything.

All the answers were in the Christmas cards, she'd decided sitting in the hall outside her dad's room. The images of the cards flitted through her head, like she was in a Hallmark store browsing the racks. They held the name of who killed Conrad Delaney and Abigail Thornbridge and Samuel Reynolds and Jacob Wallem. That had to be Jacob in the chimney, killed before the others. Randy had radioed her that when the body was pulled out, the face sort of looked like a picture they had of Jacob. And if the cards held the *who*, they also held the *why*. Could she unlock the motive if she took yet one more pass through the cards?

There was a gas station/quick mart in downtown Rockport, and she stopped to fill up the rental, talking to herself the entire time about the cards. Inside she bought three boxes of prepackaged dough-nuts and the biggest cup of coffee they had; she found the coffee in the sheriff's department a half step above awful.

Piper dropped two of the doughnuts boxes on the dispatcher's desk. "For anybody who's hungry," she said. The other remained tucked under her arm. "I'll be in—"

"—the break room?" This dispatcher came on at eleven, when Teegan left. His name was Drew Farrar, somewhere in his late thirties. He'd injured himself working at the Rockport power plant and had a prosthetic leg. Her dad had told her with the settlement and disability, if he'd wanted it, Drew could have managed to not work another day in his life. He used the settlement to buy a house, but he passed on the disability and instead took the dispatcher job, wanting to stay active, and proving that he certainly wasn't disabled. Piper had promised to move him to the seven to three shift when or if it opened. "Where all the Christmas cards are, right? The break room?"

"Yeah."

"You had your radio on in the car. I heard you talking about the Christmas cards. You really think you can find the killer by the cards?"

"Ooops."

"The catches on some of those car radios are finicky, lets me hear everything if you don't click it just so." He paused. "How's your dad?"

She shrugged. "The nurses say good."

"But you're not so sure."

"Cancer came back, now this heart attack. I suppose 'good' is relative. I'm hopeful. Listen, I can't chat, I've got—"

"Dog needs walking," Drew cut in. "Nobody else here, I can't leave the board. But if you'll man the phones for just a couple of minutes, I can walk—"

"Dog?"

"Teegan said Randy brought in a three-legged beagle from one of the crime scenes. Says it has to stay here, that it's evidence."

"Really?"

"It's in a little kennel in Randy's office. Teegan said she walked it a couple of times. Apparently it pees a lot. If you'll handle the board for a few minutes, I'll—"

"I'll walk the dog. Thanks, Drew."

"Can I have it, the beagle, when it's not evidence anymore? Been thinking about getting a dog. I can relate to that one. It won't make it out of the shelter."

"I'm thinking yes, but we'll check with Randy when he comes in. I don't think Jacob Wallem had any relatives in the area." And who knew if Jacob had a will that detailed plans for his dog.

"When's Randy coming in?" Drew looked anxious about getting the dog. "Oh, and you should check this printout. JJ found some death report from Henderson she flagged and made some calls on. Was sitting in Teegan's 'in' basket. I couldn't help myself. You better read it."

Piper juggled the coffee and her box of doughnuts, and grabbed the printout.

"About Randy, Sheriff?"

She wasn't sure when her detective would show up. While the deputies worked in rotating factory-like shifts of seven to three; three to eleven; and eleven to seven, the detective kept mostly nine-to-five hours. These past several days had thrown the schedule out of whack, though, and she'd have to address overtime and her budget. "He should be in before the funeral. Mentioned he wanted to go to that."

"Yeah, I watch *Blue Bloods*. You can get clues, seeing who shows up at funerals."

She leashed the beagle and took it along the border of the parking lot. "And why are you evidence, Merry?" Piper turned too quick around a light post and the dog smacked into it. "Sorry sorry sorry." She bent and scratched its neck. "You're evidence because you're alive. Our killer only throttles people. So I guess my dad has a bit of furry evidence nested on his kitchen floor."

Back in Randy's office she spotted two evidence bags of cards on his desk, one labeled Reynolds, the other Wallem. He should have put them with the other cards, but he also should have at least spoken to her at the hospital. She'd seen him dash into her father's room and come out in less than five minutes, talk to Oren and leave. Randy had been in a hurry to go somewhere, and not home. She knew he was putting in long hours on the CCK.

"Hey, Drew, did Teegan say what Randy was working on last night?"

"Nope. But Teegan did say she'd tried to get him on the radio before her shift ended. She didn't know if she should feed the dog again. Said he'd turned off his radio. Cell phone, too."

Balancing the box of doughnuts under her arm, coffee in one hand, and bags of cards in the other, Piper used her elbow to flip on the lights in the break room. Two tables, one with Abigail's cards, the other with Conrad's, the whiteboard at the end listing the victims. No suspects yet.

She spent the next hour and a half studying the cards uninterrupted, going through notes Randy and Oren had typed up, eating four doughnuts—she'd been careful and hadn't taken the messy powdered sugar box—finishing the coffee, and filling the cup with the less-than-stellar stuff from the department pot. Piper decided to spend her own money on a good coffee maker for the office, as caffeine seemed to be a requirement.

Oren came in before seven.

"How's Paul?"

"The nurses say good."

"I called Randy. He's not answering his phone." He padded in and looked at the whiteboard. "Randy was onto something last night. I could smell it on him."

"I saw you talking to him in the hall outside my dad's room yesterday. Did he give you a clue what he's looking at?"

"Nope."

"Are you sure he's—"

"He's a good detective. He's onto something, and he's being secretive because he doesn't want to share. Stinks." Oren was clearly miffed. "He thinks catching a serial killer is part of some big game show and that it'll net him a prize and a kiss from Vanna White if he guesses all the letters. Those notes of his you're looking at... probably not complete. He's probably holding something out of them so I can't connect the dots."

That realization hit Piper in the gut. That's why Randy hadn't put the cards from the past two murders in with the others. There was something in one of them.

She pointed to the new table she'd set up, half of it covered with cards from Samuel Reynolds's place, the other half, separated by a yardstick, with cards from Jacob Wallem's. She'd been sitting in the middle.

"Shit," she said.

"And two is four and four is eight." Oren hung his coat and hat on a hook and pulled a chair up opposite her. He did not meet her eyes. She was surprised he was in the same room with her, seemed he had basically avoided her presence since Day One. But this is where the cards and the clues were, and so she knew he didn't have much choice.

"There's a vacancy coming in Vanderburgh. I wondered if anyone from here was nosing around," Piper said. "Gut feeling Randy is."

"I wouldn't know about that."

"Know or say?"

He didn't reply, and started studying the Wallem cards, which Piper knew he hadn't seen since he'd not been to that crime scene.

"Look at this." She passed him the printout from the Henderson police report.

SUSPICIOUS DEATH

HPO Case Number: 0P05-33-645

PIO Number: 10-4-21

Date: December 10

Time: 0657

Place of Occurrence: Atkinson Park, Henderson, KY

Victim: Thomas Olbert, Henderson, KY (DECEASED)

Description of Incident: Henderson police and Henderson County Sheriff's Office homicide detectives are investigating the suspicious death of a twenty-six-year-old man. Paramedics and deputies responded to a call shortly before 7 a.m. regarding a medical situation. A parks department employee preparing for the annual Candy Cane Hunt found Mr. Olbert impaled on the horns of a deer decoration in the park's holiday display. Mr. Olbert was pronounced dead on the scene. The Henderson County Medical

Examiner is conducting an autopsy to determine the cause of death. Initial observation is Mr. Olbert, a seasonal parks employee, was getting an early start on hiding candy canes, fell, accidentally impaled himself on the antlers, and was discovered by another parks worker.

INVESTIGATORS FOR HPD: Det. Ira Dammann and Sgt. Harry McConnell

THIS REPORT PREPARED BY: Selina Northquist-Baker/PIO

Scrawled in pencil underneath was a note from JJ: checked with the coroner's office, COD is strangulation, death between 9 p.m. and midnight the night before. Investigation is ongoing. They've marked it a homicide, but have no suspects. Dammann reported a red mug was found nearby, no mention if it said Merry Christmas or if there'd been anything in it.

Oren let out a low whistle. "Killed on the ninth. That would be before Jacob Wallem, right? But it might not be related. Doesn't say it was a Merry Christmas mug. And doesn't fit the pattern, wasn't posed at a house."

"Yeah. But it's a guy impaled on a reindeer antler." Piper pushed up from the table and dropped her coffee cup in the trashcan. She shuffled to the doorway. "Drew, try Randy's radio again." She reached into her pocket and pulled out her cell phone, punched in Randy's number —one of the few she'd memorized and not programmed in. It went straight to voicemail. She hurried back to the table and plucked up a card, turning it so Oren could see.

It was one that had been sent to Jacob Wallem, a cartoon design with Santa, his sleigh, and reindeer poised on the roof of a snow-covered house. But Santa was tangled in the reins of the sleigh and was leaning over, his suit caught on the antlers of the first pair of deer. A word balloon above his head said "Merry 'hic hic' Christmas." The inside greeting read: Have A Cup Of Good Cheer. Just Don't Drink Too Much Of It. A scrawled note: *Jake, I'm staying at the Harbor Light House Shelter until I can get back on my feet, getting some hours from the parks, managing to send out a few cards this year, not buying gifts though. Good seeing you at Thanksgiving, thanks for having me. Such a nice house*

you have. Someday, eh? I'll call you when I get a phone. Hugs and fist
bumps, Tom

"Shit," Piper whispered.

"He wasn't posed at a house because he didn't have a house. He
was homeless. But he was posed to look like the card he sent, leaning
over a reindeer."

"I'm going to call the detective." Piper put the card back on the
table. "Randy found something in these cards, Wallem's or Reynolds's,
that I'm not seeing. Maybe something that connects all of them
together. Maybe this reindeer card." She tugged her fingers through
her hair, wanted to holler, slam down her fist. But she kept her
composure; the Army had taught her that, to not appear ruffled in the
face of frustration. "It's in front of us, Oren. I just—"

"Nothing!" Drew called from the other room. "Can't get Randy,
but I'll keep trying."

"What the hell did he see that I can't?" Piper moved around the
table, looking at all of them, flipping each one open.

"He's a good detective," Oren said softly.

"So says you and my dad." She stopped and leaned over another
card. "But if he's so damn good, why keep his discovery a secret?
What's good about that? There's not a damn good thing about that. In
fact, that's absolutely rotten police work, Oren. Unconscionable. If he
wanted to go for the Vanderburgh opening, I'd make sure he got a
letter of recommendation."

"Solving a serial killer case would go a hell of a lot farther than a
letter of recommendation, and maybe take him a hell of a lot farther
than Vanderburgh County," Oren shot back. "Those doughnuts up for
grabs?" He nodded toward the open box sitting on the end of
the table.

"Please. Eat them." Piper was stopping herself from going for a
fifth. She needed to fit in these uniforms. She also needed to cancel
dinner tonight with Nang, but figured she could do that in person.
He'd probably go to Conrad Delaney's funeral, claimed they were
friends. She tried Randy's cell phone again. "Randy said he'd be at the
funeral."

"Told me he wasn't sure about that," Oren said. "Pretty good doughnut for something out of a box."

"Shit."

"And two is four and four is eight," Oren said again.

Piper remembered the expression. It was one her grandfather had used. He was a cribbage player, and she thought it referred to scoring awful on a hand. Oren was old enough to be her grandfather, she thought. Sitting in the ER hall last night, she'd thought a lot about the sheriff's department, guessed that Oren wasn't retiring because he was waiting to see if she passed the sheriff's exam in the spring. If she didn't, the county board would name him to fill the vacancy, that's just how it worked. He was a vulture, circling for the job. Despite her lack of experience with Indiana law, Piper figured she could pass the test. Did she want to?

Piper felt her face coloring and took a deep breath. Never lose control, the Army had taught her. Never ever. What the hell was Randy thinking? Thinking about himself, not the department, and most certainly not about chain of command. A sheriff, unlike a police chief, was responsible for all the deputies 24/7—liable for their personal conduct. And Randy's conduct was sucking swamp water.

"I'm calling the State later this morning," she said. "Right after the funeral. We need help on this."

"Figured you would." Oren still hadn't met her gaze. "But if Randy's got something, you should wait, until the end of the day or at least until you talk to him. How would it look, your very first case as sheriff, calling in the State? Not sending a good message to the people who voted for you. But that's just my opinion."

It was a jab, Piper knew, veiled as advice. But it was a successful jab. Oren wanted the department to crack the case. She wanted to throw it back to him and say, *How would it look, a crusty old fart with forty years in law enforcement, not able to solve a multiple-murder case? Forty years and zippo on this one, eh Oren?* She tried Randy's cell phone again. Nothing. Went to the doorway.

"Drew, do we have GPS tracking software? Do we have a GPS locator? We've got something, right? It's how you found my Taurus."

She didn't bother asking Oren, as antiquated as he operated he probably didn't know what GPS was.

She walked to Drew's desk. "No luck with Randy on the radio?"

He shook his head.

Piper noticed that Oren was standing in the doorway of the break room, eating another donut and making no move to conceal his curiosity.

"Not all the cars have GPS, Sheriff. Some of the deputies opted out. Go figure, they thought it would be like spying on them, and your dad didn't push it. He liked to keep everybody happy. But it's a good idea, a locator for the department. It's pretty cheap. Even the Rockport Police has it, and the State can be back up if the original system breaks. I can find us an online supplier."

"There's nothing standardized?"

"CALAE has been—"

"The Commission on the Accreditation of Law Enforcement Agencies," Oren supplied.

Drew nodded. "They've been trying to standardize things across the country, get us to buy the same equipment and stuff. It'd be a big help, I think."

"So we've got no way of finding him? The car?" She heard the whir of some office machine in the background, someone sending a fax.

"I'll contact OnStar. Randy's one of the few cars that has a GPS system." He paused. "We ought to have a Facebook page, too, Sheriff."

Yeah, that would be handy, she thought. One more thing for her to-do list.

"Call the detective in Henderson, will you? I want to get a copy of everything she has on this case, email or fax, doesn't matter. I want it ASAP. Tell her it's related to our murders." She put the printout in front of him and stabbed a finger at Detective Ira Dammann's name.

"You gonna be here a little while, Sheriff?"

Piper shook her head. "I'm going to take another pass through the Wallem house." What she didn't say was if Randy had found something... maybe that something was from that crime scene. "Call OnStar right now, have them locate Randy's car. I want to know where the son of a bitch is. Then call me when you've got it. And I want our own GPS locator ordered by Monday and something in place to get GPS in everything we drive."

"Yes, ma'am. Sheriff."

Piper would find the money in the budget, buy it herself if she had to. She turned to Oren. "Take another look at the Christmas cards. Find out what we're missing. After Wallem's, I'm going straight to the funeral."

"I'll see you there, Sheriff Blackwell."

"Oh, and walk the dog in a little while."

"Sure thing, Sheriff Blackwell."

THIRTY

R andy's phone went to voicemail for the umpteenth time; Drew had tried to ping it before she'd left the office. She knew that cell phones could be pinged in an emergency to give an approximate location, but the phone had to be active and have a signal. No such luck. Randy had shut it all the way down.

"He's disconnected," Oren had said. "He's figured it out, and he's going to get the guy."

Piper hadn't considered that something bad might have happened to Randy, but now that thought crept into her head. She'd almost been killed herself when rammed off the road a few days ago—and she still ached from the experience. Or was her detective so hell-bent on grabbing glory that he'd severed connections from the world until he'd gained his prize, like Oren suggested? Oren certainly was convinced it the latter; Piper had never seen the chief deputy so pissed off. But if Oren had figured it out, wouldn't he have done the same thing as Randy?

Did she have any respect in the department?

Was this a mistake?

If it was, Piper could easily correct it come April. She could purposely fail the exam.

A path had been shoveled from the street to the front door of the Wallem house, which smelled only slightly better this morning. In the laundry room she found a box of well-chewed stuffed dog toys. She took it with her, intending to send them through the washing machine to get the stench out. Piper figured the toys belonged to the dog, nothing wrong with giving them back to her. A walkthrough yielded nothing else, another look at all the decorations—finding a couple of beagle ornaments on the tree that likely came from the store in Santa Claus—and a small address book in the desk; she put that in an evidence bag, grumbling that Randy should have done that.

Piper locked up and left.

Minutes later she made a quick call to the hospital and was put through to her father's new room. He said he was fine and once more encouraged her to catch the bastard. Then Piper turned her cell phone to vibrate, put it in her front shirt pocket, and went inside the funeral home. Maybe Randy would show up anyway, and she'd rip him up one side and down the other for dropping out of contact. She hoped Oren was wrong and that her detective had not been holding anything back, though not bagging the address book was sloppy, especially when Christmas cards apparently linked everything.

In a way, she could understand Randy's actions. Randy had been with the department fifteen years, and she'd been here five days. Understand, yes. Accept, no. The Army had taught her the importance of chain of command. Maybe she ought to fire his ass and get a new detective. Piper wanted more diversity in the department; this could be a good opportunity.

The music in the main chapel was somber, typically the case for funerals, she knew from experience. She'd been to a few military services, however, where they'd played upbeat stuff that the fallen soldier had favored, *25 or 6 to 4* to name one instance.

The room was fairly crowded. According to interviews, Conrad Delaney had kept to himself and was a lonely man. But obviously he had touched a lot of local souls. She saw Dr. Annie Neufeld in the front row, head turned and talking to someone behind her. Chris and Joan Hagee sat midway back, Chris on an aisle, fingers drumming on his knee. Nang was in the back row, dressed in a dark gray suit, pale blue shirt, and a tie that had tiny spaceships on it. A few seats were empty on either side of him. Piper moved forward and inched into his aisle.

"May I?" she asked, indicating a chair.

He nodded. "Please."

She sat and hooked her coat over the back. There were flowers, but not all that many, a spray across the casket, which was closed, though Piper thought it hadn't needed to be. Conrad Delaney's body had been in fine, frozen condition. She'd move up after the service and look at the tags on the flowers, see who sprung for them. A large arrangement at the head of the casket was all big white blooms with sprigs of greenery, and a smaller one at the foot was full of red and yellow carnations and mums. There were two plants on pedestals off to the side, and the requisite peace lily on the floor near them. She couldn't smell the flowers this far back, but she picked up Nang's aftershave and the competing fragrances of two middle-aged women in front of them.

Piper had been so very busy the past handful of days that she'd not been able to personally meet with all the people at Chris Hagee's party; she wondered how many of them were here. She recognized a few faces in attendance, when they turned this way and that to see who else was in the chapel. But she couldn't put names to them. Was one of them the killer?

She spotted Anthony Delaney walk in from a side door and sit in the front row next to Dr. Neufeld; his was the only bald head in the room. Another young man followed him and sat at his shoulder, probably Zachary, though he didn't fit the description Oren had painted.

"About dinner," she whispered to Nang. "I can't—"

"I understand." Piper had to strain to hear his voice over the murmurs of the crowd and the organ. "You are busy with all of this death."

"Yeah."

"It is unfortunate to be so busy because of death."

Death. Four bodies in Spencer County. One in Henderson, Ky. She needed to go there and talk to the detective in person. Let them know their homeless man in the park was likely the first victim in the serial killer's string. How did Henderson connect to Spencer County?

She thought about that. The first victim. Why was the homeless man first? Or were there more before him? Eleven mugs purchased the first week of December.

The homeless man had mailed a few Christmas cards, at least according to the one he'd sent Jacob Wallem, funny cartoon cards, so he had a morose or humorous take on the holidays. And how did a homeless man connect to Jacob Wallem and Samuel Reynolds and Conrad and Abigail?

"You're young to be faced with all of these troubles," Nang whispered.

She'd been faced with troubles in her tours in Iran.

Young? She hadn't been too young for Iran. But was she too young to be sheriff of Spencer County? Oren and Randy would say yes, as would probably everyone in the department except for JJ.

Age wasn't a factor between the victims. The homeless man, hugs and fist bumps Thomas Olbert had been twenty-six; Samuel, twenty-seven; Jacob twenty-eight; then it jumped thirty-seven years to Conrad, aged sixty-five; and jumped another seventeen years to Abigail, eighty-two.

"The day I met you," Piper said, keeping her voice low, "in your quick stop, a man came in wearing an Indianapolis Colts jacket. Any chance you remember that?"

Nang nodded.

"Do you know who he was?"

Nang pointed toward the front. "Zachary Delaney, Conrad's son."

The music stopped.

The Pastor stood. "If we have been pleased with life, we should not be displeased with death, Michelangelo wrote, since it comes from the hand of the same master."

Oren slipped into the row across from her, taking off his hat.

The pastor was from Sweet Abby T's church, Oren had told her when the funeral notice ran. Conrad hadn't attended church in many years, but his wife had gone to that church. The pastor was officiating at Abby T's funeral tomorrow. Business booming because of the killer. She wondered if Oren had found anything in the cards while she was at Wallem's place. She'd ask him after the service.

It's in the cards, Piper thought again. *It has to be. CCK CCK CCK. What am I missing?*

The cards tied it all together; she just couldn't find the thread. Randy had found the thread and kept it secret. But he was a trained detective. She'd trained as an MP. He had fifteen years of experience. She had five days.

"Do you know what Zach drives?" she hushed.

"Silver pickup. Why?"

"Not maroon?"

"It has a red door, replaced from an accident. Why?"

Her phone vibrated as the pastor motioned everyone to stand. She pulled it out and looked at the screen: Drew. She'd call him back. Maybe he'd found Randy.

A woman perched next to the organ started singing *Amazing Grace.*

Piper's mind spun like a kaleidoscope, pictures of cards forming and shattering, reforming and replaced by faces of the victims. Anthony Delaney had known all of the victims save for Thomas Olbert from Henderson. Or had he also known Thomas? They were only two years apart. Maybe Thomas hadn't always been from Henderson.

Maybe Anthony Delaney was the one thing they all had in common.

And thereby maybe Zachary Delaney, too.

Zachary Delaney was the man in the Colts jacket, drove a silver pickup, which could have looked gray in the snow storm. A red door that could have looked like a flash of maroon.

The man standing to Anthony's left was dressed in a dark suit, with short hair. She'd heard from Oren and Randy that Zachary Delaney looked like a hippie. But anybody can clean up, especially for a funeral. The guy in the Colts jacket had looked a little scruffy, but familiar. Had he been familiar because she'd seen pictures of him in Conrad's house?

"That's Zachary? Next to the bald man?"

Nang nodded.

The song ended. Zachary looked behind him to take in the attendees. Piper shivered. It was the same face from Nang's store. Cleaned up nice and proper. Their eyes locked for a moment, then he turned back to face the front.

The pastor quoted Revelation. "God shall wipe all tears from their eyes; and there shall be no more death, nor crying, neither shall there be any more pain: for the former things are passed away."

Her phone vibrated. Drew again.

She smiled at Nang, and slipped out of the chapel room.

Two men in black suits stood in the funeral home entrance, looking out the glass doors to the parking lot, ready to welcome any latecomers. Beyond them a white hearse waited to take Conrad's body to the cemetery. Directly behind it was a metallic blue Ford with a 'funeral' flag on the hood, just like the car she almost hit coming out of her driveway early this morning. Another suited man in the parking lot was attaching more of the flags to cars. Piper hadn't planned on attending the burial.

"Whose car is that?" she asked the men. She pointed to the metallic blue Ford.

One shrugged. The other said, "Son of the deceased."

That would be Zachary Delaney.

What happened to his silver pickup? Damaged in the crash, probably replaced it, she thought, knew deputies would be looking for it.

She found a niche near the restrooms, a blank spot of wall between two large urns of mums, and called Drew.

"Found Randy?" she asked, keeping her voice low. Piper had a hard time hearing him, organ music from the chapel was also piped out here. The woman started singing *Bridge Over Troubled Waters*.

"His Crown Vic anyway," Drew said. "Took longer than it should have. We really should get this software, Sheriff, less than a hundred bucks. Gotta be in the budget, right? I could order it today. Track everything ourselves."

"Where is he?"

"What?"

"Randy. Where is Randy, the Crown Vic?"

"Its coordinates, actually. I'll text over a couple of addresses you can find with your GPS, the Vic pings smack in between them, not at any address. It's right across the bridge, in Owensboro."

Piper waited for the text, hearing the organ crescendo beyond the closed doors. The singer kept it to one verse; the music stopped. She looked at the screen and called Drew back. "Are these residences? These two addresses? Do you have names to go with the addresses?"

"Just a minute."

Since her car accident, Piper hadn't been able to search the Internet on her phone; she'd probably have to break down and get a new phone with all those advertised bells and whistles.

"Still checking. Did I interrupt the funeral?"

"Nope, funeral's still going, you just—thankfully—interrupted my listening to it."

"Sorry. I don't like funerals either. Sorry, but you said to call if—"

"It's okay, I don't mind. Oren's in there, representing the department." She heard computer keys clicking, figured he'd set down the phone right next to his keyboard. The clicking stopped.

"Got it. One address is a furniture store, but it doesn't look like it's in business anymore. The other address is an apartment complex, well, maybe a motel. Something like that. Found a pic on the Internet, looks kinda dumpy, a rent-by-the-week thing. Doesn't have a website, I got the pic from the yellow page listing. I'm sending it over."

Something niggled at the back of Piper's mind, something she'd read in one of the reports that Randy or Oren had presented, probably Oren if Randy had been holding back. Rent-by-the-week. Rent-by-the-week. Rent-by-the—

"Shit," she said, not able to make the connection.

"What?"

"Nothing, Drew, thanks."

241

"I'm working a double today by the way."

"Fine."

"Sheriff, Randy still doesn't answer on the radio. But according to the OnStar, his car's been in the same location—that spot I sent you—for more than twelve hours. Maybe he's got a girlfriend or—"

"I'll talk to you later, thanks for your help."

"Sheriff. Buck Hannoh came in half an hour ago, dropped his resignation letter on the desk."

"Shit."

Piper crept back into the chapel. The row behind Oren was empty. She edged into it, sat, tapped him on the shoulder, and whispered.

"Rent-by-the-week. Owensboro?" she asked a little too loud. A woman in front of Oren shushed her.

"That'd be Zach Delaney."

"I think he's our killer," she whispered. "In fact, I'm sure of it." Then Piper stood and looked to the front row, instantly locking onto Anthony Delaney's baldhead. The seat next to him was empty. "And two is four and four is eight."

"You really think he's our doer?" Oren asked softly, as he stood, too. "Zach? Randy said Zach didn't have the wherewithal."

"Shhhhhh!" from the woman directly in front of Oren.

"Yeah. He's our thread, Oren. Somehow."

"Zach slipped out the side door a few minutes ago, about the same time you left. Guess it wasn't for a bathroom break." Oren eased out of the row.

Piper slid to the other row, grabbed her coat, and whispered, "Later," to Nang.

THIRTY-ONE

In the parking lot, the metallic blue car that had been behind the hearse was gone.

"Peeled out of here," one of the suited men said. "Didn't even take our flag off. Surprised you didn't hear him. Some people can't handle funerals."

"He was alone?" Piper demanded.

"Yeah, clipped our hearse on his way out."

"Did you get the license plate number?"

"Damn straight, Sheriff. Or close to it. I don't know if this is a 5 or an S, had some ice hanging down." The man showed his hand. He'd written it in ink.

Piper pulled out her cell phone, not wasting the heartbeats it would take her to reach the radio in her car. "Drew. Drew. Drew!" He answered. "Broadcast this license number to our deputies and all police in the area. A BOLO on a metallic blue Ford Focus, older model, license number 5490-5B99, it might be SB99."

Piper almost sent Oren back to the office, but backup was a more prudent idea, as was taking his four-wheel drive car.

"Want me to drive, Sheriff Blackwell?" Apparently he anticipated her plan.

She pointed to his Explorer, and once in the passenger seat she was on the radio to Drew again. "State police, too, Indiana and Kentucky. Say the driver—Zachary Delaney—is wanted for questioning, and that he's probably dangerous. The car might have a funeral flag on its hood. Was last seen on Main in Rockport. Send someone—Marsh if he hasn't quit—to pick up Anthony Delaney at the cemetery. He'll be there shortly. Let him see his dad put in the ground, then take him to the office and have him wait for me."

Next, she radioed JJ. "High school yearbooks, JJ. Zachary Delaney didn't graduate from high school, but go to the library and pull the books from eight years ago, that would have been Zachary's senior class. You're looking for Thomas Olbert. Call me back."

The radio crackled with a report about a traffic stop on the highway near the monastery, a van in a ditch. Minutes later, with reports of two big dogs running loose near Fulda, and repeated BOLOs about Zachary Delaney's car.

Piper would indeed fire Randy's ass. Randy had connected the dots to Zachary Delaney and hadn't bothered to tell anyone about it. That didn't make him a good detective; that made him a stupid one. And she was liable for his stupidity.

"I thought he had an alibi that was verified," Piper said. "Zachary Delaney. The report said he had a verified—"

"Verified by Buck Hannoh," Oren said. He turned the flashers on to help them cut through the scant traffic, but kept the siren off. No use alerting Zachary, Piper realized.

"Buck. Great." Who had turned in his resignation this morning, and was probably looking at the Vanderburgh County opening. "Shit."

Oren added, "But Randy thought Buck was maybe skimping on work, just going through the motions. He mentioned that last night."

And Randy hadn't bothered to mention that to her. No respect for chain of command. No respect for her. Could she blame him? Most certainly. *Randy Gerald had better hope the Vanderburgh Sheriff will pick him up for that coming vacancy, because he's history in Spencer County.*

"That car's not going to be easy to find," Oren said after the dispatcher put out another BOLO on the Ford Focus. "A county boy, he knows the back roads from here into Kentucky."

"Yeah, he's heading to Kentucky," Piper agreed. What was likely the first victim—a homeless man speared on a Christmas decoration—had been killed there.

I should have figured this out. Should have interviewed Zachary, skipped the autopsy... which I ended up missing.

"Should've figured this out," Oren grumbled. "The pieces were there."

Neither said anything else for the hour drive until the radio crackled with Drew's voice still issuing alerts and picking up reports of no sightings.

Then JJ called Piper on her cell. "Got it, Sheriff. Rockport High School yearbook. Thomas Olbert, eight years ago. I checked ten years back, too. Anthony Delaney, Samuel Reynolds, and Jacob Wallem were all in that same graduating year, and apparently in the same shop class and on the varsity track team together."

"Money?" Piper mused, not meaning the question for Oren. "It can't be about money, killing all of them. A homeless man has no money."

He answered anyway. "It's always about money, isn't it? Why I'm still in the department, wanting to draw a paycheck. Money. Why Zach Delaney would kill his dad, so he'd inherit everything."

"But if it's about money, why the hell kill all those people? And why pose them to look like Christmas cards? It can't *just* be money."

Oren shrugged. "Okay, we're still missing a piece or two."

They found Randy's Crown Vic a block from the address Drew had texted, in an alley behind a boarded over furniture store in a section of Owensboro's old downtown, where traffic was light and open businesses were few. The spot had no address, which is why Drew had provided two to place it between. It hadn't been hard to find.

Randy was in the trunk. Handcuffed, strangled.

P-e-t-e-c-h-i-a-l, Piper thought. She felt punched in the gut. Her detective, the man who'd fussed over her the night she'd been run off the road, stared blankly up at her, his legs curled around his evidence kit. Why had Randy been so stupid to let this happen?

How many times since she'd started work as Sheriff of Spencer County had it been difficult for her to breathe?

"He was a good guy," Oren said softly.

But he'd been a foolish one.

The rest was a blur, radioing Drew and the Owensboro police and coroner.

"Stay here," Piper told Oren. "I'm going to that rent-by-the-week." She had the address, one of the two Drew had sent.

"You need backup," Oren said.

"He won't be there," Piper returned. "But I bet that's where Randy found him."

She took off at a run, reaching to her side and feeling the grip of her gun… just in case she was wrong and Zachary was home.

The manager remembered Randy from last night and took Piper to Zachary's room.

"He cleared out early early early this morning. Woke me up with all the racket he was making. I saw him throw his clothes in the trunk so I threw on my coat and came out to see what was going on. Told me things with his dad hadn't worked out as planned and so he had to move on, but that he was going to the funeral first. I told him no refund on the rent he'd paid. He was paid up until the end of the month, paid me with a stack of tens and twenties." The manager nodded repeatedly like one of those drinking birds on a tavern windowsill. "Told your deputy that last night, about the tens and twenties. Zach, he told me I can have whatever he left in the room. He wasn't a bad sort, Zach. Not really. A quiet renter most of the time. What kind of trouble did he get himself into?"

Piper didn't reply, just opened the drapes so light could stream in. It was an old, worn place, not quite a dump, but close enough to it in her opinion. It smelled fusty. The bedspread was SpongeBob Square-Pants, the pillowcase had Spiderman and Captain America on it, making it look more like a child's room than an adult's. Again she mentally pummeled herself; she should have talked to Zachary a few days ago rather than going to Conrad's autopsy. Piper thought she'd made the right call at the time... but she missed the autopsy because the coroner started early, and she missed gleaning something from the Zachary sit-down that maybe Randy had picked up on. She'd been on the job then less than forty-eight hours at that time, was in over her head and had made the wrong call. But kicking herself in the brain now wouldn't accomplish anything. And her having interviewed Zach would not have saved the Christmas corpses... though it might have saved Randy.

Don't beat yourself up about this. Soldier on. Learn from it.

She saw the little ceramic tree on the desk.

"He said I can have whatever's here," the manager repeated. "That little tree, I can have that." The manager had left the door open and was standing in the threshold. The cold air flowed in. She heard sirens.

Piper saw the stack of Christmas cards. "Not the cards," she told him. In her haste she hadn't brought an evidence bag, so she kept her gloves on. "You don't get those." She didn't give a shit about anything else... it was the cards.

"I'm thinking about what he might have in the refrigerator. Don't want it to go to waste, you understand. That'd be sinful. He usually had some beer."

Piper opened drawers, finding them empty, the closet empty save for an oversized bag from the store in Santa Claus, and at the bottom of it a box containing three red Merry Christmas mugs.

Eleven mugs, he'd bought.

Five victims so far.

Three mugs not used, so eight accounted for.

That equaled potentially three more murder victims.

Piper growled.

"The food, can I take that now?"

"Wait," she told him. "And don't come in here." Her cell phone chirped. Oren. "What? Sure, get over here, apartment 2A, the door's open. Need a couple of evidence bags and your kit. Radio JJ, I want her down here, lights and sirens so she makes good time. Put someone in the car with her. I don't care who. I want two of our guys here."

Piper went back to the cards and spread them out, not as deftly as she would have without the winter gloves. One from Conrad. She flipped it over, saw it was signed *Dad*. No message. One from Abigail Thornbridge. She nudged it open; signed *Abby T*. One from Jacob Wallem, again nothing inside but a signature, *Jake*. Same with the triple snowman card from Samuel Reynolds, *Sammy*.

"There!" She found a cartoon card just like the one the homeless man had sent to Wallem, Santa tangled in reindeer antlers. Inside, the signature *Tommy*.

Twenty cards, ten of them signatures only. These she separated.

"Excuse me. Gotta get in here." Oren had made good time, but he'd only been a block away. She suspected he'd been pulling in the parking lot when he'd called her. He pressed past the manager. "Owensboro coroner showed up with the cops. Fast. Seems they'd been listening to the BOLOs."

"Here," Piper said. "This is Zach's kill list."

"Christmas cards."

"He killed the people who didn't write him a note inside the cards they'd sent him. That's how the sick son of a bitch picked his victims. Here and here and here and here, and the homeless man. The homeless guy, Olbert, he sent Zach a card, too. And these other five cards, signatures only... I'll wager three of the senders are dead, because that's how many goddamn red Merry Christmas mugs are not accounted for." She waved a hand behind her to indicate the bag with the mugs in them. She'd brought it out of the closet and set it on SpongeBob's face.

"So Randy came here hoping to catch him, and—" Oren said.

"—somehow got caught instead. That's not a smart detective." Piper stepped back from the desk and tugged off her gloves, pulled out her cell phone and called up the menu; it was easier to operate with her bare fingers. "Drew. Anybody in there with you? Marsh? Put him on." She paused and watched Oren pull out two evidence bags, one for the cards with only a signature, one for the more thoughtful and breathing people who had written notes.

As she talked to Drew, she stepped in the bathroom, opened the medicine cabinet. All it contained were two empty prescription bottles, one for Prozac, the other for Clozardil. "Awesome," she said softly, recognizing the latter medicine. A civilian employee at Fort Campbell always carried it in her purse, told Piper Clozardil was for her bipolar problem. "Maybe Zach has been off his meds a while."

She came back into the other room, still talking to Drew.

"While you have him on the phone," Oren cut in, "tell him to have everyone switch channels on their radios. The radio's missing out of Randy's car. I bet Zach's been listening to us, knows exactly where we are."

"And two is four," Piper hissed.

THIRTY-TWO

Piper took the Audubon Parkway west out of Owensboro. The GPS told her it would take thirty-four minutes, but she'd make it in far less. The lights flashed, no siren, and she topped the speed limit by twenty. There was no ice on the road, and the snow on either side was light, as if the blizzard of a few nights past had stopped at the Kentucky line.

She was driving Oren's Explorer, and had thought about leaving him at the rent-by-the-week; he could have caught a ride back with JJ, who'd radioed she was on her way. But Oren had pressed her.

"Randy went after this guy alone, Sheriff Blackwell, and look where that got him," he'd said. "You need backup. Zach's damn dangerous."

Piper had acquiesced, not because of what Oren said, but because of the look in his eyes. They gleamed. She suspected her chief deputy didn't give a damn about her safety or being backup—maybe wouldn't mind if she was killed so he could take her job—he was just hungry to catch this guy. Likely the biggest case in his forty-year career, and he didn't want to be left behind. So she decided not to leave him behind. She just wished they liked each other a little; his company would be more tolerable.

"I'm driving," she'd told him.

He didn't argue, and he didn't talk during the short trip. The radio chatter, on another channel, was all about Randy Gerald, the rent-by-the-week efficiency, and the serial killer that had plagued Spencer County, Indiana.

She took a right onto Main when they reached the downtown, passing a resale clothing store, buildings for lease, and a shoe store with a SALE sign in the window. Henderson, with more population than all of her county, didn't have much more of a business district than Rockport. Most of the retailers were out on the strip by the bridge. Some historians claimed that prior to WWI Henderson had more millionaires per capita than any other city in the United States. Tobacco had been the reason, with warehouses and farms that closed when high tariffs were imposed after the war. The little city's economic boom reversed.

Piper had been through the town many times, as a child with her father attending the annual bluegrass festival, which was still one of the largest in the country, and then later when she went to Fort Campbell for basic training; the base was a straight shot down from Henderson.

She'd never been to the police station, but she knew where it was on Barrett. She parked in the side lot and headed in, Oren, still quiet, behind her.

Detective Ira Dammann was short, about Piper's height, but was likely twice her age and had fifty pounds on her, her shirt straining at the buttons as evidence. She had close-cropped stark white hair, bright green eyes, and a nose that seemed a little too small for her face. Her smile was engaging and her handshake strong and dry. Piper had called the Henderson Police Department on the way and fate was generous, Ira was in. She agreed to wait for them.

"It's open, that's for sure," Ira said of the case. She had a deep southern accent, hinting that she had roots a good way southeast of Henderson. "No suspects. Thomas Olbert had been homeless, though he was staying at the shelter at the time of his death. No relatives in the area, a sister in Indianapolis who claimed the body and had him cremated, his mother deceased. The sister said the father took off on the family when they were kids; she had no clue where he was, neither did she care." Ira paused. "But the sister cared about Thomas, said she had tried to get him to move to Indianapolis, to stay with her and her husband and get him into rehab."

"But he wouldn't," Piper surmised.

"No. It might have saved him. In more ways than one." Ira nudged the coroner's report across the table. They sat in what passed for the department's cafeteria, coffee in the middle of the table, steaming cups in front of them. Oren was drinking his. Piper was too preoccupied.

"Death by strangulation," Piper said, reading the cause. "Blunt force trauma to the head first. The impaling was done post-mortem."

"Probably wacked him because he put up a fight," Ira suggested. "Strangled him when he was down."

"Late stage cirrhosis of the liver," Piper continued.

"Coroner said he was obviously a heavy drinker, or had been. The shelter said he was going to AA but kept tripping up. Cirrhosis would have got him before summer, most likely, but someone sped up his demise. Sad end for someone so young." Ira sat back from the table and gave Piper the up and down. "Heard about your election, Ms. Blackwell. Quite the news item."

Piper kept reading the reports Ira provided. Oren looked over her shoulder.

"Do you have any files on Zachary Delaney? He used to live here, said he had some drug problems while he was here, and—"

"Got those files coming for you," Ira interrupted. "Saw it on the wire, you figuring him the doer in the Spencer County murders. So I had the files pulled. You're thinking he did Olbert, too?"

"There was a red Merry Christmas mug with the body, right?"

"Right."

"Yeah, we're thinking he killed Thomas Olbert, too."

"The files, they don't leave the room, Sheriff." Ira stood. "I'll be at my desk, you need anything. Stop by on your way out."

As if on cue a woman in a khaki suit walked in with a thick manila folder. Her name badge read Sgt. Angie Muller. She appeared to be in her mid-thirties, face sharp angles and planes and expression hard-looking. "Ira says you want this. It can't leave the room. Let me know if you need copies of anything."

"Thanks," Piper said. "Angie... do you remember dealing with Zachary Delaney?"

She gave a nod. "Was listening to the stuff on the scanner out of Owensboro and it piqued my interest that you're looking for him. Zachary? I remember him. He used to live around Henderson a few years back. Zach had some run-ins here. A lot of run-ins, actually. I arrested him three or four times. Drugs mostly, nothing major, annoyances really, some noise complaints, parking tickets. A lot, but nothing really awful. He didn't do time for any of it. I read his file over again just before you came. Looks like he was a troubled kid, wrong kind of friends, couldn't quite find his way."

"Maybe he found his way to a very dark place," Piper told the woman. She passed Oren half the papers in the file, and they started reading. A dozen pages in, she stopped and used her cell to call JJ and then Drew... they reported no sightings of either Zachary Delaney or the blue car.

"The monk's here in the office, Sheriff," Drew said. He dropped his voice to a conspiratorial whisper. "He's cross-legged on the floor, meditating or something. Hasn't a clue where his brother would run to. He seems real shook up about all of this, and swears Zach wouldn't hurt anyone."

"I don't think Anthony knows his brother anymore," Piper said more to herself. "He's been away too many years."

Several minutes later, Piper pushed her part of the file away. "The addresses are all over the place, Oren. Apartments. No list of friends or associates. And two is four."

"And four is eight," Oren said. "I might have something."

He reached into his pocket and pulled out a narrow notebook. Piper saw it didn't have many blank pages in it. He flipped to the front and started paging through. She caught names printed and under-lined: Chris Hagee, Joan Hagee... must have been from the scene of Conrad's murder, when he talked to the people at the party. After several pages, he stopped. Zachary Delaney was underlined. He ran his thick finger down his notes, which were mostly illegible to her, a sort of shorthand scrawl. He'd typed them up, into the computer, and Piper had read through them, but she didn't recall everything. Too many names, too few days to take it all in, too many murder victims. Five days on the job, and she felt as worn out as if she was going through the rigors of basic training again.

"Here," he said. "I got it pretty much word for word. Wrote it down after Zachary left. He used to deliver *The Gleaner* on rural routes. That's the little Henderson paper, a daily."

"I know what *The Gleaner* is."

"He drove a black Civic he called the Batmobile and bought a trailer at a small park in the sticks. He probably meant somewhere in this county. Henderson's bigger than Rockport, but there are lots of rural places. Some folks still make moonshine around here and call clumps of houses 'hollers.'"

Piper pulled out her phone again, got up and went to a table that held a cardboard box full of Christmas decorations that had been taken down. Near it were stacks of Styrofoam cups, sugar packets, and napkins—and a phonebook. She leafed to the yellow pages, then punched in a number, made a request, got pushy and was connected to someone at *The Gleaner* who managed employee records. She repeated her request and tapped her foot, walked back to the open file, then started pacing.

A moment later, she whirled and pointed to Oren's notebook, rattled off an address and repeated it. Oren wrote it on a blank page.

"The only recorded address they had for Zachary Delaney. It's a trailer park, but the secretary said she doesn't think it exists anymore, a subdivision went in somewhere nearby."

Oren looked at the address. "Some good fishing back in there, lots of creeks, a few big ponds. There's a road that runs between Graham Hill and Zion, dinkburgs you'd call them. That's probably where your trailer park used to be. But if it ain't there anymore I don't see—" He slapped his hand on the table and the pages fluttered. "Maybe it is still there."

"What?"

Oren whistled. "Something I didn't write down, but remember. Zach said he had a live-in girlfriend that was a bad influence on him. They called it quits and he gave her the trailer. 'I go back and check on her every once in a while… to see if she's still there,' he said. I suppose it's worth a looksee, Sheriff Blackwell."

"We've got nothing else," Piper said. But she tried Drew and JJ one more time to make sure. "You're driving this time. You seem familiar with the area."

"That was years ago, the fishing," Oren said softly. "Decades. Me and Annie and Conrad, when he turned sixteen and could drive and wasn't worried about gas money. Wild geese are prime for chasing in the winter in the sticks, Sheriff Blackwell."

Piper started to like Oren… but just a little bit.

THIRTY-THREE

T he sky was the color of cold ashes, like one big cloud had settled in a dome over Henderson County, but it hinted at rain rather than snow, the temperature above freezing.

Piper looked at her watch: 4 p.m. She'd been up twelve hours, but it felt like days because of the scant sleep she'd grabbed at the hospital. Still aching from her accident, she wished she would have grabbed a bottle of aspirin out of her desk drawer and chugged a few. At least, she thought, she was in too much pain to drift off. It gave her an edge and kept her alert.

"Gonna be dark soon," Oren observed, as he pulled the Explorer to the side of the county road. They'd already made one pass by the overgrown drive and had come around from the other direction. "According to your address, it'll be back in there and up on that little hill. Can't be anywhere else, past the ditch and through the trees. Don't want to pull up into the drive in case he's there. Don't want to spook him. And I don't think he'll be able to see my Ford here because of the trees."

Piper got out and checked her gun, a Sig Saur P229. She went to the back of the Explorer, and reached over the evidence bags of Christmas cards from Zach's room and the unused Merry Christmas mugs, and grabbed a Smith & Wesson rifle then closed the hatch. The rifle was light; she guessed about five and a half pounds, with a strap that let her sling it across her back.

Oren started down the ditch ahead of her. Beyond it and past a sprawling pond, perched on a rise, were six trailers in various states of decay. It could have passed for the set of an apocalyptic movie, Piper thought. As much rust as paint, held together by dicey welds, all of them looked uneven and probably had been damaged repeatedly by strong winds. She doubted anyone had lived in any of them for a few years. The weeds were brown and knee high, and a small tree had grown into the side of the nearest trailer. She grabbed Oren's arm.

"Wait a minute."

"They look like bones," he said. "Skeletons of homes. It'd work for a *Walking Dead* episode."

Oren watched that show? She thought it a reasonable description and could picture zombies lurking.

"I think my wild goose chase isn't going to get us anything except muddy boots, Sheriff Blackwell. Looks abandoned. Not a vehicle in sight. Maybe we should go back to—"

"Shhh!" she cautioned him. Piper edged ahead of Oren, staying in the ditch, crouched, and peeked above the other side. Hard to see from this vantage point because of the high weeds, but she thought a light shone in one of the busted trailers. Couldn't see it now, might have been the sun poking through a gap in the clouds. She looked up. No gap, just the solid gray dome. "I think someone's here. And they might have spotted the Ford."

"What about *his* Ford? The blue one. I don't see any cars. 'Spose something might be parked behind a trailer, though."

Not likely, Piper thought, as she turned off her cell phone. The drive leading into the abandoned trailer park that they'd passed was heavily overgrown, and as much mud as there was from melted snow she would have noticed tire tracks.

However, a section of the ditch near Piper had tire tracks in it, and they looked recent, as if someone had driven off the road and into and up a shallow part of the channel. She pointed them out to Oren.

"Interesting," he whispered. "Don't know why the hell someone would drive through a ditch."

"If it's him, he's armed."

"Yeah, I know. *If* it's him, he's got a department-issued Sig Sauer, and a rifle."

Randy's weapons had been missing out of his Crown Vic.

Piper crawled up onto the other side, laying flat. "Stay here, until I motion for you." A pause. "I need you here and your eyes on the third trailer from the right. I'm not going to be able to see much of it for a while. And if there's trouble, I need you near the radio to call the Henderson Sheriff." On the drive here, she'd called the sheriff. There was a mutual aid agreement between that department and hers, and she'd secured an okay to pursue her suspect here.

She started a low crawl through the weeds, the ground cold and damp, and bits of mud oozing up through her gloved fingers. After a moment, she tugged the gloves off as they'd become too encased. Basic stealth training, two tours in Iraq, downrange assignments, this crawl was easy for her—though unpleasant and slower going than she wanted. It added aches to her aches. The smell of wet earth from the melted snow was strong and seemed to settle on her tongue.

She crept along, noting that the breeze was significant enough to rustle the weeds and high dead grass. Milkweed stalks stuck up in artful patterns and bent in the wind, the pods long ago burst open. Perfect. The ground cover moving with the wind meaning her passage might not be noticed. Finding the tire tracks, she followed them and saw that they went right into the big pond.

"What the hell?" she whispered. Rising up on her elbows she looked at the tracks again to be certain, saw boot prints next to them, the prints smeared like someone had slid. Slid while pushing the car into the pond. "What the hell?"

Flattening again, doing a low crawl to the edge of the water, the bank a mix of mud and sand, the surface reflected the gray of the clouds overhead. She kept staring and the details came a little clearer; the hood of the car appeared to be a foot below the surface of the water, and next to it was a pickup—maybe the one that had run her off the road.

"Jesus," she whispered, continuing to stare. There was another vehicle down there, a little farther out. She risked it and pulled the small flashlight from her belt, turned it on and aimed it at an angle. Three vehicles all told in the water, two cars and a truck. The car farthest out was murky, weeds grown up all around it, but she saw the large stylized outline of a bat on the hood. The Batmobile, Oren had referenced. The car closest both to the edge and to the surface had a little flag on the hood. She couldn't read it, but she knew in her gut it was from the funeral home, the Ford they'd been looking for. Putting them in a pond was apparently a good way to hide them.

Piper flicked off the flashlight, low crawled back to Oren, and told him what she saw. "Call the sheriff for backup," she said, keeping her voice softer than it probably needed to be. The weeds were making a shushing noise in the breeze. "I'm going to take a closer look at the trailers. I swore I saw a light in the third one from the right. And if he's in there I don't want him running before the Henderson deputies get here. And tell them no lights, no sirens."

"Yes, Sheriff Blackwell," Oren said.

That hadn't sounded quite so patronizing as usual. She noticed he'd unsnapped the catch on his holster and had retrieved the other rifle from the back of the Explorer. He turned and climbed up the other side of the ditch, back to his car. Where Oren had parked, trees between it and the trailers, she agreed that there was a good chance it was not visible from the trailers.

She might be able to surprise him. Zachary Delaney had to be there.

"Catch the bastard," her dad had told her. She hoped to do just that, but she wasn't going to be stupid about it, had no intention of ending up like Randy. She'd not come alone, and backup would be here in minutes.

Piper was soaked by the time she reached the closest trailer; the moisture from the ground had seeped into her slacks and chilled her skin. Her fingers had cramped from the cold and were black with mud. She'd crawled a lot on downrange assignments in Iran, but it had been over sand and dirt, and the heat had been a bother, not the cold. One set of conditions was no better than another. Her heart thrummed in anticipation. Odd, she thought, feeling so alive when everything about this skirted death—the victims, the threat Zachary posed, losing her detective. It had been the same sensation when she and her men had searched for Taliban members, the peril of death making life sweeter somehow.

There was trash scattered amid the weeds, the coil from a bong, crumpled cigarette packets, smashed aluminum cans—a mix of beers and A&W. Crawling closer, she felt broken glass slice at her legs. She maneuvered and looked to see that she'd pulled herself across the remnants of beer bottles.

Piper's muscles felt like fire, though her teeth chattered from the cold. She cursed herself for not seeing a doctor after the accident. Her aches had doubled, and now her head pounded to add to her misery. Still, she felt the excitement. She crawled into a thicker clump, no longer able to see the trailers, but she knew where they were. Piper had visually memorized their positions. On some of her downrange assignments, when they slithered into compounds and neighborhoods at night, she'd had to rely on her memory of what she'd seen in daylight hours. She was a good judge of distance.

In a handful of minutes she was at the base of the nearest trailer. The unit she wanted was roughly in the center of the apocalyptic scene... at least that's where she swore she'd seen a light. Crawling to the busted steps, she saw no tracks—save for the prints of small animals that were likely living underneath the trailer. The air was foul here with rust, rotted vegetation, a trace of old oil and gasoline, evidence people had lived here quite some time ago.

As she made her way to the next trailer, and then the next, she wondered how soon the local sheriff deputies would arrive, and whether Oren had called JJ. Teegan should be on shift now. Closer, and she heard thunder. A heartbeat later she heard rain falling against the patchy skin of the trailers.

She felt it *tat-a-tat-tatting* against her back.

This trailer she hunkered against was precariously tipped, the skirt gone to reveal supports rusted through and twisted. It was smaller than the target trailer, but it provided enough cover that she could crouch next to it and peer above the weeds. Getting up from being prone was arduous.

Someone's in there, she knew for certain when she saw a light coming from a side window, which hadn't been visible from the road. It flickered, a lantern or candle, clearly no electricity was running to these things anymore. From her vantage she saw slabs of concrete arranged like domino patterns between the weeds, hints that there had been well more than a dozen trailers here at one time. The planning had been poor, she thought, putting the neighborhood on a rise. Southern Indiana and into this part of Kentucky was called Tornado Alley. Scattering trailers and mobile homes on a hill was like asking God to "come and get me."

The target trailer had curtains, and a flimsy panel near a large front window moved. The person inside would have a clear view down to the drive, and maybe to the road, but likely couldn't see the Explorer or Oren. She sucked in a breath and dropped to a low crawl again, worked her way to her target and lay flat beneath the front windows. She reached to her side for the Sig and shrugged the rifle off her back and left it. She shimmied to the front door and saw boot tracks in the mud leading to concrete blocks that served as a front stoop, muddy prints on them. It was evidence someone had walked through the mud and into the trailer. Didn't look like the prints had gone back out. Had Zachary thought to hide here for a few days, then venture out and pick up a new vehicle somewhere? If Oren hadn't recalled Zach's comment about visiting to his old trailer to check on his ex-girlfriend, Piper would have had no clue to come here. Zachary might have slipped their grasp.

Wait for backup. Wait. Wait.

Piper heard a click and the sound a window makes sliding open. She looked up and saw the barrel of a rifle point out above her. He wasn't aiming at her, couldn't see her, but he saw something, the nearby weeds keeping whatever he was interested in hidden from her view. He let off two shots in rapid succession, and she nearly jumped. Piper didn't know if he hit anything or anyone, didn't know if Oren had decided to come closer or if the backup had arrived and drawn Zachary's attention. She could see only a sea of brown weeds twitching in the breeze.

Two more shots and she heard a "Damn!" coming from the trees. She rose up and saw Oren grab his chest and drop to his knees. Another shot hit him in the shoulder and he fell back.

Shit! Piper nearly ran to Oren, a part of her wanted to.

But the wiser part was a trained soldier who acted swiftly. She dropped and rolled away from the trailer for a better angle, shooting up into the window and through the siding right beneath it. Piper saw Zach's rifle barrel wag, and with a *clunk* it dropped inside the trailer. A muffled groan and a "goddammit" told her she'd at least wounded him.

Piper had to make sure, though. Eliminate the threat, then go to Oren. She rolled back up against the trailer and skittered to the concrete block porch, all the while listening, hearing her heart and the sound of the rifle being reloaded, the sirens. Saw the barrel stick out of a window in the center. He was away from the door. Wounded, but no idea how bad. *Not bad enough*, she thought. He was able to hold a gun, was still a threat.

Piper leaped onto Zach's porch, vaulted across the threshold and landed inside in a crouch, aiming the Sig up and firing when she saw her mark. The light was dim, coming from a lantern behind Zachary, but it was enough to see by and to hit what she was aiming for. Piper'd shot him in the shoulder. She shot again now, striking the fleshy part of his arm, again and she struck his hand as he was turning the rifle on her. She could have killed him, a shot to the head or the chest. Piper would have done that on a downrange assignment—wholly eliminate the target.

But she wouldn't be able to talk to a dead man. She fired once more, striking his leg. The gun fell from his fingers and he hollered while she tried to look around him to see if they were alone. Oren had mentioned a girlfriend.

Zachary's yell turned to a scream of rage and pain, and despite his wounds, he lunged.

"I don't want to kill you, you sonofabitch!" She stood and brought her leg up, and slammed her heel into his stomach. She kicked again and he fell back, striking his head and bloody shoulder on the edge of an old wooden table. His screams grew wilder, a wounded animal.

Piper followed, ramming a foot down on his stomach. Randy's Sig was stuffed in Zach's belt, and with his good hand he tried to reach for it.

"Don't, you bastard!" she warned. "Don't even breathe."

He reached for the Sig anyway and she planted her other foot on his good arm, preventing him. He struggled, nearly setting her off balance, but she kept him down. Piper wanted him alive.

"Kill me," Zachary pleaded. "Do it. Kill me. Kill me. I'll find Duke. I'll be with Duke. Send me to Duke, you bitch!"

Piper didn't know who the hell Duke was, but she wasn't going to kill him. Dead, he couldn't fill in the gaps.

He continued to ramble, his struggles a little less, the pool of blood spreading. There was a disturbing madness in his eyes caught by the lantern light. The sirens stopped.

"You sick bastard," Piper cursed. "You sick—"

She heard the pounding of feet, someone shouting, a voice she didn't recognize.

"Sheriff Blackwell!"

"In here," she called, keeping the Sig trained on Zachary's face. "My chief deputy's been shot. He's—"

"Alive. We got him. Ambulance is coming."

She felt the floor quiver, people coming in. "Careful," she cautioned. "This place could fall in."

"Suspect down," someone said behind her, probably into a shoulder mic. One more thing Piper wanted to get for the department. "Send a second ambulance."

A man squeezed next to Piper; he wore a Henderson County sheriff's uniform. There wasn't much room inside the trailer, broken furniture, crates, an aisle running down the middle of the mess, and her and Zachary Delaney in the center of that. Just past them, in a chair next to the lantern, were the desiccated remains of a woman.

"That'd be the ex-girlfriend, I'm thinking," Piper said. She shivered. The corpse was wearing Piper's gold necklace.

Apparently Zachary Delaney had come here from time to time to check on his dead girlfriend.

How the hell did he get my necklace?

"Impressive, Sheriff Blackwell," one of the deputies said. "Front page stuff."

THIRTY-FOUR

SATURDAY, JANUARY 6TH

Piper sat at the end of her father's bed and breathed deep. Flowers everywhere, the air smelled good, like she was inside a florist's shop. She ached, every inch of her, and her fingers and toes felt a little numb. Still not recovered from her car crash, she'd sliced her legs crawling through the abandoned trailer park, and strained muscles she hadn't tested since leaving Fort Campbell. They'd patched her up in the ER in Henderson, and JJ had dropped her back at her apartment shortly before midnight—after they both checked on Oren. The chief deputy was going to be in the Henderson hospital for several days.

Eight hours later, she'd woke, tended to a few things at the office, and come to see her father.

Her New Year's resolution: find the closest YMCA and buy a membership so she could stay in military shape… after she allowed herself this weekend off to rest.

Paul Blackwell was propped up in bed, his lunch tray in front of him. He'd eaten most of it. He beamed at her.

"God, but I'm proud of you," he said for the fourth time.

"It was money," she said. "At the heart of it, just money." Piper and the Henderson County Sheriff had ridden with Zachary in the ambulance, and after he was read his rights, Zachary said he had an attorney but wasn't going to call him just yet. He spilled to her. "Zachary was fired, Dad, from Plank Manor at Thanksgiving; they cited shoddy work. He'd asked his father for some money so he could pay rent until he found something else, maybe unemployment hadn't kicked in or wasn't enough. Conrad turned him down, and Zachary decided to kill him for spite and so he could inherit everything. Apparently it wasn't the first time Conrad had refused to give Zachary money. But it was the last."

Paul made a face. "Then why kill all the others? Did Zach try to get money from them, too?"

"We're still sorting that out. He had some mental issues, hadn't taken his prescriptions for a while. That might have played into it. I think he killed all the others as a sick smokescreen, picked his victims because they didn't bother to write him a sentence on the Christmas cards they sent. In the ambulance Zachary said, and I quote, 'those people were lazy and deserved a Christmas death.' He said anyone who'd buy cards and pay postage and couldn't even add a sentence deserved to die. He thought he made a statement by posing them to look like the cards they'd sent. And he tried to swipe their address books so his name wouldn't pop up. Like I said, we're sorting it out."

"Wow."

"Oh, and he might have killed his former girlfriend from a few years back. He wouldn't comment on that, though we'll know more when the Henderson coroner uh—"

"Talk about a cold case," Paul said. "Double wow."

Piper nodded. "Apparently he'd seen enough cop shows on TV to think if he made it look like Conrad was the victim of a serial killer, we wouldn't look at him for the murder, and he could inherit it all without worry. So I'm guessing he bought the Merry Christmas mugs because he wanted a 'signature.' No idea why he didn't kill the dogs and cats."

"He was nuts."

"Well, yeah, he had issues. I call him a sick bastard… a damaged one. But I think he'd been damaged for a while. Maybe it was all the drugs, leaving home, dropping out, more drugs. It'll probably come out in a trial... trials. He's facing charges in Spencer County, Henderson County, and in Owensboro. We have to sort through jurisdictional issues." Piper listened as a medicine cart softly clattered by. A nurse came in and looked at the machine connected to Paul, took his pulse, then backed out without a word. "Yeah, Zachary wasn't all there. But I think he's sane enough that his attorney—Harlan Cook—won't be able to put up a credible defense. A serial murderer? He's not walking."

Paul laughed. "Harlan Crook?"

"Cook. I said Harlan Cook."

"Good attorney for Zachary to have signed with." He pushed the tray away. "You're not in your uniform."

"Hell of a first week on the job, Dad. I'm taking the day off. I deserve it. Thought I'd spend some of it with you, then I'm gonna run down to Henderson and visit Oren. We started getting along yesterday."

"He's a good man."

"Yeah, yeah. I get that. I'm taking tomorrow off, too."

"What about Wrinkles? If you're here—"

"Anthony's watching him for a few days."

"I like that dog," Paul said. "I like that dog a lot. He's got character. I want to get the hell out of here so I can get back to my dog." A pause. "So what else can you tell me? Something I haven't picked up from hospital scuttle?"

"Zachary's probably going to be in the hospital as long as you... in Henderson. I put three bullets in him, and he lost a lot of blood. Nothing he won't survive." Piper tipped her head back. "Zachary told us the names of three more victims... who also sent him Christmas cards with just a signature. One in Spencer County, which we would have found when the snow melts; Zachary had packed her *inside* a snowman. JJ's on that one. The woman had a cat, a very skinny one that is recovering at Oren's vet. The other two victims were from the outskirts of Henderson—and they'd been dead quite a while, dating back to a day after Zachary bought the mugs. Dr. Neufeld said she was happy the Henderson County coroner had to deal with those souls."

"Impressive," Paul pronounced. "You're so damn impressive. Don't know how you'll top your first case."

"I don't want to top my first case," she returned quickly. "I don't want Spencer County to face another serial killer. Not while I'm here anyway. And I don't want another week like this ever again. I'd like it to go back to being Sleepy Spencer County." She got up from the bed. "I'm gonna get me some coffee. Then I'll be back, and you can tell me about some of your cases until—"

"—until my meds kick in, I fall asleep, and then you go see Oren?"

"And then I'm going out for dinner. Home cooked, something called—" She paused, trying to remember how Nang had pronounced it. "Bún Thịt Nướng, and pear wine. I'm not sure, but I think it might be a date."

ACKNOWLEDGMENTS

I thank Randall Lemon for his Christmas cards that inspired this tale; Sheriff Jim McDurmon and attorney John Rudisill for sharing their knowledge of Spencer County; Bob Jenkins of Fort Campbell for providing background on the Screaming Eagles MP division; Paula Lawlor for her devious demises; and Vicki Steger, William Gilsdorf, Lee Goldberg, and Raymond Benson for lending their discerning eyes.

Spencer County, Indiana

It's a real place, about as far south in Indiana as you can go. The towns, roads, and some of the businesses I reference in this novel exist. There really is a Santa Claus—it is nestled between the Ohio River and Interstate 64; on my latest visit to the Christmas store there I picked up some fudge and a Boston terrier ornament that I had personalized. Rockport is about twenty miles away. I've fictionalized the county, taking considerable liberties. I used to live in Indiana—

Evansville, during my newspaper reporter days. Spencer County isn't far from there. The place is a good home for Piper Blackwell and company.

AFTERWORD

I write ... a lot. Currently mysteries.

And I write with dogs wrapped around my feet. I get to wear sandals or bedroom slippers to work, and old, comfortable clothes.

When the weather is fine I get to write on my back porch. I love summer.

I started getting published when I was twelve, studied journalism at Northern Illinois University, and then went to work as a news reporter...eventually for Scripps Howard, where I managed their Western Kentucky Bureau. Getting itchy feet, I moved to Wisconsin and went to work for TSR, Inc., the then-producers of the Dungeons & Dragons game. I wrote Dragonlance novels for several years. I've been on the *USA Today* bestseller list, wrote a book about spousal homicide with F. Lee Bailey, picked up three Silver Falchion literary awards, and won a chili cook-off.

I've written thirty-eight novels, most of them fantasy and science fiction, more short stories than I care to count, and I've edited a lot of magazines and anthologies.

But now it's all about mysteries...thrillers, suspense, and uncozy-cozies. I had to change genres because my feet were itching again and I needed to do something different with my writing life.

I am a geek, a gamer, and a glass-fuser. I love dogs and museums and books, and I write about those things in my monthly newsletter.

Readers can sign up for the newsletter on my website: jeanrabe.com. I have an active Facebook page, where I probably post too many pictures of my dogs.

ALSO BY JEAN RABE

From Boone Street Press

The Bone Shroud

The Dead of Winter

The Dead of Night

The Finest Creation

The Finest Choice

The Finest Challenge

Upcoming

The Dead of Summer

From WordFire Press

The Cauldron

Pockets of Darkness

The Love-Haight Casefiles (with Donald J. Bingle)

Plus dozens more - find out more at www.jeanrabe.com!